D0953074

DEATH'S OTHER KINGDOM

A HARRY BROCK MYSTERY

DEATH'S OTHER KINGDOM

KINLEY ROBY

FIVE STAR
A part of Gale, Cengage Learning

Detroit • New York • San Francisco • New Haven, Conn • Waterville, Maine • London

GALE
CENGAGE Learning

Set in 11 pt. Plantin.
Printed on permanent paper.

LIBRARY OF CONGRESS CATALOGING-IN-PUBLICATION DATA

Roby, Kinley E.
  Death's other kingdom : a Harry Brock mystery / Kinley Roby.
  — 1st ed.
    p. cm.
  ISBN-13: 978-1-59414-791-3 (alk. paper)
  ISBN-10: 1-59414-791-4 (alk. paper)
  1. Brock, Harry (Fictitious character)—Fiction. 2. Private investigators—Florida—Fiction. 3. Human trafficking victims—Fiction. 4. Human trafficking—Fiction. I. Title.
PS3618.O3385D45 2009
813'.6—dc22   2009016130

First Edition. First Printing: September 2009.
Published in 2009 in conjunction with Tekno Books and Ed Gorman.

Printed in the United States of America
1 2 3 4 5 6 7 13 12 11 10 09

For Mary

"Those who have crossed
With direct eyes, to death's other Kingdom
Remember us—if at all—not as lost
Violent souls. But only
As the hollow men
The stuffed men."
(T. S. Eliot, "The Waste Land")

1

Rigoberta Quirarte sat very straight on the back seat of the white van, clutching a stained woolen shoulder bag containing everything she owned and trying to make sense of what she was seeing out the filthy windows. She had been traveling for a week, at first on foot and then by bus and plane and prayed that she was nearing the end of her journey.

The two men in the front seat, a heavy white man with a face like a dented shovel and the tall Hispanic driver with a livid scar where his left eye had been, made no response to her questions, asked in halting Spanish. Since leaving her mountain, she had found no one who understood her *Quiche*. When the men spoke to her, they called her *puta*. The insult angered her, but because they were dangerous, she said nothing to provoke them. In any case, they seldom spoke to her.

Rigoberta was dark, with brown eyes and long, straight black hair, tied back at the nape of her neck with a piece of red yarn. Exhausted and heartsick for the children she had left behind, Rigoberta faced the weariness by telling herself she had been weary before. As for the pain of being separated from her children, it was a pain that she must endure. If, in the end, they joined her, she would be repaid.

It was some consolation that she was no longer on the plane. The night before, she and eight other men and women had been driven in the middle of the night to a dark airstrip and bundled into an ancient Cessna with no running lights. The flight was rough, and several of those crowded into the baggage space were ill. When she got off the plane, half sick herself and smelling of strangers' vomit, the one-eyed Mexican yanked her out of the group and took her to the white man, held his nose and said, "Stinking *chola.*"

The white man had laughed and passed her the black slacks and jersey she was now wearing. Deeply shamed and angry, she was made to change in front of the men while they laughed and said things she knew she was fortunate not to understand. They made her leave her many colored skirts, which she had been wearing ever since she left the mountain, on the trampled dirt.

She remembered that moment with a sharper pain as she stared at the pastel-colored houses, palm trees, bougainvillea, fichus, and hibiscus trees, and a forest of incomprehensible signs crowding against the roar of the highway on which she was riding.

She spoke no English, only Indian Spanish and *Quiche,* her native tongue. When she was six, she had been sent to the village school, which she had attended sporadically for two years, but after that she was kept home in her parents' thatch-roofed hut, to care for the children that had come after her. There had never been enough books in the school to go around, and the youngest had to wait their turns. Her turn had never come.

When she was twenty, her husband had been killed in a rockslide on the mountain where he had been searching for a lost sheep. Her husband and an older brother and his family had shared their farm, but Rigoberta refused to go on living on it without her husband to protect her and the children. Neither of her parents needed to ask what she feared.

Her parents still had children to feed and could not support her and her two children. She could not appeal to her husband's parents. They had both died the previous winter of tuberculosis.

"Old Menchu needs a woman," her mother suggested.

Rigoberta shook her head.

Her mother went to the village priest, a pale, bald, soft-spoken man in his 70s with large, square hands, and asked what they should do. The question did not surprise him. Very little did. Trained as a medical doctor and called belatedly to the priesthood, he had come to the northern highlands of Guatemala in the late 1960s where within a year he had embraced liberation theology. After that he became both a doctor and a priest. For nearly forty years he had been a survivor of the place itself and scores of attempts by government death squads to kill him.

At the height of the fighting in the 1980s, the slaughter of the Indians in Huehuetenango had been terrible. When the death squads began murdering nuns and priests, the Church pulled stakes and abandoned the people to their fate. But he had stayed, to live *con el pueblo,* and now he knew he would never leave. Who would replace him?

"Your sister is still in North America?" he asked.

"Yes."

"Do you know where?"

"No."

"Does Manuelo?"

"Perhaps."

He sighed. The Indians trusted no one. Why should they? They took communion and his medicine, lit candles in the church, and were no more Christians than their goats. Was he? He no longer knew. Perhaps he prayed to the mountains. Looking at her, despair, disgust, anger, resentment, cynicism, pity all tugged at his mind, offering solace, but as he had always done he turned away from those consolations.

"Tell him to bring me the address," he said.

Later that day, her husband came, carrying an envelope. He was a bent mummy of a man in a filthy conical wool hat. His face was blackened and seamed by the weather and by the harshness of his life. The knuckles of his calloused hands were swollen with arthritis, and he limped and could have been any age. The priest knew he was fifty-three, an old man in that country.

"Would your wife's sister take Rigoberta?" he asked, after the formal greetings.

"Perhaps, with her husband's permission."

"Would she go?"

"Possibly."

"Shall I write to him?"

The man nodded.

Leaning forward, the priest placed a hand on the man's bony shoulder, looking steadily into his eyes. "If she goes, the children must stay here," he said. "They may be able to go later, but that is not certain. Will you and your wife care for them?"

"It will not be easy."

The priest shrugged.

"She will be in great danger until she reaches your brother," he said. "Many have left and never been heard from again."

"Many die here," the man said.

The priest nodded. They continued to stare at one another for a moment, sharing an awareness that required no words. Then the priest said, "I will write the letter."

In time he received a reply from the man's brother, telling him that if Rigoberta could get there, he and his wife would take her in. As for her children, perhaps she would later be able to pay to have them smuggled into the *Estados Unidos*. He also said that on her journey she must follow the instructions he had sent her, do as the men she would meet told her, but to trust no one.

"It goes without saying," her uncle concluded, "she must carry a knife and when necessary use it."

The priest smiled bitterly, recalling lines from Auden: "That girls are raped, that two boys knife a third/ Are axioms to him . . ." He reread the instructions, counted the money folded into the letter, and sent his housekeeper to fetch Rigoberta, wondering as he did so whether he was her savior or her executioner.

The van turned out of the roar and hiss of traffic onto the East Trail into the La Ramada housing development, paused, and then turned right on Calle Felicidad, making a slow and smoky progress along the deserted, potholed street and finally rolling to a stop at number 11264.

Rigoberta sat up straighter, staring hard at the house. She guessed it belonged to her uncle and started to get out.

"Stay put," the white man snapped.

With her heart racing, she waited. It had taken her a long time to get here. She could wait a little longer. Accustomed to cold, she began to sweat as the sun's heat seeped into the van.

Like all the other houses in La Ramada, number 11264 was a squat, single-story white box with a gray shingled roof and sagging car port, sitting blankly in a square of mostly dead grass. There were no trees to be seen, but there was a leafless forest of tilted and bent television antennas on the roofs of the houses.

The white man climbed out of the van, squinting in the sudden glare. Rigoberta flinched as he slammed the door and, with his jaw thrust out, lurched toward the house. Gathering her courage, she asked the driver if this was her uncle's house but got no answer.

She saw the front door open a crack. Some words were exchanged, then the door closed and the man came back to the truck, climbing in with a curse.

"What?" the driver asked, still looking at the house.

"They're short," the white man said.

"How much?"

"Five hundred."

The door of the house opened and a man was framed briefly in it before he slammed it shut.

"*Chinga tu madre!*" the tall man exploded.

"She's dead," the white man said with an ugly laugh. "Get us out of here."

"We'll wring her fucking neck and drop her in their fucking yard," the tall one growled in English, jamming down on the throttle and swinging the van in a screeching circle.

"Was he my uncle?" Rigoberta cried, not having understood any of their exchange.

The white man turned, thrusting a thick arm over the back of the seat.

"Shut up," he said.

The menace in his voice required no translation.

I must do this myself, she thought in desperation. As the turning truck thrust her against the door, she pushed down the handle and was flung out of the careening van. The ground rushed up at her. Curling around her sack, she struck the soft dirt at the edge of the street in a puff of dust and rolled onto the sparse grass.

For a moment she lay dazed, the wind knocked out of her. Then the world stopped spinning and, gasping for breath, she saw the van skid to a stop. For a long moment, the sight of the white man jumping down from the truck and breaking into a lumbering run toward her, froze her with fear. Then, remembering her children and determined that she would not die, she scrambled to her feet and ran stumbling toward the house. The man had emerged again and was beckoning to her and shouting encouragement.

Glancing over her shoulder, she saw that her pursuer had halted and was pointing a gun at her and also shouting, but she did not understand what he was saying. The beckoner had vanished. First, she felt the searing pain in her right leg then heard the blast of the gun and fell, screaming. The man in the house reappeared with a gun and began shooting at her attacker.

There was a shout of pain, and she turned to see the white man stagger backward, grasping his right shoulder, and break into a shambling run for the van. Then Rigoberta saw the van's driver step around the back of the truck and begin shooting with a gun that made an entirely different noise. Windows began to shatter and the doorframe was ripped into splinters.

She thought with a loss of hope that she would be killed. Surrendering to the pain in her leg, she prepared to die, but the next second she heard firing from several houses and, raising her head, saw the one-eyed man dodge back behind the van.

The Anglo had dragged himself into the van, and a moment later it started forward, surrounded by a deafening clatter of gunfire that seemed to come from everywhere, then jerked to a stop. The Anglo fell slowly out of the van onto the dirt. The man she had first seen in the door hurried toward her, still holding his gun.

With their guns pointed at the van, two other men from the house to Rigoberta's left ran forward, dragged the fallen shooter to the back of the van, and threw him into it. Then they pulled the dead Mexican from behind the wheel, and tumbled him in on top of the Anglo. Then they drove away. A moment later, a car pulled into the street and followed the van.

Speaking rapidly to Rigoberta as he worked, the man shoved his pistol into his belt holster, drew a knife from inside his shirt, and began cutting the bloody cloth of her slacks away from the wound. Because of the pain and shock, it was a moment before Rigoberta realized she could understand what he was saying.

"Uncle Cavek, is it you?" she asked through clenched teeth.

"Yes, it is I," he told her.

A woman dressed in wide, multicolored skirts and carrying a yellow bucket and a roll of white cloth rushed out of the house and ran toward them.

"There is good news," he said when she reached them, wiping his knife on a clump of grass. "The bullet missed the bone."

"Welcome to El Norte, Rigoberta," the woman said bitterly, dropping to her knees and starting to sponge the wound. "As you see, people die here too."

2

After a mostly sleepless night, Harry Brock was sitting on his lanai, cleaning his CZ, the pungent smell of gun oil permeating the lanai. Beyond the dirt road and the swamp east of Puc Puggy Creek, an enormous red sun was rising out of the low-lying mist, promising another scorcher. Just yesterday, Harry had grumbled to Tucker LaBeau, his only human neighbor on Bartram's Hammock, that May was getting to be as hot as July.

Located on the western edge of the Everglades, the Hammock was a low, flat, lozenge-shaped island about three miles long and two wide, at the confluence of Puc Puggy Creek and the more sluggish flow from the Stickpen Cypress Preserve. Several miles north of Avola and connected to a remote County Road by a rickety, hump-backed wooden bridge, the thickly forested Hammock was a state game preserve. Most of it was part of Tucker LaBeau's farm. The rest had been owned by a developer who built a house on his part of the Hammock as an investment and leased it to Harry.

Years earlier, shortly after Harry had moved into the house, he was hired to investigate a murder that put the developer in jail. The state confiscated the man's land, turned it into a protected area, and began pressuring Tucker, a man well on in years, to sell his farm. Tucker made a counteroffer. Having no family, he agreed to deed his farm to the state for a modest cash settlement and the right to live there until his death, at which time the entire Hammock would become a part of the Stickpen Preserve.

The Fish and Game Department agreed and offered Harry a new lease on his house with the stipulation that he take on the job of keeping the island free from squatters, poachers, drug runners, and orchid hunters. Saved from eviction, he signed the lease with relief.

If any place in southwest Florida retained the characteristics of its pre-Columbian world, Bartram's Hammock did, and it was unlikely that any other two people were better suited to live there than Tucker LaBeau and Harry Brock.

Harry loved the Hammock. Twenty years earlier he had drifted onto the island from Maine, where, while carrying out his duties as a State Game Warden, he had shot and killed a man who was trying to kill him. In the ensuing public outcry, he was charged with murder, tried, and found innocent, but bowing to political pressure, the Department fired him.

His wife Jennifer, furious with him for having risked his life over a dead deer, divorced him and separated him from his son and his daughter. By the time he found the Hammock, he was almost ready to take the big jump, but through the quiet and patient ministrations of Tucker LaBeau, the healing peace of the Hammock, and the work that began coming his way, Harry gradually rekindled his interest in living.

In general, the years since that dark time had been happy ones for Harry, except for his penchant for falling in love with good women and then losing them. After Jennifer, he had married Katherine and adopted her two children. Pregnant with his child, she had left him because he refused to give up being a PI. After living through her first Florida hurricane, Cora, the most recent woman in his life, had left Avola.

She spent a few weeks in New York and then decamped for the Bahamas. She had now been gone for six months, and during her call the preceding night when he had said he missed her and asked when she was coming back to Avola, she left the question unanswered but invited Harry to join her as her guest on an extended Scandinavian cruise, to which Harry had countered by saying he was planning a canoe trip on the Puc Puggy Creek and asked her to come with him, promising to do all the paddling and provide the Deep Woods Off. Cora did not say, "Love you," before hanging up.

It was one of those "act in haste" things that Harry spent the rest of the night regretting in sleepless leisure, but he was too stubborn to pick up the phone and try to patch up Humpty Dumpty.

Harry was sliding the CZ into its holster when Captain Jim Snyder and Sergeant Frank Hodges turned off the sandy road into his driveway in a Tequesta County Sheriff's Department's cruiser, pulling a funnel of dust behind them. Harry stood up, a man of middle height, uneasily climbing into his middle years, still fit, with cropped, graying hair, and a deeply tanned face. Because he was a PI, other people's troubles had a way of becoming his, and he suspected it was trouble that had brought Jim Snyder and Frank Hodges to his door.

"Hey, Harry," Hodges called as soon as he was out of the car. "You had breakfast yet?"

Hodges's mind was never far from food.

Jim Snyder, who encountered the world with the restrained gentility of his Tennessee mountains upbringing, suffered in mostly silent disapproval his sergeant's brashness. Jim was six-three, lean as a rake with closely cut hair so pale it was nearly white. His long, solemn face usually expressed pained astonishment at the human capacity for folly.

Hodges, on the other hand, was surprised by nothing. What he lacked in Jim's height, he made up for in girth, and his bustling advance across the lawn, broad red face beaming, was a study in contrast to his Captain's long, sedate strides. Harry watched the men approach, grinning in appreciation of their differences.

He never saw Jim loping along without imagining him in a frock coat with a Bible under his arm and Hodges, with a donut in his hand. Hodges got to the door first and wrung Harry's hand.

"Coffee's hot," Harry said, "and there's a couple of crullers left."

"Don't indulge him, Harry," Jim said in a moonshine drawl so thick it attracted the attention of the mockingbird in the wisteria vine at the end of the lanai. "He's supposed to be dieting."

The three men went into the kitchen, listening to Hodges's heartbreaking account of the piddling breakfast he had eaten.

"And that's so far behind me," he said, looking at his watch, "that it's down below the horizon."

"What's up?" Harry asked when they were seated with coffee and the cruller box open in front of them.

"Plenty," Jim said, frowning and shaking his head, "and it's giving me fits."

Harry looked more closely at Jim and saw that he had lost weight he couldn't afford to lose, and his face was marked with sadness.

"It started with a white Chrysler van we found out on Panther Trace with two dead men in it all shot to pieces," Hodges said around a cruller. "If you had poured a pail of water over the front of them, it would have all run out their backs."

"Who were they?" Harry asked.

"A Mexican by the name of Hernando Rodriguez and Henry Gee Baker, an Anglo from Laredo," Jim said.

"*Porqueria malo*," Hodges said. "They've got rap sheets longer than two rolls of toilet paper."

"We think that's why they switched their specialty from drugs and murder to human trafficking," Jim said, "that and the fact Florida is an expanding market."

"What were they doing out on Panther Trace?" Harry asked.

"That's where you come in," Hodges said, dusting the last of the powdered sugar off his hands.

"I know you're shorthanded," Harry said, glancing from Hodges to Jim, "but if you're thinking about deputizing me . . ."

"Don't get all huffy," Jim said, inching his coffee, which he had not touched, a little farther away from him. "I don't want you deputized. That's the whole point of this. I don't want anyone to know you've got anything to do with the police."

"That coffee must be stone cold," Harry said, pushing back his chair, noticing that Hodges hadn't touched his either. "I'll just make us a fresh pot."

"Oh, no!" Jim and Hodges chorused, throwing up their hands. "We're good. We're good."

"It's not that bad!" Harry protested.

"No, it's worse," Jim said, "but don't worry about it."

He rubbed his head and frowned, an action that told Harry he was seriously worried and not about the coffee. Hodges was eyeing the cruller box.

"Up until a few months ago," Jim said, "we assumed the up-tick we've been watching in the number of people being smuggled across the Gulf was due to increased surveillance along the Mexican border, but now it looks as if we were way behind the curve."

"How do you mean?"

"Slavery," Hodges said and took another cruller.

"You keep on and you're going to end up in the hospital," Jim told him.

"It's only my second," Hodges protested.

21

Harry had not heard about the van, but he thought it was more likely the shooting was over a drug deal gone wrong than slavery.

"Haven't there always been instances in Tequesta County of Mexican women being kept as house servants and not paid?" Harry asked, hoping to distract Jim from his futile efforts to reduce Hodges's calorie consumption and get a sensible discussion going.

"Yes," Jim agreed, "but those situations usually get straightened out as soon as the woman tells her priest or the check-out person in her grocery store about it. What's going on here is a whole lot worse."

"What's different?" Harry asked, having discounted Hodges's *slavery* remark as typical Hodges exaggeration.

"One thing is the level of violence," Jim said, shaking his head. "This van thing is a sample."

"And it's getting worse," Hodges put in.

"Frank's right," Jim agreed. "Nobody shoots anybody just once anymore. They're turning one another into colanders."

"How does human trafficking come into the van shootout?" Harry asked.

"We think Rodriguez and Baker either trespassed on some other traffickers' territory or tried to cheat the people they were dealing with," Hodges replied.

"That's right," Jim added. "The thing is, the Feds are telling us that it's mostly women, young women, some as young as twelve and thirteen, who are being bought and sold."

Harry noticed that his friend's ears had turned red, which always happened when he was upset.

"Was there a woman involved?" Harry asked.

"Probably. A road crew working near the entrance to La Ramada," Jim said, "saw a white van go into the complex with two men and a black-haired woman in it."

"The bad part," Hodges added, "is they moved on before the van came out."

"It's not much to go on," Harry said, becoming bored with the story then asking in an effort to show interest, "Are these Mexican women?"

"We don't really know," Jim said. "Reports we've had from Miami say that many of them are coming from Guatemala. Many of them are recruited in the poorest parts of the country and told they'll find jobs as housekeepers or farm workers. If they're men, they're told they will be given construction jobs. They're all told they will be earning at least seven dollars an hour, which in their world is a fortune. In Guatemala, Indian girls are working in American factories for as little as a dollar a day."

"We're not really talking about slavery, right?" Harry demanded, still not convinced.

"Oh, yes," Hodges protested. "That's just what we're talking about."

Harry started to make a scoffing response, but Jim cut him off.

"That's how I responded when I first heard about this thing, but it's likely the men in the van were selling the woman they had with them or delivering her for sale."

"Selling her!" Harry said, his voice rising.

"Get used to it," Jim said.

"But you haven't found the woman," Harry said.

"Nope," Hodges said, peering hopelessly into the empty cruller box.

"And there's no Guatemalan community close to where you found the dead men?" Harry asked.

This conversation was making him very edgy. Slavery in southwest Florida? How could that be possible?

"No, there's not, but there is one on the East Trail about ten miles south of where we found the van," Hodges said.

"La Ramada," Harry said.

"You know the place," Jim said hopefully.

"A couple of years ago," Harry said with a grin, "the Bonner Ford Agency sent me in there to reclaim a Ranger for back payments. When I found the house, there was nothing left but a cement slab and a pile of ashes. Nobody knew anything, not even that there'd been a fire. It's not where the beautiful people come for fun in the sun."

"And it hasn't changed much since then, except maybe got worse," said Jim.

"I'm guessing that you found prints in or on the van that didn't belong to the victims," Harry said.

"Three sets, one in the back seat and two, aside from the dead men's, in the front," Jim told him.

"You're thinking the set in the back seat belongs to the woman and the rest to the men who drove the van to where you found it?"

"That's about it," Hodges said.

"What do you want me to do?" Harry asked Jim, suspecting that getting the whole answer was going to be like inching into very cold water.

"We've been working on this for a while now," Jim told him, displaying uneasiness, "and found out that if you send a cruiser or plainclothes officers with badges and guns into any of these communities, you get no answers to your questions, find no one who speaks English or Spanish, and very few who will even open a door. These are extremely suspicious, careful, and, from what I saw in that van, dangerous people."

Harry leaned back in his chair and swore silently.

"And you want me to go in there unarmed and get someone

to talk with me," he said, finding nothing pleasurable in the prospect.

"Better you than me," Hodges said with a wide grin.

3

For several days Rigoberta's wound caused her intense pain, mitigated by Percocet and heroin, cautiously administered by her aunt Agata, a small, black-eyed woman with a sense of humor as dark as her hair.

"A little of this will hasten your healing," she told Rigoberta with a sly smile, holding up the syringe and tapping it. "Too much will hasten your death."

Within a week Rigoberta was hobbling around on a home-made crutch and helping Agata with the children. She no longer needed the heroin and very little Percocet. Her appetite returned and with it an interest in living. Unfortunately, she also began to think of her children and to miss them.

"You will soon be able to work," her uncle said. "We must make plans."

"Will I stay with you?" Rigoberta asked.

"No. You need to earn money. I will put you in a place where you can learn English, which you must do if you wish to bring your children here."

"Is this place I am going to very far from here?" Rigoberta asked, chilled by the thought that she might have to begin traveling again.

"No," her uncle said quickly, calming her fears, "but you will not see us much because you will be working hard. But, from time to time we will talk to you, to be sure things are going well."

There was something about her uncle's voice that disturbed her, but her relief at learning she would be near him and her aunt made her forget whatever had concerned her.

"What kind of work will I be doing?" she asked.

"Sewing, I think, which is good because you can sit down as you work, and the leg will finish healing more quickly."

She was so absorbed in what her uncle was saying that she did not notice that her aunt was not looking at her but sitting with her head down, staring at her lap, and nervously smoothing her red and yellow skirt across her knees.

"I don't have many clothes," Rigoberta said, already thinking about what was before her, "and I have no money. What I had, the men who brought me here took."

"That will be taken care of," her uncle said with a dismissive wave of his hand. "You can give back the money spent on your clothes from what you are paid."

Rigoberta smiled for the first time in a very long time. A faint blush brightened her cheeks and put a sparkle in her large, dark eyes, making her suddenly beautiful.

"And then I will begin to save dollars to bring Mireya and Manche here, and we will be together again. Perhaps they will go to school."

"Certainly," her uncle replied. "All children go to school here. It is a requirement."

Rigoberta was startled out of her sleep at three in the morning by her aunt shaking her shoulder.

"Come," Agata said. "We must hurry. Hugar is waiting."

"Who is Hugar?" Rigoberta asked, still groggy with sleep.

"Never mind. As soon as you have eaten, you will be taken to the place where you will work."

Rigoberta looked at her aunt and saw that she looked frightened or angry. "Aunt Agata," she said in a whisper, grasping the woman by the wrist. "What is it?"

"Nothing," Agata insisted, pulling herself free and avoiding meeting Rigoberta's gaze. "Come. Relieve yourself. Wash. Put your things into your sack. Eat. There isn't much time."

She scuttled out of the room. Feeling both excited and frightened, Rigoberta scrambled out of bed. Her uncle came to get her as she put the last of her things in her satchel.

"From now on, Rigoberta," he said sternly, taking her arm and leading her firmly through the house, "it would be best if you did not ask questions or talk at all. When we get to the place you are going, I will leave you with the people who will be responsible for you. Once you are there, do as you are told. Say little. Work hard. Things will go better for you if you remember my advice."

Rigoberta was suddenly afraid, and her heart began racing.

"I want to say goodbye to Aunt Agata," she said.

"There is not time."

Continuing to hold her arm, her uncle hurried her out the front door. A long, dark van was waiting in the street, its headlights off.

"Wait," Rigoberta said, pulling back, suddenly filled with dread.

The van, the darkness, her aunt's disappearance, her uncle's haste, all set off alarm bells in her head. "Where are you taking me? What is happening?"

"You are being taken to where you will work, where you will begin your new life," he answered in a harsh whisper, pausing, thrusting his face close to hers. "Don't give me any trouble. Think of your children. You are an illegal. If you're caught, you will either go to jail or be sent back to Guatemala. Is that what you want?"

"No."

"Then come along and remember what I have told you."

Frightened but unwilling to believe he would do anything to

harm her, she allowed her uncle to hurry her toward the van. In the van's feeble light, she saw four blindfolded women huddled on the seats. Rigoberta gasped and tried to turn back, but her uncle pushed her onto a seat and wrapped a black cloth around her head.

"Uncle!" she cried, but he silenced her.

"No one is going to hurt you," he told her. "It is for your own protection. Remember, do as you are told. Work hard and it will all go well."

With a leaden heart she heard the door slam and felt the van jerk forward, knowing she had been betrayed.

4

After Jim and Frank Hodges left, Harry locked away his CZ and decided to walk to the bridge. He was pushing open the screen door on the lanai when his house phone rang. Swearing under his breath so as not to tempt the mockingbird, he went back into the kitchen.

"Harry, it's me."

The voice jumped Harry's heart like a shot of adrenalin.

"Katherine," he said, stirred by both pain and pleasure.

Katherine. In an instant of total recall he saw her as he had first seen her, standing on his doorstep with two thin, exhausted young children, looking for Will Trachey, her absconded husband. She was then a penniless woman in her early thirties, at the end of her tether. But as she stood looking at the screen on the lanai door, the sun behind her made a glorious nimbus of her long, red-gold hair, highlighting the most beautiful green eyes he had ever seen. Half an hour later they had found her husband, shot to death, in his cabin at the end of the Hammock road.

Harry now knew he had fallen in love with Katherine Trachey the moment he saw her, but it had taken him a while to admit it. But after almost losing her to Jim Snyder, he finally got his head straight enough to tell her how he felt. Shortly after that they were married. But love's old sweet song, he now thought bitterly, had ended on a very sour note. Still, that didn't really matter because he had never stopped loving her.

The thoughts vanished as quickly as they had come. He braced himself. Katherine was not given to making casual calls.

"Are you all right?" he asked.

"Yes," she said in a way Harry recognized as conditional.

"The kids?" he asked as calmly as he could with his stomach churning.

He had adopted Minna and Jesse when he married Katherine, and she was pregnant with Thornton when they separated. She and the children lived in Georgia, which was too far away for Harry's taste.

"Which one is it, Katherine?" he asked, his dread growing in the silence on the line.

"Minna," she said and stopped.

"Has she been hurt? Katherine, say something. Is she in the hospital?"

"No."

Harry's patience was about to snap, but he took a deep breath. It always happened this way with Katherine, who was laconic at the best of times. The worse she felt, the harder it became to find out what was bothering her, and pressing her froze her into a deeper silence.

"Can I help?" he asked.

"I don't see how."

Not being there for her and all, he thought but stifled the sarcasm and said, "Minna and I have always gotten along pretty well. It might be worth a try."

"I'm angry with her and being angry makes me feel worse," she said.

"Oh?"

It was, he thought, like one of those bad dreams in which you want to run and can barely move your legs. Feeling that his head was about to burst, he said, "How bad is it? What's happened?"

The silence at the end of the line was broken by the choked sounds of someone trying not to cry and failing. Through all the grief, stress, and emotional turmoil that had led up to their finally splitting, Harry remembered Katherine never cried. Alive, Willard Trachey had put her through a course in neglect, abuse, and abandonment from which she had graduated, having shed most of her tears. If she was crying now . . .

"Cry it out," he said as gently as he could, hating it that he was not there to comfort her, trying at the same time to find the words to ask if the child had been . . . what?

"She's been . . . assaulted." Katherine's voice was ragged. "It could have been worse," she told him, choking back the tears.

"Was she . . . ?"

He couldn't finish the sentence.

"No. She has some bad bruises. He didn't . . ." She left it there, her voice breaking, and Harry caught the words between the half-stifled sobs that kept welling up.

Relief washed over him.

"When did it happen?" he asked.

"Three nights ago. He stopped her on her way home from a chorus rehearsal. He was parked just below the bridge in a white van. Minna said it had passed her a few minutes earlier just after she got off the late bus. She said he was standing beside the van, looking at a map with one of those pocket lights when she started to pass him. The van's lights were off."

He knew the road. There were woods and no houses near the bridge. Harry's anger forced the words out before he could check them.

"Why was she . . ." he began.

Katherine's voice rose in an explosion of her own anger.

"Do you think I haven't told her never to walk home from the bus in the dark? She had her cell. She was supposed to have called me. I would have been waiting."

32

"I know you would," he said quickly, struggling to sound calm. "Why didn't she call?"

"It was a warm night. She'd been in school all day. She wanted to walk." Katherine's voice lost its force, but the pain was audible. "You know how she loves being outdoors."

"Yes," Harry said. He did know. She and her brother had spent half their lives outdoors when they lived on the Hammock. "How did she get away from him?"

"He knocked her around some getting her into the back of the van," Katherine said, speaking quickly in a flat voice. "Then she stopped struggling, and when he came onto her, she yanked his head down and bit his nose. When she got back here, she was covered with his blood. She told me that when he yelled and pulled back, she let him go, pulled a leg free, and drove her heel into his stomach while he was coming up off his knees. The kick knocked him over backward. She scrambled over the front seat and out the door before he could get out the back."

"Then she ran like a deer," Harry said, cheering her on.

"Right into the woods and up into Grady's hollow," Katherine added. "She and Jesse know every inch of that place. A posse couldn't have found her in there if she didn't want them to. In another fifteen minutes she was home."

Harry's next thought terrified him.

"Has Minna been tested . . . ?" He couldn't quite finish the sentence.

"It's too soon, Harry," Katherine said in a fading voice.

"The blood she swallowed won't infect her," he said quickly.

"Unless there was a lesion somewhere in her mouth," Katherine said in a bitter voice.

"Was that checked?"

"Yes," the doctor said he couldn't find any." Katherine stopped. "But any cut or scratch wherever the blood went . . ."

Katherine couldn't finish the sentence.

"When can she be tested?" he asked.

"They can do the PCR test ten days from contact," she responded, "but it's not a hundred percent reliable. At twenty-eight days they can do the HIV Duo test, which includes the antibody test and the p24 antigen test. That's the one that will tell us if she's infected."

"How is she?" Harry asked, not wanting to linger on what Katherine had told him.

"Not good, Harry. She's gone all silent. That's not like her. Jesse is worried. She won't even talk to him. After she told me what I've told you, she just stopped talking. She lies in bed and stares. She gave the doctor a bad time. She doesn't want to be touched, not even by me. And when I ask her if she wants to go back to school, she just shakes her head. I'm frightened, Harry."

"I think she'd better start talking to a therapist," Harry told her. "This is too much for her to deal with all alone. And it's not your fault she's shut you out. From what I know, it's what you'd expect."

"I know that, but she won't see anyone. And she's as stubborn as you are. It's terrible to be shut out like this. I've always looked after her, except when you and I were together and I had you to help. You're right, you know. You two were close right from the start. I wish . . ."

Then she went silent.

"I'll come down," he said. "I can be there before dinner time." But only after a damned hard drive, he thought. Georgia wasn't just around the next bend in the road.

"Oh, God no, Harry!" Katherine cried. "No! It would be too much. Please don't!"

He swore silently at himself. He hadn't been thinking about where he and Katherine were in their lives.

"OK. How long before school closes?" he asked, changing direction.

"About two weeks."

"Then bring her here, Katherine. You and she come. Let Jesse and Thornton stay with your sister until school closes, then they can come too."

"No, Harry. Jesse's won an internship in marine biology at Woods Hole for the summer. He's got his heart set on going."

"Good. Let him go. It's the best thing that could happen. But you and Minna come here. She'd feel safe here."

She started to speak but he interrupted her.

"No, don't say no. Think about it. Sleep on it. Can I talk with her?"

"I'll ask her."

There was a pause, then Katherine said, "She's asleep, Harry. I don't want to wake her."

"Fine. When she wakes, tell her I love her. Then say that I heard Benjamin the alligator last night for the first time this year. Tell her Tucker sends his love and wants to see her, which is true. Katherine, persuade her and yourself. Maybe together we can work a healing."

"All right, Harry. I'll think about it."

Then she was gone.

5

Katherine's call left Harry badly shaken. Among a host of other wounds, it opened up the past, which he had more or less buried. But for the moment he was locked in the present, painful shock of absorbing what had happened to Minna.

Thinking of Minna, he remembered Boots, the cat that Minna at the age of three had wanted more than anything else she had ever thought of. She had grown old and slow, and in February, a coyote had killed and eaten her. Harry could remember when there were no coyotes in southwest Florida. Everything did not get better with time's passing. That grim reflection dragged his mind back to Minna.

After hanging up, surges of anger pumped through him. For one wild moment he thought of packing a bag and his gun and going after the son-of-a-bitch who had attacked Minna. He would find him and blow his fucking head off.

When he came to himself, he went to the sink and filled a glass with water and drank it. By the time he had emptied the glass, the spasm had passed, and he began to think again. But his responses were circular—fear and concern for Minna, a compelling urge to do something, and a lurking sense of helplessness that had him racing up and down emotionally like a monkey on a flight of stairs. In the end he decided there was nothing he could do but wait for Katherine's call. *If* she called. What would he do if she didn't? He began to be angry again, this time with Katherine, and stopped himself. He looked around the kitchen and told himself that there was no need of being a bigger fool than he had to be.

"There's only this to do," he told the open window. "I've just got to go on, and that's what I'll do."

For a few seconds, Harry considered canceling the walk and writing insurance company surveillance reports instead. The crushingly boring assignments kept him solvent, but the morning was too beautiful to waste indoors. Pocketing his cell phone, he put on his Tilley hat, which was so stained and tattered that *Oh, Brother!*, Tucker's mule, now lifted it off his head at every opportunity and dropped it on the ground.

The sun was burning the mist off Puc Puggy Creek, and flocks of ibis and other waders were passing overhead, wings whistling, spreading out across the swamp in search of fish, frogs, snails, lizards, small crabs, and the hundreds of other wriggling, creeping, crawling, swimming creatures that fed them. The dense, dark, liana-hung forest crowding up to the white, sandy track was full of bird song, and Harry breathed in with pleasure the rich scent of damp earth and trees and flowering shrubs.

His spirits, however, remained subdued. The Hammock was his world and he loved it. It was unfortunate, he thought, that Cora was no longer there to share it with him. Although if he were honest with himself, he would admit that she had never been really enthusiastic about the place.

"It's lovely, Harry," she'd told him when he suggested that she move in with him, "but it's like living in a zoo that's way out of control."

His knew his plan had crashed when she asked him what she would do with her paintings.

Harry admitted she had a point. Every wall that wasn't a window in her four-thousand-square-foot beachfront penthouse in the Silver Sands was covered with contemporary oils, watercolors, and collages. She even had some late Stieglitz photographs—"For contrast," she said.

She made the comments and asked the question shortly after putting her hand on an eight-foot blue indigo snake as thick as her forearm. The reptile had been hunting in the wisteria vine at the south end of Harry's lanai. She had reached out to move some foliage in order to take a quick peek at the five young mockingbirds in their nest in the vine when a shining length of the vine convulsed under her hand. The snake, with lunch in mind, was also looking for the fledglings. Cora had leaped back screaming, and the snake, deaf to her screams but appalled by the touch of her hand, had catapulted out of the vine and onto the ground and slithered away in swift, glittering flight.

Harry lost more points for laughing when, having come running, he saw the snake in flight and Cora standing in the glider, still hitting high C.

"Did you ever see anything more beautiful than its skin?" he asked after he had lifted her down from the glider and held her until she stopped trembling.

"It was a huge *snake*, Harry!" she shot back, angrily pulling her dress back into place. "Nothing about a *snake* is beautiful until it's made into a belt."

Well, he thought, emerging from the memory with a sigh, that pretty much summed up her relationship with the natural world. He gave his attention to his walk.

Earlier in the year, a young female otter had made a den near the bridge and given birth to three pups. He had first seen her in late December, and at that time she was probably halfway through her two-month embryonic gestation period. Judging by the fact they were catching fish on their own, Harry thought the pups were now just about four months old.

They were, he guessed, sleeping in their den after a night of feasting on crabs and fish, leaving Harry alone on the bridge, which was all right, but he had wanted to see the family going about their watery business. Outside of Tucker's recalcitrant mule, Oh, Brother!, and his dog, Sanchez, otters were the only animals he knew with a sense of humor.

Staring down the small river, hearing the colonies of night frogs fading into silence, he forced down his impulse to begin thinking again about Minna and turned to the problem of getting the inhabitants of the Ramada housing estate to talk with him. But first he needed some help.

He checked his watch and frowned. Eight forty-five was very early for Ernesto Piedra, who, like the otters, usually slept late, but not for the same reasons. Harry dialed his number anyway.

Ernesto had long ago given up cutting cane and sweating in bean fields. Now he worked nights, when he *did* work, relieving people who were asleep of unessential items such as rings, watches, gold chains, and excess folding money. Like Robin Hood he stole from the rich, but unlike that socially conscious thief, Ernesto distributed the money from his fenced objects to the women who were bringing up what he delicately called his *responsibilidads*. His responsibilities had increased to the point that he now had to work four nights a week for the children, leaving only three for the mothers, *las madres*, as Ernesto called them.

"*¡Hola!*," a weak voice responded.

"Sorry to wake you, Ernesto," Harry said, trying to keep his amusement out of his voice, "but I need your help."

"So early?"

"What if I buy you lunch and discuss my problem?"

"Estrella has my car."

"I'll pick you up at twelve. Go back to sleep. Go back to sleep."

La Gallina Lenta was a tiny restaurant at the end of a narrow, unpaved street in a cluster of small houses, sheds, and lean-tos with hens and their chicks and the occasional strutting rooster wandering freely in the street and between the buildings. Harry found the twisty street and its dusty sunlight as well as its inhabitants very much to his liking.

"You are one very weird *gringo,* Harry," Ernesto complained, stepping carefully around the chicken droppings, "Why do you like these *sitios campesino?*"

"It's a relief from the rest of Avola," Harry replied. Not quite true—he simply *did* like local eateries.

His companion only shook his head in disapproval.

It had been a while since Harry had seen Ernesto, and he thought the slender, handsome man with his curly black hair and soulful eyes was beginning to show some wear. Threads of silver streaked his hair, and he was thickening a little around the middle.

"When they were seated at a tiny, Formica-topped table beside an open window in which a yellow tomcat with a torn ear and various other scars of battle was lying in the sun, sleeping off the night's excesses, Harry called Ernesto's attention to the cat.

"In cat years," Harry said, managing not to grin, "he's a little older than you. See what's ahead of you?"

"Very funny, Harry. Why did you drag me down here?"

"I need to talk with some people in the *La Ramada* housing project off Forty-One East. Do you know it?"

"Guatemalans," Ernesto said without enthusiasm.

"Do you know anyone there?"

"Ernesto shook his head."

"How about going in there with me?"

"It would be a big waste of time," Ernesto told him.

"Why?"

"No one would talk to us."

"Don't tell me they don't speak Spanish," Harry protested,

recalling what Jim and Hodges had said about them.

"They speak it all right and English, too, most of them, but not with you and me asking the questions."

A small, dark woman with a long, black pigtail and a red and yellow apron asked for their orders.

Harry chose the quesadillas, and Ernesto, rice, beans, and pulled pork with green chilies.

"Mucho caliente," Harry said.

Ernesto looked at the woman and smiled. "Si," he said, *"pero, muy bien."*

The woman blushed and smiled back. Harry watched the exchange with a mingling of amused pleasure, envy, and admiration.

"You ought not to be let out without supervision," he told Ernesto when the woman was gone.

Ernesto sighed and looked sad again.

"The source of all your *responsibilidads,*" Harry said, laughing.

"Exacto," Ernesto agreed.

"Back to my problem," Harry said. "What do I do?"

"Find someone who speaks Quiche."

"Quiche?" Harry asked.

"A Mayan language, spoken by many of the mountain people there."

"Guatemala," Harry said, bringing a nod from Ernesto. "Do you know anyone who speaks it?"

"Our waitress," Ernesto answered with a grin.

"I don't think I'd get far with her Quiche," Harry said, "and she doesn't understand my English."

"No. Let me work on it. I will call you."

They ate their lunch, and as they were leaving, Harry mentioned Jim's comment about the increased number of shootings the police had to deal with. Ernesto nodded.

41

"Everyone has a gun and is ready to use it," Ernesto said grimly. "It has become so dangerous that I may have to give up you know what. More and more, I fear for my life."

Harry dropped a hand on Ernesto's shoulder and said, "With good reason, *amigo.*"

"There are times when one wonders," Tucker said to Harry sadly, "what we're coming to."

Harry had just finished telling Tucker what had happened to Minna.

Tucker sighed, shook his head, and added, still solemn, "But I suppose the truth is we're the same mix of good and bad we've always been, and in some the bad is real bad."

He pushed back from the table. June bugs, a month early, were banging against the screen door, drawn out of the darkness by the lamp burning on the table.

"I'm going to have a glass of plum brandy. Can I pour you one?"

"Yes, and fill the glass."

"I remember a couple of lines of irreverent poetry that seem to fit in here," Tucker said, getting to his feet, " 'And malt does more than Milton can to justify God's ways to man.' The ale isn't ready to drink, but I think the brandy will do."

When Tucker set the brimming tumbler in front of him, Harry said, "I can't stop thinking about what happened for more than a few minutes at a time, and, worse than that, I can't do anything but wait for Katherine to call."

"Proliferation," Tucker said, sipping his brandy.

They were sitting at Tucker's kitchen table, the remains of dinner spread out before them.

"What?" Harry asked.

"It's like what your tongue does when you've chipped a tooth. It keeps going back to the chip over and over until it just about

42

wears you out."

"The mind," Harry said with a wry smile, "keeps revisiting the event."

"That's it, and the negative feelings proliferate."

Harry was about to say *respond* when the moonlit peace of the surrounding night was shredded by piercing screams, squeals, and roars, punctuated with the sound of things snapping, ripping, and being torn apart.

Both men came onto their feet running. Harry was out the kitchen door first because Tucker detoured past the fireplace to grab his shotgun and a handful of shells from the shelf under the gun. Harry had his CZ in his hand as he crossed the back stoop, trying to locate the source of the eruption.

"It's the garden," Tucker said, having cleared the stoop. "I'll bet you I know . . ."

Harry lost the last part of what Tucker had said as the old farmer broke into a run and disappeared around the corner of the house in the direction of the barn and the garden. Close on Tucker's heels, Harry broke out of the shadow of the house into the full moonlight and was nearly run down by Oh, Brother! who came thundering out of the barn and shot past the two men and plunged into the garden where Harry could see dark figures leaping and racing and making horrific sounds that raised the hair on Harry's neck.

In the next moment Harry heard Sanchez yelp with what could only have been pain.

"Those devils!" Tucker shouted, pulling to a stop and firing two blasts from his shotgun into the air above the garden.

Half deafened by the gun's roar, Harry kept running and was in the garden before he understood what was happening.

"Pigs!" he shouted in astonishment. "There's pigs in the garden!"

"Watch yourself!" Tucker said, stopping beside Harry. "Their

43

teeth are like razors. Where's Sanchez?"

There were pigs running in every direction, making more noise than a train wreck, and in the middle of the fray was Oh, Brother!, plunging back and forth like a black avenging angel, kicking, striking, and occasionally putting his teeth into a pig's backside if it wasn't moving fast enough.

"I can't see him, but I heard him yell," Harry shouted over the din.

Then it was over as suddenly as it had begun. Oh, Brother!, Harry, and Tucker were standing in the eerie silence of the garden as the last pigs vanished into the woods.

"Where is he?" Tucker asked Oh, Brother!.

The mule swung around and trotted over to the far side of the garden and put his head down into the broken corn plants.

Tucker dropped onto his knees beside the dog, lying sprawled on the dirt and broken plants. In the moonlight Harry could see that Sanchez's side had been ripped open in a long, horizontal wound that was bleeding freely.

"Harry," Tucker said in a tense voice, "I need towels. He's cut badly."

"Right," Harry said, already turning, "and I'll call Heather Parkinson."

"We'll need her," Tucker said.

Harry holstered his CZ and ran back to the house, taking Tucker's shotgun with him. Once inside, he called the vet. After asking a few questions, she told him she was leaving as soon as she could get her gear into the truck, after which Harry grabbed the towels, Tucker's five-cell flashlight, and the large bottle of hydrogen peroxide Tucker kept under the kitchen sink and raced back to the garden.

Sanchez lifted his head when Harry arrived, but he was obviously in pain and dropped it again, giving up on being sociable.

"He's losing blood the whole length of him," Tucker said in a low and worried voice, getting to work with the towels and disinfectant. "Fold and roll this second towel and lay it on mine as I unroll this one. The more pressure we can keep on the tear, the more we slow the bleeding."

While the two men worked, Oh, Brother! stood over them, watching and from time to time looking at the woods in the direction the pigs had fled.

"What cut him like that?" Harry asked.

"One of the sows raked him with a tusk by the looks of the wound," Tucker replied, sitting back on his heels. "We're lucky there wasn't a mature boar in that herd."

"Much larger tusks," Harry said.

"He'd have ripped the guts out of him," Tucker agreed.

"You know," Harry said, looking up at the mule, "I think it was Oh, Brother! who saved Sanchez. I think the pigs were swarming him when Oh, Brother! put his stick into them. He kicked one of them right out of the garden. I wouldn't be surprised if in the morning we find it dead out there."

Sanchez, who had been stoically enduring everything Tucker had done to him, suddenly began to whine and try to get to his feet, but Harry and Tucker held him down, and after a couple of minutes, he gave up and collapsed again, panting in short, quick breaths.

"We've done what we can," Tucker said, "but it's not enough. If she doesn't get here soon . . ."

Just then Parkinson's pickup rumbled up the driveway, its headlights pitching and bobbing. She jolted to a stop with the truck's lights pouring over them.

"Let me see him," she said, pushing Harry out of the way and more gently but still firmly moving Tucker to one side.

She began by gently lifting the end of the towel off his shoulder.

"Something did a good job on you, fella," she told the dog,

dropping the towel and looking into his eye with a pen light and getting her hand under the towel to feel his heart beat.

She rummaged for a moment in her bag and came out with a syringe and gave him an injection.

"That will make you feel better," she said, "and now we're going to get you into the house, and we're going to do this carefully and very quickly. Harry, get your hands under his shoulders. Tucker, you reach under back here. I'm going to take his head."

She moved around to the front of the dog. "At the count of three: one, two, three, and up. Now go. Go, Harry! Oh, Brother!, get the hell out of the way!"

It was an odd-looking group that scrambled across the garden, heading in a kind of crippled crab run for the kitchen with Oh, Brother! crowding them from behind. They had some trouble getting through the door, but, mercifully, the injection had put Sanchez beyond pain, and once inside, Parkinson said, "Hold it."

Letting the dog's head dangle for a moment, she swiftly cleared the table of its dishes and glasses and, lifting the dog's head again, said, "All together, onto the table with him and set him down carefully."

Blood had soaked the towels and was soon dripping off the table.

"Boil about a quart of water and organize some lighting around the table while I get a couple of bags from the truck," Heather told them, running for the door with her brown hair flying out from her Red Sox cap.

"She's no bigger than a wood mouse," Tucker said, when the screen door slammed behind her and he began gathering table and floor lamps, "but she's got more courage than any two other people I know."

"Remember how she walked into that cage with Weissmuller

and sank that knock-out needle into him while he was snarling and growling and tearing his trap apart, trying to get at her?" Harry asked, filling Tucker's electric kettle and plugging it in.

"I do, but she's got her hands full here," Tucker said with a sigh, looking at the dog as he set a floor lamp at each end of the table. "If she saves him, it will be a miracle."

"She'll do it," Harry said, trying to sound convincing. It shouldn't have been difficult; Heather Parkinson's encounter with Weissmuller, the wild dog Tucker tamed, was only one of many near miracles performed over the years by the diminutive veterinarian.

He was almost as worried about Tucker as he was about Sanchez. The old farmer was pale as the moon. Heather came rushing back into the kitchen, carrying two battered cases.

"OK," she said, a little short of breath, banging down her cases and unpacking them on the chairs she had pulled out from the table. "I'm going to have to shave all around that wound, clean it again, and then stitch it up. Once that's done, I'll have a look at the rest of him."

"What are his chances?" Tucker asked, his voice a bit shaky.

"I'd say fair. He's lost a lot of blood."

She interrupted what she was saying to scrub her hands in the sink, then pull on a pair of surgical gloves.

"He's showing signs of stress," she said. That's what the panting is all about—but no major arteries are severed, so I'm not too worried yet."

"Listen up," she continued, striding toward the table. "I'm going to clamp that wound shut, but that's not going to fully stop the bleeding. Harry, get over here and use these sterile rags to mop up the blood so I can see what I'm doing. Here we go."

"How can I help?" Tucker asked.

"You bring me things from those bags when I need them."

"Is it all right if I stroke his head?"

Heather glanced up, giving him a quick smile.

"Can't hurt," she told him.

"He's still bleeding too much," Tucker said after the clamps were in place.

"It looks worse than it is. Try not to worry," she told him.

The kettle was whistling. She stopped what she was doing to pour some of the water into an enamel pan.

"Hogs," she said suddenly, glanced again at Tucker, and plunged an ancient shaving brush into the pan then whipped it around in an equally old blue and white china mug and began lathering Sanchez's side. "If we don't get a handle on them pretty soon, we're going to be worse off than Hawaii."

Harry guessed that she was trying to distract Tucker and gave a silent cheer. She put aside the mug and brush and lifted a heavy safety razor out of one of her cases, and set to work shaving the dog.

"The latest estimation," she said without looking up from her work, "is that there are about 500,000 wild hogs in this state. Have either of you ever seen one in the woods?"

"I've seen a lot of them and eaten my fair share," Tucker replied. "The Spaniards brought them in here. I believe the first came with Ponce de Leon and Hernando de Soto, who came ashore in what's now Charlotte Harbor in 1539."

Harry suppressed a grin. She had found Tucker's obsession with the state's history and was working it beautifully.

"That's it," Heather said, nodding and giving her razor a final rinse. "Then Eurasian boars were imported into the upper states for game animals in the nineteenth century."

She set aside the razor and pulled off her gloves, going on talking as she examined the wound.

"Their number isn't the entire problem," she said. "They're host to brucellosis, tuberculosis, anthrax, and half a dozen more pathogens, which are not good news for cattle or people."

She stood up and stretched her back.

"OK, now for the stitches," she said when she was finished. "Harry, work with those rags just ahead of me, and when I say the word, you take out the next clamp. The blood's going to run a little more freely. Just don't faint."

"I'll try not to," he said with a straight face as they bent to their tasks.

"Some go down like a tall tree falling," Tucker observed.

"Tell me about it," she said, tying off the first stitch.

As she worked, swiftly and efficiently, she went on talking to Tucker, and Harry found himself joining in the conversation. As he grew more accustomed to what he was doing, he became aware of the sounds of the surrounding night. Beyond the stoop, Oh, Brother!, clearly concerned about Sanchez, was walking back and forth restlessly.

An uneasy wind rattled the palm fronds, and the tree frogs and insect orchestra, backed up by the hooting of a pair of barred owls, filled the woods with their eerie music.

Listening to the night sounds, Sanchez's labored breathing, and Heather Parkinson talking about pigs as she worked and all the while anxiously watching Tucker, who was paler than ever and still silent, Harry thought bitterly that order and tranquility were ephemeral, not that it was a new idea. He found that the destruction of Tucker's beloved garden, coming as it had on the heels of the attack on Minna, was both a shock and a harsh reminder of the fragility of humans and their constructions.

"Harry," Parkinson said, "I saw two glasses of that plum brandy on the sideboard. Give one to Tucker. Tucker, you drink some of it and don't stint, you hear me?"

"I don't see . . ." he began impatiently.

"Drink it," she told him. "Harry—get back here."

As they worked on the dog, Harry, glancing at Tucker now and then, was relieved to see that the brandy did seem to have put a little color in his cheeks. The relief he felt reminded him of just how much he loved his old friend.

Caught in that thought, Harry remembered Blake's line: "The invisible worm/ That flies in the night . . ." and shivered.

"You're not going to quit on me are you, Brock?" Heather demanded.

"Not yet," he said, grateful for the distraction.

Working beside her held back the darkness.

Ten minutes later Parkinson said, "He'll do," stepping back from the table, her shirt soaked with sweat and a hank of hair plastered to the side of her face. "Let's lift him off the table, Harry. Tucker, get something for him to lie on."

Tucker hurried off and returned with a brown woolen blanket, which he folded and laid on the floor beside the stove.

"Put him there," he said. "When he wakes up, he can look out the door and see Oh, Brother!"

At the sound of his name, the mule snorted softly. Heather laughed.

"Racehorses sometimes have a dog for a friend," she said, "but Oh, Brother! is the first mule I've known to have one."

When Heather had washed and changed her shirt and come back to the kitchen, her hair freed from her baseball cap, Harry was scrubbing the table, and Tucker was sitting cross-legged on the floor beside Sanchez, stroking the dog's head.

"He's going to be fine, Tucker," she said a little sharply, fists on her hips. "but I'm not so sure about you. Up! Up! I want you in bed. Harry can do whatever's left to be done. Sanchez will sleep for a while, and so should you."

"I'll stay," Harry said to Tucker, already protesting. "Heather's right. You need bed rest."

Tucker got slowly to his feet, fending off Harry's and Heather's efforts to help him. His thin shoulders sagged and his face was gray with weariness, but his voice was still strong.

"Heather," he said, "without you, Sanchez wouldn't be alive. Thank you. There aren't words to tell you how grateful I am."

"Wait until you get my bill," she told him, pulling on her cap. "You'll think of something to say. Harry, help me carry my gear back to the truck."

6

Two days had passed since the first battle of the Pig War—Tucker's description of what he saw as an evolving event—and on a morning proving to be as hot as the rest, Harry was reluctantly settled at his desk, working on the hated reports, although they were kicking sand in his face.

"What would Boswell have been without Johnson?" Tucker had asked him earlier when Harry complained about them.

"A happier man," Harry told him, but too pleased with the good report Heather had given Tucker on Sanchez's condition to pursue the matter.

Reprieve from report writing came in the form of a call from Ernesto Piedra.

"I have found someone who speaks Quiche," the young man said.

"You don't sound too happy about it," Harry said. "Have you been missing sleep again?"

"*Very funny*, Harry," he said sourly.

"OK, I'm sorry. What's the matter?"

Harry regarded Ernesto as a temperamental artist working in a difficult medium and treated him gently.

"There is a problem."

"It's usually money."

"With Soñadora is no *dinero*."

"Who is he?"

"Is no he!" Ernesto protested. "Is she. *Mujer mucha*."

"Did you ever meet one who wasn't 'much woman'?" Harry asked with a laugh. "What's her problem?"

Ernesto laughed, surprising Harry because it was something he almost never did.

"The problem is you, *amigo,*" Ernesto said, wrecking Harry's grin.

"How can it be with me? I don't even know her."

"She knows you. You are *un hombre blanco.*"

"You're having too much fun here," Harry said, deciding Ernesto was pulling his leg.

"*Si, pero* I am not making jokes. Soñadora is other."

Harry paused and said, "Do you mean *different?*"

"Very different."

"But she can speak Quiche and English?"

"And Spanish."

"Will she talk to me?"

"Possibly."

"Do you have her number?"

"No, but here is an address."

Feeling more depressed every moment, Harry drove slowly along a seriously potholed street in one of the poorest sections of East Avola and stopped in front of a low stucco building with paint peeling off the walls and bare, cracked wood showing on the window and door frames. A barren gravel rectangle occupied the space where the lawn should have been. Only the black iron grates protecting the windows looked new.

Getting out of the Rover into near silence, broken only by the sour cawing of a fish crow, Harry paused on the dirt yard and looked around, feeling the skin on the back of his neck crawl. The place smelled of dust, heat, and hard times. The neighboring buildings, partially visible through the tangles of dusty brush separating them, appeared to be as sullen and neglected as number thirty-seven.

Resisting a strong urge to clamber back into the Rover and get the hell out of there, Harry walked briskly to the scarred door set in a tiny recessed porch in the front of the building. A square of bleached cardboard hung from a nail driven into the door, bearing the word *Salvamento.*

As he wondered who or what was being saved, he pointed his keyless entry at the Rover and pressed the lock button. Then he knocked on the door.

"Entrar!"

He opened the door and stepped into a room loud with the voices of five clearly Hispanic women speaking Spanish on telephone connections while typing in front of computer screens. The clatter of the key pads and the rattle of an air conditioner stuck in one of the back windows added to the din. A sixth woman, facing the door, had risen from her desk to greet the visitor and did not seem at all happy with what she was looking at.

She was light-skinned, slender, and dressed in an orange blouse and blue, pleated skirt, caught at the waist by a wide black belt with a heavy silver and jade buckle. Her black hair hung over her left shoulder in a thick, shining braid. Harry was trying to make an ethnic connection when she spoke.

"Can I help you?" she asked in slightly accented English, walking toward Harry as if to keep him from coming any further into the room.

He noted that she moved with exceptional grace. A dancer? he wondered, noting her intensely black eyes. The moment she spoke, conversation in the room stopped, and the women turned to look at him. The sound of the air conditioner seemed to double in volume.

Harry looked around the room, crowded with computers, a fax machine, a couple of dozen old and dented black metal filing cabinets, and tables piled with more files. He could not imagine what these women were doing. For a wild moment he thought he had stumbled into a betting parlor.

"I think I've made a mistake," he said, slightly disconcerted by the dark eyes bent on him and the sudden silence.

"Are you looking for someone?" she asked.

Harry turned back to her and saw for the first time that she was beautiful. There was no other word for it. Her high cheekbones, shining hair, and large, startling black eyes kept Harry staring longer than the situation called for, and he stumbled over his words a little, trying to redeem himself.

"Yes, well, I am, but I don't . . ."

"See her here, Mr. Brock?"

For a moment a slight smile softened her austere features.

"You must be . . ." he hesitated again.

"Soñadora Asturias."

To Harry's relief, the hum of voices rose around them again, and the women returned to their work.

"I'm afraid you are very busy," Harry told her, thinking all the while that it would be very easy to lose himself in those eyes, all the time doing exactly that.

"Yes, I am," Asturias replied with some edge. "Ernesto was not very clear about why you wanted to talk with me."

Harry pulled himself together.

"It's complicated and will take some explaining. Perhaps, you would let me buy you lunch."

He would have said more, but she glanced at her watch and said, "There's a place not far from here. I'll give you half an hour, and I'll buy my own lunch."

"You don't let strangers buy you a meal?" Harry asked.

She stepped past him, pulled open the door, and waved him through it.

"No, I don't," she said.

The restaurant was very like the one where he had eaten with Ernesto, and Harry liked it immediately. It was only lacking the one-eyed cat, he thought with some amusement, and the chickens weren't allowed to wander around, picking up crumbs from under the tables.

"You're not afraid the food will make you ill?" Asturias asked him as they were sitting down.

"I figure if you're eating here, I'm safe," he said but didn't get a smile.

Harry looked at the card that served as a menu and found he couldn't read anything on it.

"Nahuatl derivative," she said. "Shall I order for both of us?"

"Yes. It would be better than ending up with boiled chicken's feet."

"Do you think that's what Indian people eat?" she asked.

Harry laid down the card, folded his hands, and looked at her in silence.

"They don't," she said.

"Is that an apology?" he asked carefully.

"What do you think?"

She put her own menu down. Harry met a gaze devoid of warmth and thought that her eyes, beautiful as they were, were flat as a snake's. The burning sensation in his face in response to her question told him all he needed to know about where this conversation would go in the next three seconds if he didn't change directions.

"I'd better tell you who I am and why I'm here," he said. "You know my name. I'm a P.I., and I live on Bartram's Hammock."

"In a house leased to you by the state," she added. "Your

only neighbor is an elderly man by the name of Tucker La-Beau."

"Did Ernesto tell you all that?" Harry asked, unsure whether or not he was pleased.

"No. I'm very careful who I allow near me."

Captain Jim Snyder, Tequesta County Sheriff's Department," he said, carefully monitoring his voice, "asked me to go into a Guatemalan section of Avola and ask anyone who would talk to me for information about a particularly bloody double homicide that the police believe took place in their community. They will not talk to the police. Although it seems farfetched, Captain Snyder is convinced the men were killed while transporting a woman being sold into slavery. I agreed to help, but I don't speak either Spanish or the Indian language spoken there. I called Ernesto Piedra. He gave me your address."

It was a long speech, and giving it calmly cooled Harry down.

"You have a quick temper," Asturias said.

"It's childish, but I don't like being disliked."

"Especially by women?"

"Probably. Can we move on, or would you prefer to declare victory and go back to your office?"

"Do you know what we do in my *office*, as you call it?"

Apparently, she doesn't answer questions, Harry thought.

"It looks like a betting parlor," he said, then added, "Which is OK with me."

Asturias flushed, clenched her fists, started to speak, stopped herself, and suddenly dropped back in her chair and burst out laughing. It was infectious enough to make Harry smile.

"What's funny?"

"You are," she said, motioning to the shy young girl in a colored skirt who had led them to their table and was now hovering by the bar.

Asturias gave their order in a swift flow of words that were incomprehensible to Harry.

"We are called *Salvamento*," Asturias said when the girl left. "But we gamble in lives, not souls."

She was no longer expressing amusement. Harry was puzzled.

"I don't . . ."

Asturias gripped the edge of the pine table with both hands as if trying to keep herself or it from levitating.

"How is it possible for people in this Anglo world to be so ignorant?" she said, her eyes narrowing with anger or disgust.

Her passionate denunciation startled Harry, and not knowing what she was so furious about made him wonder how stable this woman was.

"Whoa," he said, holding up both hands, palms facing her. "I haven't got a clue what you're talking about."

All the while this conversation, flawed and frustrating as it was, was unfolding, Harry, unaware of what was happening, was opening the door into Soñadora Asturias's intensely private world. Fully awake to her presence, and floundering between anger and fascination, he hung, his breath almost suspended, wondering whether or not she would take his head off.

She paused, her face bright, her eyes burning, and released her breath in a long sigh. Then she let go of the table and planted her arms on it.

"You really don't know, do you?" she asked after a lengthy pause, her voice dropping an octave.

"No," he said, watching her closely. "Tell me."

After a brief pause, she said, her voice growing slower and softer and freighted with pain, "We are working to rescue women, mostly women but some men, who have become slaves. In a twenty-mile radius from where we are sitting there are at least five hundred people living in the utmost degradation, who have lost their freedom in this way."

Harry found what he had heard almost impossible to believe,

in part because, if true, it was so horrific there was no way to fit it into his concept of life in southwest Florida. How could what Jim and now Soñadora Asturias had told him be true?

"How can you know this?" he asked.

"Through a great deal of hard work," she answered crisply, "and what you're really saying is, 'I don't believe it.' "

"Captain Jim Snyder of the Tequesta County Sheriff's Department told me people were being smuggled into Tequesta County from Mexico and Guatemala and sold like animals. It doesn't compute. Where's the economic incentive?"

"In the free labor," she replied.

Their food came. Harry glanced at his plate in disappointment. Chicken, corn, beans, tortillas.

His face must have registered the letdown.

"Taste it," she said.

He started with the corn. It was delicious. He said so.

"They grow their own," she said, putting down her fork and digging in with a spoon. "This was picked less than an hour ago," she told him, her mouth half full.

Having reminded himself that this was Florida where gardens produced all year, he paused to watch her eat and grinned.

"What?" she asked, pausing, her spoon just short of her mouth.

"You," he said and gave himself two points. Later he would think that perhaps her single-minded attack on the food may have had a dark beginning.

She ignored his sally and said, "Eat."

He did not need encouragement. The food was excellent.

When she had cleaned her plate, she described the efforts *Salvamento* had made in the past two years to trace the people from the Mexican and Guatemalan villages who had left for the States and apparently vanished. In the process they had uncovered a labyrinth of criminal trafficking connections, stretching from Panama to the United States.

"All of us in the organization have either had someone in our own family or known of someone who went missing. In the beginning we had only rumors to substantiate our suspicions that these people had been kidnapped. We found that almost none of the lost ones had died en route to this country."

"I'm surprised you could find that much," Harry said, thinking how easy it must be for a poor person to vanish in Guatemala and Mexico.

She nodded. "You are assuming they would not be seeking attention, and no one would be paying attention," she responded.

Harry saw by the sharpening of her voice that he had been guilty of another chicken feet mistake, but she passed over it.

"It is an ironic fact that, all too often, only when someone dies does she become conspicuous. The police appear. Reports are written and filed. At first, we found only the ones who had died."

"How did you find out what was happening to the ones who hadn't died?" Harry asked, interested now in Soñadora's story.

"Am I boring you?" she asked at once, leaning back from him, her face stiffening.

"No," he told her. "I'm putting myself in your place, wondering how I would have solved the problem."

She smiled and leaned forward again.

"I forgot. You're a professional investigator."

"It would appear I could learn something from you," he said with no intention to flatter her. The problem seemed to him a very tough but interesting one.

"For months we learned nothing. We found no one, but our constant probing, talking through intermediaries to police in three countries, interviewing anyone who we thought might have encountered the lost ones, passing out cards with *Salva-*

mento printed on them along with telephone numbers where we could be reached, finally brought results."

"Let me guess," Harry said, feeling pleased with himself. "Someone, who had been cheated out of some money, called and told you what had happened to one of the missing people."

"That happened later. Our first proof came from a very brave thirteen-year-old girl from a tiny village in southern Mexico. She was smuggled into the country and sold to the traffickers, who sold her to a brothel. Eventually, one of her customers gave her one of our cards. She kept it and when she escaped and after a week of hiding days and walking nights, finally got up the courage to call us. For nearly a year she had been kept as a sex slave in a brothel not a hundred miles from here. One of the doctors we use found that by some miracle she was HIV free and had contracted no serious sexual diseases. We kept her under wraps until we were sure she had not been followed. Then we sent her home."

"You didn't call the police?" Harry asked in surprise.

"Once we knew she was safely in her village, we told the police in Punta Gorda what we had discovered. They acted quickly, made arrests, tried the people running the operation, and gave them long prison sentences."

"You don't sound very pleased with the outcome," Harry said, waiting for a smile and seeing only Soñadora's face grow more somber.

"There were eight more women in that house between eighteen and forty-two. They slept and worked on bare mattresses in a room fifteen feet square. They were fed two meals a day. The pittance they were paid all went back to people running the operation who sold them cigarettes, cocaine, and candy, and fined them if they spent too much time in the toilet, if they kept lights on after three A.M., if they refused to do something a customer wanted done, the list was very long. The forty-two-year-old woman who had been there three years had almost forgotten how to talk."

"What happened to them?" Harry asked.

"They were turned over to the Immigration people and imprisoned all over again as illegal aliens. We are working to get them released and returned to their homes, but the bureaucracy is almost impenetrable, the laws draconian, and the department woefully understaffed."

She paused, frowning. "It is all complicated here because we cannot deal directly with the police or even tell them who we are."

"I'm sorry," Harry said, feeling both responsible and angry.

She shrugged.

"The good news is that at long last the police have begun to admit we have a problem, probably because like your Captain Snyder the side effects of human trafficking, general mayhem of the sort usually associated with drug smuggling and distribution, has begun to surface in their jurisdictions."

"Will you help me with the Guatemalans?" he asked.

She frowned and shook her head. Harry was sure she was going to say no, but something entirely different must have been occupying her thoughts.

"Yes," she said after a lengthy pause, "but we may both end up dead."

7

Still blindfolded, Rigoberta was pulled unceremoniously out of the van and told in gutter Spanish to stand where she was. There were cries and protests from others, who, she supposed, were also being treated as she had been. A moment later, someone roughly planted her right hand on the shoulder of the person in front of her. From its thickness, she guessed it was a man's. A voice told her to walk.

As she set off in a shuffling gait, clutching her bag in her free arm, a woman began to cry.

"*¡Cállate!*" a man shouted.

The command was followed by a loud slap. Someone gasped in pain. Rigoberta guessed the woman who had begun crying had been struck to silence her. What kind of place was this where her uncle had sent her? She suddenly remembered her aunt's evasiveness and refusal to look at her while Rigoberta prepared to leave. Had her aunt known what was going to happen to her? Even approved? Was it possible?

The line stopped and Rigoberta bumped into the man in front of her. Someone bumped into her and grunted.

"*¡Continuar!*" the same harsh voice commanded.

The shoulder she was holding slid up and out of her hand, and at the next step her foot struck a riser.

Steps, she thought and climbed them one at a time, being hurried along by those pushing up behind her. Then someone fell and there was more shouting and confusion. The air had changed when she reached the top of the stairs, and she surmised they were inside a building of some sort. She wanted to push up her blindfold, to see where she was, then thought better of it. She would know soon enough.

She was pushed back by the others crowding into the new space, and a moment later she found herself pressed against a wall. More confusion, raised voices. Then several voices began repeating, "You, *you, you.*"

More cursing and protests. She assumed that some of the people were being taken out of the group. Then a door slammed, and a woman's voice, firm but not harsh, told them to take off their blindfolds. Blinking in the sudden light, Rigoberta jammed the blindfold into her sack and through squinted eyes took in her surroundings. She was in a room with ten other women. It had yellow walls, two barred windows, and a single, bare light in the center of the ceiling. Except for the bars on the windows, it was an ordinary room. Perhaps I am in a house, she thought. The woman began to speak.

"I am Maria," the woman said in Spanish. "I already know your names. Answer when I call yours."

She was a large woman with graying-black hair pulled back into a bun behind her head. Rigoberta watched and listened closely, trying to understand all that was said and equally determined to know the person she was dealing with, because she knew intuitively that this woman held the answer to what was going to happen to her. She carried a list in one hand and a cell phone in the other. One of the first things Rigoberta would learn about Maria was that she was never separated from the phone.

By the time Maria had read the last name, Rigoberta was able to repeat the names and attach each to a person. Most of the women were young—younger, she thought, than she. Three were Anglos, and she could not judge their ages as easily. They had thin, stringy hair, narrow faces, and dark-ringed, sunken eyes. Rigoberta wondered if they were *tuberculoso* or, possibly, *addictas.*

What Maria told them did nothing to lessen her fears. They would work. They would be fed and paid. They could buy whatever personal items they required, but for an unspecified length of time, they would not be allowed to go outside. When some of the women protested, Maria said, her voice hardening, "The restriction is for your protection."

"From what?" one of the dark women demanded in Spanish.

"The police. Now Gomez will show you your beds. He will waken you at five. Work begins at six."

A hulking Mexican, carrying in his right hand what looked to Rigoberta like a long ruler, came into the room, grinning at them. For a moment Rigoberta thought he was simple minded until she saw the expression on his face as his eyes slid over each of the women, herself included.

Rigoberta and the others were herded down a narrow hall and into a small, bare room with eleven mattresses arranged on the floor, leaving only enough space to walk between them. There were two windows, both heavily barred and whitewashed. She walked to the first corner on her right and sat down on the mattress, then turned to face the door. She would have a wall at her head and on her left side. It was something.

When the eight women had chosen their mattresses, Gomez, waving the ruler at them, said in a deep, rasping voice that if they needed a bathroom, they were to knock on the door. Only one at a time could go and for no longer than five minutes. With that he closed the door, shutting off the ceiling light. The room remained dimly lit by a nightlight plugged into an outlet in the wall halfway between Rigoberta and the door.

"What brought you to this shit hole?" the woman beside her asked.

Rigoberta said *Hazel* to herself, identifying one of the Anglos, sitting cross-legged on her mattress, her dress pulled carelessly above her bony knees.

"No *habla englesa*," Rigoberta answered.

Hazel, snapping her gum, tried again in rough Spanish.

Before answering, Rigoberta wondered why she wanted to know, then, too preoccupied with what had happened to her to care, replied, "To work, to bring my children."

"Where you from?"

"Guatemala."

"Thought so. Indian, right?"

Rigoberta nodded, finding herself grateful to be speaking with another woman, one close to her own age.

"Why are you here?" she asked.

Hazel grinned. "I needed to get out of sight quick."

"*No comprender*," Rigoberta said.

"*Chapas*," Hazel told her with another grin.

Rigoberta smiled. She knew about the police and the necessity to avoid them. Then, reverting to her own thoughts, she said, "I think we will be kept here."

"They'll try," Hazel agreed, "but when I've been here as long as I want to, I'll leave. If you want to go, I'll take you with me."

"We will be worked to the end of our strength, and then they will kill us."

"It won't happen," Hazel said, shaking her head emphatically.

"What is there to stop them?"

"Me," Hazel said cheerfully and flung herself back on her mattress then popped back up again.

"There's one thing to know—say, what's your name?"

"Rigoberta."

"No shit? I'll call you Riggs. That all right?"

Rigoberta nodded, a little shocked by such rudeness but

found that it pleased her.

"OK," Hazel said. "Here's the most important thing. Watch yourself with that Gomez, and if it comes to it, let the bastard screw you because if you don't, he'll beat the shit out of you and keep on doing it every chance he gets."

Rigoberta was surprised and puzzled.

"Do you know this Gomez?"

Hazel gave a bitter laugh as she lay down again.

"Riggs," she said, "I've known baboons like him all my life. You mind what I say, you hear?"

Rigoberta nodded, having no intention of having intercourse with Gomez. The thought of it made her shudder with disgust. Then she remembered her knife and felt better. Pushing her sack under her head, she slept.

8

The days inched by for Harry, while he waited for Minna to be tested. He had talked with her twice, and she had responded patiently to his efforts to interest her, but he had not been fooled. He was not getting past the barrier she had erected between herself and everything else. The energetic, funny, happy child was gone, and her place was taken by a brooding double who gazed out at the world with fear and rage. The transformation wrung Harry's heart.

Predictably, the pain and stress Katherine was experiencing had driven her back into herself, and although Harry talked with her at least once a day, it was pretty much a one-way conversation.

As for himself, he continued to deal with his own grief and frustration by working, and when Soñadora called him, to say she had carved out some time for him, he said a prayer of thanks for the distraction.

"Now remember, Harry," Jim Snyder told him when Harry came to his office and said without enthusiasm that he and Asturias were going into La Ramada. "Don't reveal that you're a P.I. Let Ms. Asturias do the talking. It's important that everyone thinks you're just her backup."

"How am I supposed to know what she's asking and they're answering?" Harry asked.

The longer he listened to Jim, the more dubious he became about the project.

"What's your cover story?" Hodges demanded.

"We haven't decided," Harry said, not having discussed it with Soñadora.

"Keep it simple," Jim warned, frowning at Harry.

"Tell 'em you're working for the *Avola Banner*," Hodges said, "and that you're doing a story on violence in the immigrant communities."

"And have the door slammed in your face," Jim said angrily, his ears turning red. "Then be gunned down before they can get out of the association."

"Those people like it when they think they're being paid attention to!" Hodges protested.

Their wrangling gave Harry time to think about Hodges's question and he waited for a break in the argument.

"We'll say we're members of a religious group—I don't have a name yet—and are trying to collect ideas for ways to bring people to church," Harry said. "That will give us a chance to bring up the issue of violence without sounding as if we're on some kind of fishing expedition."

"Sneaky but good," Hodges said at once.

"I still don't see how I'm going to know what's being said," Harry complained.

"Do you trust this woman?" Jim asked.

"Yes."

"There's your answer," Hodges said with a broad smile.

Harry suggested the plan as soon as he picked up Soñadora at the Salvamento office and headed for the East Trail. She did not like it.

"What's wrong with it?" he asked, still thinking it was brilliant.

"It would probably work," she said with apparent reluctance, "but I don't like the group part."

"We could say that we're connected to a church then," Harry suggested. "St. Jude's On the Water would be a good one. They would know nothing about it, and it's just the kind of thing the Episcopalians are always doing. They probably would have heard of them."

"I don't think I look much like an Episcopalian," she said with a sudden laugh.

Harry looked at her. She had combed out her hair and pinned it back with a tortoiseshell comb. Tumbling across her shoulders and down the back of her dark red blouse, it made a dramatic frame for her pale face and black eyes.

"Episcopalians don't have a special look," he told her with a pleased smile.

He was relieved to hear her laugh, and it occurred to him that she was a remarkably beautiful woman. He had been feeling too miserable to notice, but her laugh drew him out of himself far enough to pay attention.

"Name one you know who looks like me."

Harry couldn't tell what emotion lurked in that simple statement. She was no longer laughing.

"She should be so lucky," he said.

She turned her head from him, but not before he saw that she had blushed.

"Let's give it a try," he said, sensing that it would be a serious mistake to mention the blush to her. "It might work."

"I don't like it," she told him, still avoiding his eyes.

He had a thought.

"You're superstitious," he said. "Are you afraid that something from the Episcopal Church will jump out and bite you?"

"Do you think I am such a fool?" she demanded coldly.

"No. I think the opposite is true," he said. "I'm sorry if I've done chicken feet again."

"Chicken feet?" she demanded, obviously confounded by the phrase.

"Yes," he said, maintaining a serious face. "Indians eat chicken feet. They are also superstitious."

For a moment she stared at him, hard-eyed. Then her face collapsed into a wide smile.

"How will we do it?" she asked.

Harry finished telling her just as they were turning into La Ramada.

"You do the talking. I'll carry the literature and smile," Harry said, pulling his silver Land Rover off the street.

"You will frighten the children," she said. "Get rid of the hat."

"Right," he said, having forgotten he was wearing it.

Tossing it onto the back seat, he lifted two bunches of printed pamphlets out of a cardboard box on the floor behind the driver's seat.

"What's that?" she asked.

"Something I picked up at St. Jude's."

"Let me see."

Harry pulled one of the pamphlets out from the rubber band holding the packet together. It was an eight and a half by twelve inch sheet of heavy, glossy paper, folded three times and printed on all six of the resulting sides.

" 'Beareth all things, believeth all things, hopeth all things, endureth all things,' " Soñadora read in a flat voice, her eyes moving slowly down the page. Harry watched her with interest. "For now we see as through a glass darkly; but then face to face . . . And now abideth faith, hope, charity, these three; but the greatest of these is charity."

She looked at Harry with a puzzled expression.

"It means love," he told her. "The word *charity* means love."

71

"Oh, yes," she said. "I'll remember to tell that to the next thirteen-year-old girl we find imprisoned in a whore house and who has spent ten hours a day for the past two years on a mattress being fucked by whoever staggers through the door."

Harry didn't—couldn't—find any quick reply to that.

"Let's go," she said, dropping the pamphlet on the ground.

Harry watched her march off toward the first house and hurried to catch up with her, telling himself he probably wasn't going to see her in church on Sunday. That made him remember it had been some time since he had been in St. Jude's on anything but business.

Actually, churches gave him quite a bit of business because, more than most institutions, they had to be careful about what they were seen doing, even though it was often good work.

When they had driven into La Ramada, Harry had noticed several children playing in their dusty yards. Now they were deserted.

"Have you noticed the streets are empty?" he asked Soñadora as they approached the house.

"Yes. Are you right-handed?"

Harry said he was.

"Then keep it empty until we see what's going to happen when I knock on this door.

Harry gave her points for having noticed he was wearing a belt holster. He thought it was hidden by his jacket.

"Right," he said, thinking that if he stayed around her a while, he would improve his skills at obeying orders.

The woman who opened the door just enough to see who was on the steps opened it all the way when Soñadora began speaking to her.

"Give her a pamphlet," she told Harry a moment later, "and smile."

Harry passed the small, dark woman—dressed in colorful

traditional clothing—a pamphlet and smiled. To his surprise, she blushed slightly and looked away. After a few more minutes of rapid conversation, Soñadora said, "Let's go."

"Well?" he asked as they walked to the next house.

"You can't write anything down. The entire street is watching. I have a pretty good memory. If we live to get back in your car, I'll tell you. If we don't, it won't matter."

"I like discussing things with you," Harry said.

She expressed surprise and said, "We haven't discussed anything."

"I know," he said.

"Anglos," she said in disgust.

"Chicken feet," he replied.

The woman who was waiting for them with the door open greeted Soñadora before she and Harry reached the steps. Without waiting to be told, Harry passed her a pamphlet and smiled. She fanned herself with it and said something to Soñadora that made both women laugh.

When Soñadora backed off the steps, the woman accompanied them to the next house where they were greeted by the woman of the house, who waved in several other women who were hurrying toward them.

"What's going on?" Harry asked, growing uneasy.

"Stand up straight," she told him. "Look dignified and don't stare and don't fidget."

Stand up straight? Don't stare? Don't fidget? What the hell is she doing? Harry looked over the heads of the gathering women and tried to look serious. The conversation exploding around him had Soñadora turning quickly back and forth to face whoever claimed the group's attention. She said very little but listened intently.

Gradually Harry began to notice that one after another with no obvious intent, each of the women edged through the group until she was standing very close to him and then drifted away. When they had all done that, one of the women asked a question that set all the rest laughing. Soñadora laughed as hard as any of the rest and then gave Harry a long look that made him think she was seeing him in a completely new way. She said something. They laughed again. She turned to Harry, her smile vanishing.

"Pass out the pamphlets. Then we're leaving. Smile at them if you want to."

Harry smiled, but all the women took the pamphlets and quickly turned away, giggling as they did so.

"OK, what happened?" Harry said when he was driving them out of La Ramada.

"Nothing happened," she snapped, "fortunately for us."

"Did you find out anything about the murders?"

"No."

Soñadora pushed back into her seat, looking dissatisfied.

"But I learned enough about what's going on in there to make me very worried."

"You certainly seemed to be having a good time," he said, still irritated by all the laughter, most of which seemed to have been aimed at him.

She flashed him a sharp look and her mouth twitched.

"I told them you were my *compañero de viaje i frazada de seguridad.*"

Harry took a moment to try and sort that out.

"I'm your *security blanket?*" he asked, thoroughly puzzled.

"It means something else in Quiche," she said, and burst out laughing.

Then he got it. His face burned.

"You didn't!" he said, not knowing whether he was pleased or insulted.

"Yes, I did. I got a little carried away with my role."

"And why did all the women come to stand beside me?"

"Just to get a better idea."

He did not pursue that.

"And all the laughing?"

"I said a few other things."

She gave another sputtering laugh.

"At my expense," he said.

He wanted to feel flattered but didn't dare risk it.

"They weren't laughing at you if that's what you're thinking," she said sharply. "Indian women are very forthright and have a healthy view of life's basics. They have few illusions, except perhaps when it comes to religion. But even there they are carrying out their culturally assigned spiritual responsibilities."

Harry was still unsatisfied.

"Thanks for the anthropology lecture, but what does it have to do with what we were supposed to be doing?"

"My comments made them laugh and broke their reserve. They accepted me and spoke very frankly about what was going on in their community, especially about the increasing violence."

Harry gave up and listened.

"I hinted at the men in the white van being killed, but they skirted answering directly. Instead they mentioned that a short time ago a young Guatemalan woman had been wounded by a *blanko*. I asked where she was now. They said she vanished, which I understood to mean it was not a thing to be discussed, but that she was no longer in La Ramada."

"Did they say anything about the white man?"

She shook her head.

"Instead, they spoke nonspecifically of a sudden increase in violence. I'm pretty sure they meant that there had been killings in La Ramada, but I couldn't really press. Among these people it is a matter of not crossing boundaries. When they are ready to tell you something, they will tell you. Any pressure and they stop talking."

"You said what you heard had worried you," Harry said.

"Very much," she said, pushing back her hair with a nervous gesture and edging around to partially face him.

Harry took it that she was about to say something important to her, more important at least than the fate of the two men in the van.

"The girl?" he asked.

"Yes. I am afraid that your Captain's suspicions were well grounded. I think it is likely she was sold into slavery. But I made no progress in getting anyone in the group to say anything specific about that subject."

"That may tell you something," Harry said.

Soñadora agreed.

"Well, thanks to you, we may have possible confirmation that the two men in the van were killed in La Ramada and that they did have a woman with them that one of them tried to kill," Harry said, trying to find some justification for all their effort.

"And also thanks to my *compañero de viaje i frazada de seguridad*," Soñadora said, giving him one of her slashing sidelong glances, "I think we can say with something close to certainty that La Ramada is a link in a human trafficking chain."

9

"The test came out negative," Katherine said in a shaky voice that he felt sure was not due to a bad connection.

"Thank God," Harry said, allowing himself to lean against his kitchen wall.

It had been a very long ten days.

"The doctor said it won't be certain," Katherine said, "until the antibody test in eighteen more days."

Harry recognized that Katherine was struggling to keep herself from becoming too happy about the antigen p24 test results, but he also knew her well enough to know she was one step from refusing to take any comfort at all from the initial results.

"It's good news, Katherine. It's OK to be glad."

"I suppose so," Katherine said. She paused. "I appreciate your trying to make me feel better. You used to do that a lot."

"You didn't always like it."

"No. Minna didn't take any pleasure at all from the results of the test. She just shrugged."

"Well, I guess what happened to her in that van wrecked her world," Harry said sadly.

"And her innocence," Katherine said.

"I think I know why she won't go to school—one of the reasons anyway," Harry said.

"She's afraid everyone knows what happened to her," Katherine replied.

"Probably. My thought also is that she doesn't want to walk or ride past the place where it happened."

"Maybe," Katherine said, "but there's not much to be done about that."

"I'm going to say it again," Harry said and crossed his fingers. "Bring her down here where there's nothing to waken bad memories."

"She's got another three weeks of school . . ."

"The doctor will write the principal a letter saying she should be excused on medical grounds," Harry said, hurrying the words to keep from being interrupted. "It's not really a problem, Katherine."

Katherine was quiet for nearly a full minute, and Harry counted silently to keep himself from saying all the rest he wanted to say but knew would do no good.

"You may be right, Harry," she said, "but there's that next test."

"The Avola Community Hospital is as good as they get, and you know Dr. Benson. Esther would take care of Minna as well as any doctor you know."

"But I'm not sure Minna wants . . ."

"For the moment Minna is living in a miserable world darkened by grief and emotional pain," Harry said, pressing his advantage. "Bring her down here. There'll be five of us to help."

"Five?" she asked loudly.

"You, me, Tucker, Oh, Brother!, and Sanchez, a championship team."

That got him a small laugh.

"Harry, you're just as big an idiot as ever, but if you'll make the arrangements, I'll bring her. I'm about at the end of my tether."

"That's very good news," Tucker said. "It will be a good thing to see Katherine and Minna. Those two and Jesse are three of my most favorite people. I have missed them. What about Thornton?"

"Staying with his aunt," Harry said. "I think Katherine thought she could give more time to Minna if he stayed at home."

He started to say that he had missed them too then stopped himself. It was a fact that he did miss Jesse and Minna, but his feelings about Katherine were much more complex. Over the years they had been apart, his feelings had become a mingling of love, resentment, loss, a painful sense of failure, and, more recently, a kind of resignation that Harry chose to understand as acceptance. But in candid moments, he was not sure it was acceptance, less than certain that he had ever accepted his and Katherine's divorce.

The truth was that he had not done a very good job of finding a way to go on living without Katherine. In fact, he suspected he had not fully resolved any of the emotional issues that the loss of his two wives had left him to cope with.

"When are they coming?" Tucker asked, interrupting his reflections.

They were sitting on Tucker's back stoop. Sanchez, still swathed in bandages, was lying on a pile of rugs beside Tucker's rocker. The dog had lifted his head when Harry arrived and thumped his tail on the rugs without making any effort to get up. Oh, Brother! was standing close to the stoop and as near Sanchez as he could get, wearing his hat, dozing, and swishing flies with his tail, his head nodding in the warmth of the sun.

"In three days," Harry said, thinking that Sanchez wasn't looking very good, and that Tucker didn't look much better.

He was pale and noticeably thinner. More worrisome to Harry was the old man's failure to stand up to greet him and shake his hand. He saw that the encounter with the pigs and the destruction of his garden had done more damage than Harry had realized.

Coming up the driveway, wondering why Oh, Brother! wasn't there to greet him, he had seen to his dismay that not a lick of work had been done on the garden, and he blamed himself for not having looked in on Tucker sooner. That he had been too absorbed in Minna's troubles and in that visit with Soñadora to La Ramada to think about Tucker now seemed to him poor excuses.

"Bring them over as soon as they show an inclination to visit," Tucker said, trying to show some enthusiasm.

"You won't be able to get rid of them," Harry answered, hiding his awareness that Tucker seemed too tired and possibly ill to be truly enthusiastic about anything.

"Have you been feeling a little below average?" Harry asked, not expecting to get a satisfactory answer.

"Possibly," Tucker said. "I've been having some trouble with my right side. It hurts a lot, and I figure I must have pulled something in there the night of the start of the Pig War."

The old farmer shifted in his chair and flinched, growing paler and gasping.

"Hurts to move?" Harry asked.

"Not especially. Whatever it is just grabs me now and then to let me know it's still there."

"Any other symptoms?" Harry asked.

"I've thrown up a few times when the pain has gotten real bad, and when I'm having a spell, I have to kind of hunch over if I'm doing any walking. Once in a while it will grab me between the shoulder blades. I'm finding it easy to take plenty of rest."

"Are you eating?"

"A little. I don't seem to have much appetite."

"Have you talked to the doctor?"

"Most things cure themselves. I'm giving this a chance to do the same."

Harry knew that tone of voice and didn't argue.

Harry made several decisions. He would not tell Tucker about Minna. Starting now, he was going to look in on Tucker every day, and as soon as he could, he was going to start cleaning up the garden. This last decision was prompted as much by selfish motives as by a wish to help his friend. The sight of the wrecked garden was, for reasons he was unwilling to examine closely, extremely upsetting to him.

"How about if I make you some lunch?" Harry asked with some forced cheerfulness.

"Go ahead," Tucker said, "but I'm not sure I'll eat it."

He hadn't eaten it, and Harry had finally talked him into getting into bed. Leaving a warm cup of Tucker's chicken broth beside the bed, Harry left and once he was home called Bradley Post, Tucker's doctor, and left a list of Tucker's symptoms with his Nurse Assistant.

"I don't like how he looks or sounds, and he's in considerable pain," he concluded and wrung a promise from her that the doctor would call Tucker later in the day.

Unhappy at several levels, Harry also found a phone message from Jim Snyder, asking Harry to come in as soon as he could.

"Do you think we ought to send the EMC Unit out there and get him into the hospital?" Jim asked when Harry, on his arrival, finished describing Tucker's condition.

"I've called Bradley and have a promise he'll call Tucker before the end of the day. I'm going over, to be sure he gets some supper if he wants it."

"He's already so thin that standing sideways he don't hardly cast a shadow," Hodges said with a scowl of concern. "And if he's not eating, he's in serious trouble."

81

"He was in pretty good shape when I left him," Harry said, "but you're right. He's not eating."

"I'm sorry to hear this," Jim said, "but I guess everything's being done that needs to be done—at least for the moment. What I called you in here for was to talk some more about your and, what's her name's . . ."

"Soñadora Asturias," Harry said.

"Some name," Hodges said. "Sounds like an Indian queen or something in an opera."

Harry grinned. Coming from anyone but Hodges, the appellation *Indian queen* might have been ambiguous, but Harry knew it was just his way of saying he liked the name.

Jim simply stared at his Sergeant then went on.

"Since your and Asturias's visit to La Ramada, there's been some further developments."

"A war's broken out," Hodges said.

"Will you let me tell Harry what I want to tell him?" Jim said, his ears reddening.

"All right, all right. You go ahead. I'll listen."

"Thank you."

When Jim turned back to Harry, Hodges pointed at his own ears, his round face beaming. Harry quickly looked away, struggling to keep from laughing. Being around Hodges was, in some ways, like being back in fifth grade.

"Here's the thing," Jim said in his most serious voice. "Frank's more than half right. We have got a growing problem on our hands, and one of its centers seems to be La Ramada. I have no idea what the dimensions of this thing are."

"More killings?" Harry asked.

"Three more, but we can't identify the two men or the young woman. They're not in any of our databases."

"Are they Indians, Hispanics, what?" Harry asked.

"If I had to guess," Jim replied, "I would guess the woman is an Indian. The men are probably Hispanics."

"Soñadora was really concerned by what the women said to her about the increasing violence," Harry said. "They apparently let slip that men in La Ramada had been killed and others wounded."

"And we never heard about it," Hodges complained. "The thing that bothers me most about what's going on is that there seems to be a whole world of people doing this bad stuff and we've only been able to break open this tiny hole in the wall separating us from them. It gives me the willies."

"They're mostly illegals or criminals as far as we can tell," Jim said, "but most of our illegals, like those in La Ramada, seem to be working at regular jobs, coming home to their families. Their kids are in school. Until these shootings, there hasn't been so much as a traffic ticket given to anyone in La Ramada."

"And you're afraid of what, exactly?" Harry asked.

"That if there was criminal activity being carried out by our illegals," Jim continued, rubbing his head, "—and it looks now as though there was—it was done smoothly, without any serious conflict, probably because there was no competition, which was why we didn't know it was going on."

"Now," Hodges put in eagerly, "it looks like some organization, possibly more than one, operating north of the Texas border has decided to horn in on the operation, which wouldn't be happening if there wasn't a lot of money changing hands."

"The bottom line being that you still don't know who's doing what to whom or why," Harry said with a grin, knowing that Jim hated having something criminous and mysterious going on in Tequesta County.

Hodges laughed, slapping his knees in appreciation. Jim's ears grew red again, but he managed a strained laugh.

"That's where you come in," he said to Harry.

Harry saw that he would have been wiser not to be so smart.

"You want Soñadora and me to go back into La Ramada," he said with a sinking heart.

"It's our only door, and the two of you cracked it your first time in," Jim said, "and I need it opened."

He dropped the pencil he had been fiddling with onto the desk and waited. Hodges leaned forward, his broad face solemn.

"The Captain's right, Harry," he said. "We need the help."

Harry's first impulse was to refuse. He had enough on his mind with Minna, and while she and Katherine were with him, he had planned to limit his work to the routine tasks that would keep him away from the house as little as possible and not give Katherine cause to nail him for risking his life and exposing his family to pain, grief, and financial ruin.

There was no getting around it; it was still a sore point with him. More than anything else, it had been the issue that wrecked their marriage. Then in the midst of feeling aggrieved and badly done to, he remembered what Soñadora had said about the thirteen-year-old girl she and her team had helped to rescue from sexual slavery.

The picture of a girl Minna's age being forced to have sex with a string of rough men, some or most at least half drunk or stoned, sickened him, and he thought of what had almost happened to Minna. If there was even a slight chance his efforts could free another girl or save one from such an ordeal, why was he even hesitating?

"I can't speak for Soñadora," he said, "but I'll do what I can."

"Before this is over," Hodges said, "you may be wearing a turned-around collar. Stranger things have happened."

Jim ignored Hodges's joking response.

"Good," he said, "but I'm thinking you could be buying yourself a whole lot of trouble with Katherine. Of course," he added quickly, "it's none of my business."

Harry stood, waving his hand dismissively.

"All that was a long time ago," he said, wanting to believe it and not quite making it. "She's probably forgotten all about it."

"Not likely," Hodges told him, looking as grim as his round face would let him.

"There's no need to go there, Frank," Jim said quickly, coming around the desk to shake Harry's hand and usher him out the door. "You'll call me when you have an answer from Asturias? If she agrees, we'll work out the details. Be persuasive, Harry. We need her."

Having gotten used to the idea, Harry found himself definitely hoping Soñadora would say yes but avoided asking himself why.

10

When he got home, Harry found a message from Dr. Post, telling him to bring Tucker in at once, and if Harry got the message too late, to take him to the nearest emergency care facility. Harry checked the time and left. Tucker was still in bed. He hadn't touched the chicken broth and was obviously feeling lousy.

"Dr. Post wants to see you," Harry told him.

"I don't want to see him," Tucker replied through gritted teeth. "Besides, I don't want to leave Sanchez. He needs looking after."

"He'll manage until you get back," Harry assured him. "Besides, he's on his feet, and Oh, Brother!'s here."

Tucker scowled in silence.

"You don't have to walk," Harry said. "I'll carry you."

"I'll walk!" Tucker snapped. He threw off the covers but failed to get to his feet. "Well," he gasped, falling back against the pillows, "I seem to have misjudged the situation."

"Come on, then," Harry said, bending over the bed.

He picked up Tucker and was startled to discover how light he was. For the first time, it occurred to Harry that the old man might be seriously ill.

"Things are going to start getting better, beginning now," he said, crossing the back stoop. "Guaranteed."

The big mule accompanied Harry to the Rover. Tucker tried to laugh as Harry was buckling him into the front seat, supervised by Oh, Brother!, who stuck his head in the door when Harry was done, giving Tucker a chance to rub his nose.

"Look after Sanchez," Tucker told the mule in a voice that was little more than a whisper.

"I'm putting him right into the hospital," Post said, having finished his examination of Tucker and taken Harry into his office.

The doctor was a small, dark man, wearing rimless glasses and a white lab jacket. Harry had once done some work for Post, who, along with several other doctors in Avola, had been implicated in a health insurance scam. Post had been innocent, but it had taken Harry almost two months to discover how his identity had been stolen, to hide the real thief.

"What's wrong with him?" Harry asked.

"Before the lab work confirms it, it's a guess," Post said, "but I think it's his gall bladder."

"Surgery?" Harry asked, trying to dampen his worry at the news.

"Most likely, but, to be sure, I'll have to take some pictures and have bloodwork done."

He sighed and tapped his pen on the clipboard he was carrying.

"He's an old man, Harry. For him, having an operation is a major risk. I won't call it a gamble, but a lot can go wrong."

"Right," Harry said, beginning to feel both dread and anger. "So if he can be treated without going under the knife, it would be the way to go."

"You just need to remember the choices may not be particularly good ones," Post told him. "Leave your number with the receptionist. I may need to get in touch."

"Sure," Harry said.

"Oh," Post said, turning back, "He's worried about his dog

and his mule. Can you do anything to put his mind to rest about them?"

"I'll take care of them. Do you want me to tell him?"

Post shook his head.

"He'll be busy for a while with people putting needles in him. Also, I've got him sedated. He's dehydrated, and I've put him on a drip. But I'll tell him as soon as he can listen. Don't forget the number."

Harry gave the girl at the desk his number and left, telling himself it was only a precaution. But he didn't believe it.

Despite the clattering air conditioner in one of the whitewashed windows, the room where Rigoberta and the other seven women worked at the sewing machines was stifling. At one end of the room, Maria sat at a desk on a raised platform that allowed her to watch all of the workstations. From that vantage point she called out the name of anyone lagging and placed a check beside her name. If one received more than three check marks in one day, Gomez dragged the weeping and protesting woman out of the room and beat her with his ruler. Rigoberta and Hazel received no check marks. Rigoberta worked the way she had worked all her life, doggedly, her mind empty.

Once out of the room, some of them screamed, and some didn't. As the days passed, fewer and fewer made any sound at all.

"At this rate," Hazel told Rigoberta one night, "two thirds of this bunch will be knocked up within a month. Then what do you think is going to happen?"

"What?" Rigoberta asked.

She and Hazel were sitting on a couch in a corner of the room where they ate and spent their free time between work and lights out. Old Florita, the aged and bent deaf mute who cleaned and helped in the kitchen, was shuffling toward them, picking up empty Styrofoam cups and other trash. When she reached Rigoberta, she bent down, stuck something into Rigoberta's shoe, and shuffled on.

Rigoberta waited a moment then reached down and found a folded piece of paper in her shoe. She closed her hand around it and made a display of pulling open her sack and rummaging inside it, dropping the paper in as she did so.

Hazel was teaching Rigoberta English, and Rigoberta, to her surprise, liked learning and was advancing quickly. At one point when they began, she had suddenly laughed.

"What's funny?" Hazel asked.

"I still don't have a book," Rigoberta told her.

Then she leaned toward Hazel and said softly, "Florita stuck a piece of paper in my shoe, Now, it's in my bag."

Hazel took a quick look around the room. No one was watching them. Hazel pulled out her cigarettes, took one, and said to Rigoberta, "Give me your bag. I'm out of matches."

Rigoberta passed it to her. Hazel pulled it open and peered inside, then reached in, unfolded the printed paper, gave Rigoberta back the bag, and said loudly, "Shit."

Then she jumped up and went to one of the women who was smoking and lit her cigarette.

"What is it?" Rigoberta asked when Hazel returned.

"It's a printed flier from St. Jude's, a church in Avola. It's got numbers for a women's safehouse on it."

"Why did she give it to me?" Rigoberta asked, shoving the flier back into her bag.

"She's working with about half a deck. Who knows? I'm more interested in what's going to happen to the women who get knocked up and can't work those damned sewing machines like they're doing now. They'll be yanked out of here."

"So it will be a way out for them?"

Hazel gave a short bark of laughter.

"All the way out would be my guess."

"*Muerta?*"

"Dead," Hazel repeated grimly in English.

Rigoberta was not surprised.

"*Trabaja de esclavas.*"

"That's right. Slave labor."

"I will kill him first," Rigoberta said.

"That's the spirit," Hazel said approvingly. "Back to school. The days of the week."

Rigoberta smiled. She liked Hazel. Hazel took no . . . what was the word? . . . *shit* from anyone. Then she remembered her children, and a darkness slid over her mind, but, eyes narrowing, she pushed it back. At the right time, which they would know when it came, she and Hazel would escape. Perhaps she would use her knife.

11

After leaving the hospital Harry drove to the *Salvamento* office. As usual, the women all stopped working to stare at him.

"What do you want, *Señor* Brock?" Soñadora asked him, coming forward as she had done before, to meet him a few steps inside the door.

"I'm glad to see you too," Harry said, stung by the ice in her voice.

She stopped before she had quite reached him, her eyes hard, her face stiff.

"Were you expecting something more?" she said after a significant pause.

"Let's just forget it," he said. "Do you have a few minutes to talk with me in private?"

Speaking in a low voice, stripped of expression, she said, "I forgot. You become angry easily with those who don't like you."

Oh, good, Harry thought, *here's where I have a chance to make a real ass of myself.*

"I really am glad to see you, Ms. Asturias," he said, leaving the poetry out. "Is it true that you don't like me?"

With her hair braided and wrapped around her head and held in place with a gold pin, exposing her neck, and a dark blue silk shawl thrown over the shoulders of her red dress, he thought she looked like an Indian Nefertiti. He was going to say so then told himself he would lose a lot of points if he did.

He waited.

She studied him with what he chose to believe was a slight softening of her features. "That would be an exaggeration, Mr. Brock," she said. "Why didn't you call?"

"I don't have your number."

"It's in the book."

"No, it isn't. And I didn't want to talk on the phone."

"*Salvamento* is in the phone book," she said.

"I know."

"Hopeless," she said and, walking past him, opened the door then followed him out onto the tiny porch.

"Is this where the executions are carried out?" he asked.

He found he was, in fact, cheered up to learn she had lifted the fatwa of dislike and was determined not to dwell on the *hopeless.*

"No," Soñadora answered. "They're usually carried out in the night and are preceded by doors breaking inward, followed by the roar of automatic weapons, accompanied by the screams of the dying. If you are small enough to be fallen on and covered by someone much larger than you and dead and if the assassins are in a hurry, you live—at least for that time."

Her voice stopped, and she stood very still, not looking at anything that Harry could see.

"Something like that happened to you," he said, chilled by her words.

"Yes. When I was six, my mother, two uncles, and several other members of my family were killed by one of the death squads funded by your government," she said in a voice flat as death.

"Terrible," Harry said, watching a lot of pieces come together. He thought of saying he had consistently voted against that government but dismissed the response as fatuous. "Where did it happen?"

"I never tell anyone where I came from," she replied. "I have no telephone number and no address."

"Did your father survive?" he asked.

She hesitated and Harry caught a change in her expression but could not read it.

"He was not there," she said.

"What happened to you after the attack?" he asked.

"I was found by a priest who had joined the resistance movement. He took me into his group, gave me a new name, and taught me English and Spanish. When I was fourteen, he arranged for me to go to a girl's school in Bogotá."

He decided not to ask why her father didn't take her. She was obviously at least half Anglo. Her coloring, her thin nose, her height, all suggested mixed parentage, and her cryptic response when he had asked about him told Harry enough.

"Is the priest still alive?"

"Yes, he's alive and, I hope, well."

"Don't you write or call him?" Harry asked in surprise.

She did not seem to him to be a person who would abandon anyone close to her.

"No. It would probably be the death of him and of me too. Enough about me. Why did you come to see me?"

"Three more people have turned up dead, two Hispanic men and a young woman, thought to be an Indian. All were shot. The police can't identify any of the bodies."

Harry wanted to stop everything and talk to her about what had happened to her, but he guessed she had said all she wanted to say about it, at least for now.

"And what am I supposed to do about that?"

Harry noticed with disappointment that her voice had gone flat again.

"Jim Snyder thinks the deaths are linked to the first shooting that we went into La Ramada to question people about."

She planted her fists on her hips.

"You're going to tell me that your Captain wants us to go in there again," she said with a little more verve, which Harry attributed to disgust.

"That's the idea," he said, thinking the idea did sound pretty feeble.

"The same cover?" she asked with a little less edge.

"That's the idea."

A glimmer of hope from her question kept him from chucking the whole enterprise.

"What will we be looking for?"

"Whatever information we can get about why the killings are occurring and, if possible, who's involved."

"Why are you doing this, Mr. Brock?"

"Harry," he said, a little huffed at the formality. "I think principally to help Jim. He's an old friend, and I owe him more than I'll ever be able to repay, but if I were being absolutely honest, I'd say maybe we should just look the other way until whoever these people are get tired of killing one another then arrest those still standing."

He was not prepared for her response.

"That would be absolutely irresponsible," she said very sharply and actually stamped her foot. "Didn't you say a young woman has been killed? Wasn't another woman wounded and hauled off to God knows where? Aren't there, in all probability, other men and women caught in this net of cruelty, misery, and violence?"

Harry tried to say "but," and was flattened by Soñadora's stampede of words.

"And," she concluded, her black eyes boring into his, "Aren't we compelled by everything decent to do something about it—not *sometime*, Harry Brock, but right now?"

He stared at her in admiration. She was even more beautiful angry than stone-faced.

"Why don't you answer?"

"Does that mean you'll do it?"

She hesitated for a nanosecond. Her face blazed, and said, "You did that on purpose, didn't you?"

"What?" he asked, slower than he should have been.

"You know what."

Then he caught on and smiled gleefully because he did know, had not planned it, and was going to take all the credit.

12

After Soñadora had agreed to help a second time, and they had settled on a strategy, Harry drove back to Tucker's place, to look after Sanchez and possibly do some work on the garden. He could, he thought, at least gather the trampled and torn-up plants and enlist Oh, Brother! in the work of hauling them away.

That settled, he had time to think about Tucker and concluded he couldn't make any plans for getting him looked after until he knew whether or not Post was going to operate on Tucker or just keep him under observation for a day or two. Stymied in that direction, Harry began thinking about Minna and Katherine, both of whom would be on the Hammock in three days.

He was both excited and worried by the prospect of having them with him, and, looking for help, he had talked with Esther Benson about Minna.

"Get her professional help, Harry, as soon as you can," she told him. "I have names. These are good people with a lot of experience."

She shook her head and made a sour face.

"Unfortunately, they get a lot of these cases. The worst thing about them is that there are lots and lots of them we never hear about, and the child is left to her own limited resources, as are her parents, for dealing with the situation. That neglect leads to very serious and often delayed mental and emotional suffering."

Harry heard that as a warning, delivered with Esther's usual forthrightness.

"I've heard you," Harry assured her. "I'll do what I can to get her help as soon as she gets here."

He stopped. There was more he wanted to say but found himself at a loss to get it out.

"Start with a name," Esther told him, glancing at her watch.

"You've probably got a patient waiting, and I know how . . ."

"A name, Harry. Let me worry about the time."

"Katherine," he blurted.

"Oh, God, of course, I should have guessed. You're going to have a significant ex in the house."

"Right, and she's in fairly bad shape. You may not remember but . . ."

"I remember, Harry. A she bear is indifferent to threats to her young compared with Katherine."

"And given her own experiences with Willard Trachey, her first husband, she's especially sensitive about sexual abuse."

"And I'm betting she's blaming herself," Esther said with a sigh.

"Something like that. I asked why Minna was walking home alone, and Katherine almost took my head off."

Esther laughed.

"There was a time when I wondered if either of you was going to come out of your marriage alive."

Harry groaned and felt the old pain of their battles.

"Just remember not to take her anger personally, and give her plenty of space."

"Would Tequesta County be big enough?" he asked.

"You'll be all right," she said and laughed again. "The thing to remember is that you two really loved one another, and, if you'll forgive an unprofessional comment, probably still do."

Harry stood up, having nothing to say to that, but Esther's

advice bolstered his courage, and he thanked her for her time.

"You're welcome," Esther said, passing him a list of names. "Be sure she sees one of these people and the sooner, the better."

Dried mud on Oh, Brother!'s legs told Harry that the mule had gone to the Puc Puggy to drink, which meant the bubbler wasn't working.

"I'll get you cleaned up as soon as I have a look at Sanchez," Harry told the mule, resting a hand on his shoulder as they walked to the barn, "and then we'll attend to the water."

Oh, Brother! had met Harry at his Rover when he drove into the yard, and talking to the mule had become as natural for Harry as talking to a person, thanks to years of listening to Tucker converse with Oh, Brother! and Sanchez and report on his conversations with them.

Before taking Tucker to the hospital, Harry had transferred Sanchez and his blanket bed from the kitchen to Oh, Brother!'s box stall where the mule could watch him. Because the stall's door was never closed and Oh, Brother! was never tied, the mule was free to come and go as he wished.

Sanchez was on his feet when Harry greeted him and even managed a grin. Wagging his tail pulled the stitches on his side and created a conflict, which the big hound had resolved by giv-ing Harry a particularly full-toothed grin. His walking was limited to a stiff and painful hobble.

"Fresh water and something to eat," Harry said, having stroked and petted the dog carefully, taking the moment to check that the bandages were all in place and that there were no signs of bleeding.

That dealt with and hay pitched down from the mow, to replenish Oh, Brother!'s hay rack, Harry went out to the garden to take a closer look at the damage. What he saw was dishearten-ing. A dozen rows of almost ripe yellow corn had been mowed down and trampled into the soft earth. The frames for the pole beans were all broken, and the rows of green beans demolished. The hills of cucumber, squash, and pumpkins were decimated. In short, Harry stood, shaking his head in the middle of a desolation. It looked to him as if some of the pig tracks were fresher than the others, but other things held his attention.

"It's all got to go," Harry told the mule, who was standing beside him, apparently assessing the damage along with his companion. "Let's get the wagon and start throwing stuff into it."

Once they had returned to the barn, he was thinking of the work he had to do and forgot whom he was talking to.

"It's been some time since I harnessed a horse," he told Oh, Brother!, realizing too late what he had done. "I mean a mule," he said.

It was too late. Oh, Brother! turned around on the barn floor and walked back into the yard.

"I'm sorry," Harry said, hurrying after him. "I completely forgot."

Oh, Brother! refused to look at him and kept turning away when Harry approached. After some further futile effort, Harry gave up and went into the house and came back with a pocket full of sugar cubes.

"Oh, Brother!," he said to the mule's rear end, "I'm sorry. It was a slip of the tongue. I know you're a mule, and I know a mule likes sugar. Do you want some?"

The mule turned around and bumped Harry in the chest with his nose. Harry stroked his neck and scratched his ears. Then he took out the sugar and shared it with Oh, Brother!.

Sanchez gave a feeble and pathetic bark.

Oh, Brother! waggled his ears.

"I know," Harry said, suddenly laughing. "He wants a cookie."

Just as Harry was giving Sanchez his cookie, he heard

something moving slowly past the back of the barn, and a moment later he heard a loud, high-pitched squeal. Harry felt the hair on his neck bristle, but to his surprise neither the dog nor the mule showed any interest.

"Pigs," Harry said, but Sanchez went on eating his cookie and Oh, Brother! only snorted softly and nuzzled Harry's shoulder.

"I'm going to take a look," Harry said, refusing to believe he'd just been told not to be concerned.

Unarmed, he went out the barn door and edged up to the corner of the barn closest to the garden and peered around it, showing as little of himself as possible. Sure enough, there was a pig in the garden, rooting among the corn stalks for ears of corn, and bouncing around her was a piglet. It was only when the sow moved to a new location that Harry saw she was walking on three legs. Her left front leg was dangling from the knee joint and obviously useless.

Harry stepped out from his hiding place, regretting he did not have his CZ. The sow, he concluded, must have been injured in the fracas in the garden. She saw Harry or smelled him and painfully made her way to the edge of the garden and slowly hopped into the woods. Harry watched her make her way out of the ruined garden with mingled feelings of sympathy for the injured animal and a strong primal urge to shoot her.

That evening he visited Tucker in the hospital and found him sitting up in bed.

"You're looking much improved," Harry said. "When are they letting you out of here?"

"Looks can be deceptive," Tucker complained. "They're going to cut me open tomorrow morning. My gall bladder is unsatisfactory, according to what Post calls 'the tests.' He said it as if he had just consulted God."

"In here, I think they're accorded the same degree of reverence," Harry said, laughing to mask his concern.

The diagnosis, he thought, must have been serious for Post to put a man of Tucker's age under the knife.

Tucker made an ambiguous sound. Then he asked about Sanchez.

"He's on his feet. I think missing you has been the spur. It's either that or Oh, Brother! has been urging him to make the effort."

Harry was pleased to see Tucker smile. Then he remembered the sow.

"There's a sow with a broken leg and a piglet foraging in the remains of your garden. My guess is that it's the pig Oh, Brother! kicked the night of the raid. I think she's been surviving on the remains of the corn and the root vegetables she's been unearthing. I'll go back tomorrow with my gun and shoot both of them."

"You said she was lame?" Tucker asked.

"A broken leg, I think."

"Then don't shoot her," Tucker said decisively.

"But she can't support herself long on what's left in the garden," Harry protested.

"You know that old trap . . ."

"Oh, no," Harry said, "Don't even think of it."

"If it held Althea, it will hold two pigs," Tucker continued as if Harry had not spoken.

Althea was a young female bear that was starving and had begun hanging around Tucker's farm. He trapped her and put her in a cage he had constructed years before to house Weissmuller, a huge dog that was killing deer on the Hammock. The experiment failed. After a good beginning, the dog reverted to chasing deer again, and the game warden shot him. Althea was more fortunate. She was eventually released a hundred or so miles north of Avola, and after returning once for a visit and being put back in the woods, she stayed away.

"You're not going to be in any condition to . . ." Harry began.

"You're going to do it," Tucker broke in. "When you've caught them, put them in the wire pen. They'll be safe there. Then after that call Heather Parkinson to look at the sow's leg. By the time that's done, I'll be home, to take over looking after them."

"What are you going to do with two pigs, Tucker?" Harry asked, not wanting to add to the old man's stress by refusing but grinding his teeth over the outcome.

"Get the sow healed and watch the shoat grow. It's going to be a lot of fun."

Harry conceded defeat.

13

The next three days were busy ones for Harry. On the first day, as soon as he knew that Tucker had come through the operation safely, he called on Dr. Rowena Farnham, Rector and Chaplain of St. Jude's on The Sea.

Farnham was a large woman with thick, white hair cut in a pageboy, a rosy complexion, and even in sneakers, stretch-waist green slacks, and a light blue sweatshirt with "One of The Sparrows" written across it in white letters, she was impressive.

"Harry!" she said, throwing open her office door in the church office building, "Come in, come in. Sit down. I've been thinking about you."

The office was strictly functional with a seriously cluttered oak desk, backed by a wall given over to floor-to-ceiling bookshelves, all crammed, with spillovers piled on chairs near the desk. Farnham cleared two of the chairs, and she and Harry sat down.

"I've been waiting for an explanation of your having taken shameful advantage of Betsy Potter, our Parish Secretary, and flattered her into giving you a bundle of hideously expensive church circulars intended to be distributed among those who were once called the deserving poor."

"Guilty on both counts," Harry said, unable to keep from laughing, "And they went to the poor. Have you got time to listen to a story?"

"Is it edifying?"

"Not in the least."

"It was quite foolish of me to ask. Go ahead."

Harry gave Farnham a short account of the work he had done for Jim Snyder and what he was now planning. Having given her a quick sketch of Soñadora Asturias without naming her or associating her with *Salvamento,* he said he would be helpless in the Guatemalan community without her.

"And you want me to give you something in the way of legitimate cover for this endeavor," she said when he finished talking.

"That's it."

She paused a moment.

"St. Jude's operates a shelter for women. We don't advertise it much for obvious reasons. In the community it's called Haven House. Betsy Potter runs it. I could provide you with some of the material we pass out to our guests."

"Guests?" Harry asked.

"I know," Farnham said. "Euphemisms abound. It might be more honest to say of it, as Frost has Warren say of home, 'Home is a place where when you have to go there, they have to take you in.' "

"Except that in this case," Harry said, "they choose to take you in."

Farnham smiled. "I like to think so."

"The material would be a perfect cover, and if anyone calls to ask about us . . ."

"You're legit."

"I owe you one."

"Here's how you can repay me," Farnham said seriously. "If this woman you're involved with is who I think she is, I've heard some good things about her. I'd like to meet her. There are people in this church who would be eager to help her."

"She's extremely secretive, Rowena," he told her, "but I'll tell her you're interested and let her take it from there."

"Publicity has two sharp edges," Farnham responded as she shuffled through her desk drawers in search of the material she had promised him. "It both protects and exposes you. I understand her concern. It's why we don't say more than we do about Haven House."

She shuffled through more papers in the box on the floor.

"Here they are," she said, coming around the desk, to pass him a sheaf of papers. "Make as many copies as you want."

"Jim Snyder will have a fit," Harry said with a grin. "Copying costs in the department are over-budget, and Sheriff Fisher is ready to crucify someone, and Jim suspects the finger is pointing at him."

"Tell him prayer helps," Farnham answered, waving Harry out the door.

Harry got home to find Ernesto Piedra asleep on the lanai steps and his car on the grass.

"Hey, amigo, Harry said, shaking the curly-headed man by the shoulder.

Ernesto jerked awake and grinned. "Hey, Harry," he said around a yawn.

"Are you in trouble?" Harry asked, helping Ernesto to his feet and pulling open the screen door.

"Como siempre," Ernesto replied.

"As always, *responsibilidads,*" Harry said dryly and Ernesto nodded. "And their mothers," Harry added.

"Siempre."

"Come in. Have you eaten today?"

Ernesto shook his head. Harry sat him down at the kitchen table and made him a thick roast beef sandwich.

"Milk?" Harry asked.

"Por favor," Ernesto said, rubbing his eyes.

"Talk while you eat," Harry said.

"There are things I have heard that trouble me," Ernesto told him. "I think someone is looking for you and Soñadora."

Ernesto paused to drink some milk.

"Who?"

"I have no names. This is a very good sandwich."

"Thanks. There's more if you want another. What does this person want?"

"Enough, *gracias*," Ernesto said, shaking his head as he finished his milk then sat back with a sigh.

"But it is very bad news. A few days ago, Soñadora and her people rescued a girl from a house where she was working without pay. The people who put her there and the people who had her are unhappy.

"Harry, somehow they have heard your name, and they do not want to give you a present—at least not the kind that makes you happy."

"Ernesto," Harry demanded, becoming impatient, "are you being difficult?"

"No, but I do not like to be the one with bad news."

"I won't shoot the messenger."

"What?" Ernesto asked, looking alarmed.

"A joke. Get on with it."

"These are *personas peligrosos*."

"How bad? Are they Guatemalans?"

"Very, and possibly."

"And you don't know who they are or what they want?"

"That is true, but what I am hearing I think it is not lies."

Harry decided to say nothing to Ernesto about what he and Soñadora were doing. The less he knew, the less risk for him. Also, Ernesto's pillow talk might be less than discreet.

"Do you think our phones are tapped?" he asked half seriously.

"¿Quién sabe?"

He had gone to look out the window over the sink.

"You live in a good place, Harry."

He moved to the door.

"Don't lose it by getting yourself killed."

"That's good advice, Ernesto," Harry told him with a straight face as they walked to Ernesto's car. "Thank you for the warning. And don't forget, you're welcome here any time."

As he drove to Tucker's farm, Harry tried to assess the level of danger in Ernesto's warning. There was the possibility that his name had been attached to reports of threats by mistake. It was also possible that someone in that criminal world he and the police had begun to explore and of which Soñadora seemed at least partially aware had identified him as the person who had visited La Ramada. If that was so, it was probable that Soñadora was also exposed.

The second possibility presented two more questions: What to do about the threats and were they sufficiently credible to make it necessary for him to tell Jim and Soñadora? By the time he turned into Tucker's driveway, he still had no answers and decided to let his mind work on them while he focused on setting up a pig trap, something that he was doing against his better judgment, but if it gave Tucker an added reason for wanting to come home, then he was prepared to do it.

Both Oh, Brother! and Sanchez were waiting for him when he climbed down from the Rover. Sanchez forgot his wounds long enough to wag his tail and then yelped in pain, settling for grinning at Harry. Oh, Brother! pushed his nose against Harry's chest and snorted softly, which, as greetings went from the mule, was a warm welcome.

"We are going to trap a pig. Two pigs," he told the animals, "and you, Oh, Brother!," he said, stroking the big mule's neck, "are going to have to stand still while I put on your harness because you're going to drag that trap into the garden."

With that he set off with Oh, Brother! for the barn, Sanchez hitching along behind. Once in the barn, the trio went to Oh, Brother!'s stall, where Harry paused in front of the mule's harness, hanging from two wooden pegs in the wall, and tried to recall how Tucker went about harnessing the mule.

"The collar goes on first," he said in a show of confidence.

Sanchez eased himself onto the floor and watched Harry as if expecting a miracle. Oh, Brother! made a show of not watching, which Harry interpreted as either a display of good manners or an unwillingness to watch what was about to happen.

Harry put the collar on upside down, and the mule snorted in alarm.

"That was just a mistake," Harry said, starting over and trying to regain lost ground. "I don't do this every day."

By now Oh, Brother! was watching very closely.

"This end goes on first," Harry told his audience, tapping one of the hames, which when put on properly snapped into place around the collar.

The problem was the harness had to go over the mule's back all at once, and when Harry lifted the harness off the wall, he found it was too heavy to just toss it onto Oh, Brother!'s back and let it fall into place, and yet he had watched Tucker do it dozens of times. To complicate matters, the mule was seventeen hands high at the withers, but Harry got most of the harness into both arms and tried lifting and pushing it onto the mule's back. The moment he took his hands off it, the harness slid to the floor.

Oh, Brother! turned and stared at the tangle of leather as if he couldn't believe his eyes. Sanchez gave a short bark that Harry thought sounded like a laugh.

"All right," Harry said, "that was a practice run. Just let me catch my breath."

He thought it was completely ridiculous that he was red-faced and embarrassed, but he was, and there was nothing to do but try again. It was while he was untangling the hames and trying to restore his composure that memory kicked in.

"OK," he shouted. "Now I remember! These go on first."

It wasn't pretty, but with the back half of the harness draped over his right shoulder, he lifted the hames over Oh, Brother!'s shoulders and settled them into the collar. Then he swung the rest of the harness over Oh, Brother!'s rump. Feeling proud of himself, he pulled the mule's tail over the strap, went around to the front, and fastened the hames under the collar.

"We're ready," he announced. "Come on."

He started for the barn door, but neither the mule nor the dog followed. They simply stared at Harry. Harry studied the harness. The strap that went under the mule's belly was hanging down.

"All right, I'll get it," he said.

Once the belly strap was cinched in place, Oh, Brother! walked confidently out of the barn to where the trap was sitting in long grass and weeds behind the wire run. Harry had to make another trip to the barn for the evener and a chain. The trap, mounted on a pair of skids, measured eight feet by four by four and was built of oak framing and heavy-gauge wire. Originally built to capture a huge dog that had gone wild, it had once held a bear and was now likely to catch two pigs.

It was a simple affair. A heavy door closed one end of the trap and could be raised in a frame and pinned open. A trip wire attached to the pin ran two thirds of the way to the front of the box and down to a hinged piece of wood on the floor of the trap. Any pressure on the board pulled the wire, which dislodged the pin, allowing the door to fall and lock itself in place.

The trap and the skids weighed several hundred pounds, but

when Harry finished attaching the chain to the skids and called out, "Walk on," Oh, Brother! started away with the huge affair with no visible effort. Without having to be led or driven, the mule dragged the trap into the center of the garden, stopped, and looked back at Harry.

"Great," Harry said, pretending there was nothing odd about the fact that the mule knew what was going to be done and where the trap should be placed.

Harry managed to unharness the mule without difficulty, and, feeling that his status in the community had been restored, hurried off to the house to mix up a pail of scraps, a loaf of bread and a quart of turned milk, and stale dog food. That done, Harry lifted the door out of its tracks, to insure it didn't fall shut with him inside, and crawled into the trap and placed the rank-smelling pail just beyond the board that, stepped on, would spring the trap.

That night Harry caught a possum and had considerable trouble getting the animal out of the box. The pail was still mostly full, and the possum planned on sleeping off its first meal and having another go when he woke up. Harry found an old ox goad in the barn and made life unpleasant enough for the possum, following him into the woods and hurrying him along with occasional jabs, to insure he would stay away.

When Harry arrived the next morning, the trap had the sow and the piglet in it. Sanchez and Oh, Brother! were standing beside the cage observing the captives.

"Well, Tucker's going to be pleased," he told the pair. The piglet was taking an interest in the three, but the sow, who had eaten everything in the pail, was lying on her side with her eyes closed.

Aside from an occasional low grunt and the rise and fall of her breath, she gave no other signs of life. Harry guessed it was her first full meal in a long time. The broken leg looked seriously infected. He turned away to fetch a canvas to throw over the cage for shade for its occupants and told Sanchez and Oh, Brother! that Heather had her work cut out for her.

Tucker came through his operation very well and woke up demanding to be discharged. Dr. Post was holding out for another night, to monitor vital signs.

"We did a lap choly," Post told Harry, "so the incisions were relatively small, but all the same, he's got some years on him, and any surgery was going to stress his system. I just didn't want to take chances."

"What's a lap choly?" Harry asked. "I thought it was his gall bladder you were removing."

"My fault," Post said with an apologetic chuckle. "*Lap choly* is an abbreviation for laparoscopy. In conventional surgery a five- to eight-inch incision is made in the abdominal muscles for access to the gall bladder. In laparoscopy, some very small incisions are made, reducing recovery time substantially. Young, healthy people can often go home on the same day of the operation. After the traditional operation, patients can expect to be five days or more in the hospital, then face several weeks of recovery at home."

"Will he be able to care for himself as soon as he goes home?" Harry asked.

"He should avoid lifting heavy objects for a while and be careful how he moves. With plenty of rest, I think he'll be fine. If no counterindicator develops, I'll let him go tomorrow."

"Can someone call me when he's ready to be released?"

"My nurse will call you."

"I've told him I caught his pigs," Harry said. "You'll probably have to tie him to the bed to keep him from walking home."

"Did some of his pigs get loose?"

"They've been running around in the woods for a while,"

Harry said, enjoying his private joke.

Wetherell Clampett, the son of one of Tucker's oldest friends, drove Tucker home from the hospital because when the call came from the hospital, Harry was at the Southwest Florida International Airport waiting for Katherine and Minna. Their plane had been on the ground for half an hour, but a mechanical problem with the port was keeping them from disembarking.

By the time they came through the gate, Harry had time to think of all the ways he had been wrong to invite Katherine to come back to the Hammock. In the worst moments he fabricated quarrels, silences, slamming doors, and Minna having to be hospitalized. But when he saw them, the clouds lifted.

"I thought you would have fled by now," Katherine told him after giving him a long hug and a fleeting kiss.

That she kissed him at all surprised Harry. She had grown more substantial with the passing years, but holding her, feeling her body against his, had restored something he thought he no longer missed. For an instant his eyes stung, and he looked hard at her. Those remarkable green eyes, even behind glasses, were as clear and arresting as ever, and her hair, collar length now, somewhat darker and streaked liberally with white, was still thick and vital.

"It occurred to me to do that," Harry told her, "but now I'm glad I waited."

"Hey, Harry," a quiet voice said, "people are beginning to stare."

"They are not," Katherine said, flushing and pulling free from Harry's embrace.

"Hey, Minna," Harry said, putting out his arms.

The tall, lanky girl stepped back from the proffered embrace. Although Katherine had warned him that she did not want to be touched, a knife twisted in his heart.

"You grow taller and better-looking every time I see you," he told her, instantly dropping his arms.

It was true. Katherine was a beautiful woman. The girl's father had been a handsome man. Looking at her and feeling her stiff-faced tension, Harry thought he could see something of both in Minna. She had her mother's eyes and her father's bone structure, but her wavy brown hair was all hers.

"I'm glad you're here," he told her. "I've missed you."

"I guess," she said and turned to the backpack she had set on the floor.

Harry and Katherine exchanged a quick look.

"We're out this way," he said, taking a couple of their bags. "It's not far, but be prepared to be hot."

"How's Tucker?" Minna asked when they began walking.

"Just about getting home from the hospital," Harry said, "minus a gall bladder."

"Is he going to be all right?" she asked.

"I think so," Harry said, relieved that she had shown interest in something.

Her eyes had a twenty-mile stare in them that scared him.

Once in the Rover, Katherine talked about some of the things that had been going on in her own life, and it struck Harry not altogether pleasantly that the woman sitting beside him had a life completely separated from his. He knew that, of course, at least that was what he had been telling himself all these years.

Coping with this new hollowed-out feeling while helping to keep the conversation going, trying without much success to get Minna to take part, and in the free spaces thinking about him and Katherine together in a house where they had once been man and wife and how she was going to take the news someone might be trying to kill him kept Harry busy from the airport to the Hammock.

14

As soon as Harry had helped Katherine and Minna carry their bags upstairs, he stopped in Katherine's room. Her bags lay open on the bed, and she was hanging clothes up in her closet. When he knocked on the doorframe, she turned and said, red-faced, "You don't have to knock on an open door."

"Do you feel as weird as I do about this?" he asked, not having planned to mention how he felt about having her back in the house.

She gave a kind of helpless laugh.

"Since you've mentioned it, I guess I do."

"Good," he said, afraid to take the conversation any further. "I thought I might be the only one. Look, if it's all right with you, I've got some work that needs attending to. Will you and Minna be OK for a couple of hours?"

"Of course we will. Are you doing this just to make things easier for me? Do you think I need some time alone here with Minna? Because if you do . . ."

It was Harry's turn to laugh.

"You find it just as hard to let anyone do anything for you as you ever did. Now isn't that a fact?"

She had been holding herself straight, and the stress of the situation showed, but now she suddenly let her shoulders drop and smiled at him.

"And you're the same old charmer you always were. Isn't *that* a fact, Harry Brock?"

"It's a compliment I haven't earned," he said, returning her smile. "The truth is I really do have some work that needs attention. If it's all right with you, I'll go, but I'll be back in time to take us out for dinner."

"Go, but I know where the kitchen is, and we'll eat here. While you're gone, if I can get Minna out of the house, I'll walk her down the road to see Tucker. Do you think that would be all right?"

"Better than all right. He'd love to see you, but be ready to see some change. The years have taken their toll, and this gall bladder thing has . . ."

He stopped himself. "I'll be back as soon as I can, and the first chance we get, we'll talk about what we're going to do with Minna. Will that work for you?"

"You've already been talking with Esther Benson."

"Yes."

"Go," she said, the smile gone, "and try not to get yourself shot."

Harry laughed, but it took some effort. He knew she was making a joke at her own expense, and extending an olive branch, perhaps even making a gesture of affection, surprised and pleased him, but the fact that Ernesto had picked up word of a real threat to his and Soñadora's safety added unwelcome irony to her words and revived in his own mind the old quarrel that had divided them.

Soñadora was seated on a bench in the butterfly garden of the Avola Botanical Gardens, dressed in a peach-colored blouse, a lime-green skirt, and matching sandals, her shining black hair spread over her shoulders and tumbling down her back. She was sitting with her legs crossed, her left forearm resting on her knee, staring into the koi pond, lost in thought. Harry paused for a moment before speaking to her, treating himself to the pleasure of just looking at her. She was really very beautiful.

"A penny," he said.

She looked up and for a moment smiled.

"A penny?" she asked. "What for?"

"I'm offering you a penny for your thoughts," he said, sitting down beside her on the stone bench.

"Don't waste your money," she answered, losing her smile. "Why am I here?"

"I've had a visit from Ernesto," he said, then sidetracked. He was watching the butterflies, fluttering and flitting around them like shattered bits of a rainbow.

"Do you have butterflies like these where you come from?"

"I don't remember. What did Ernesto tell you?"

Her face, which had been so soft while she was staring into the koi pool, was hard again.

"You're very beautiful," Harry said, "when . . ."

Perhaps it was seeing her with her sword sheathed in that fleeting moment that caused him to say it. Perhaps it was just having left Katherine and Minna and transferring some of his feelings from them to her. Whatever it was, Soñadora stepped on it.

"Is the Anglo hitting on the exotic half-breed?"

Her voice was so cold that if she had slapped him, Harry would not have been more stung.

"You must think so," he said in a flare of anger, "or you wouldn't have asked the question."

"That's not an answer."

"It's all the answer you'll get from me."

An inner struggle briefly disturbed the rigidity of Soñadora's face.

"What did Ernesto tell you?"

Harry paused, already ashamed of himself for having extended the unpleasantness. But he was still smarting from her

116

question, and had, despite his efforts to remain the injured party, begun to wonder if he had complimented her because he found her sexually attractive. Maybe you only want to paint her portrait, another voice suggested. Harry abandoned the effort.

"Ernesto said that your people had rescued a girl from a home where she was living as a slave," Harry told her. "The people who put her there, and for different reasons the people who lost her, are not happy. Your name and mine surfaced."

He had jumped up after her attack, and now he made himself sit down beside her again. She edged away from him.

"Little Miss Muffet," he said, amusement getting the better of his wounded pride.

"What?" she demanded.

"Do you know the nursery rhyme?"

"No."

"Do you want to hear it?"

"If I have to."

Harry turned to her and recited, "Little Miss Muffet sat on a tuffet,/ Eating her curds and whey/ Along came a spider/ And sat down beside her,/ And frightened Miss Muffet away."

"And you're the spider because I moved away from you," she said sarcastically.

"If you say so."

"Was I mistaken?"

"No."

"You were . . ."

She stuck.

"No, I wasn't, but you are beautiful. No mistake there."

She looked away from him and shook her head.

"What are we going to do?"

"The safest thing to do would be to get out of Avola for a while. The police can't protect you. They have no idea who might be trying to kill you. They say, quite reasonably, that

117

there's not a scintilla of evidence that anyone means you any harm."

"*Scintilla?* I don't know that word."

"It means a tiny bit of something. A trace."

They looked at one another and then both started to speak at the same time.

"Go," he said.

"I was wrong to say what I did."

"I'm not so sure," he said with a smile.

"*Tonto,*" she said, forced to laugh, then became serious. "How much of what Ernesto told you is to be believed?"

"If I really am an idiot, I probably don't know, but my advice stands."

"Are *you* leaving?"

"I can't," he told her, "I have house guests."

"You are not a serious person."

"Few idiots are."

"Enough! And I'm not leaving Avola."

"What about La Ramada?"

"We had a plan."

Harry took heart, thinking she sounded slightly less hostile.

"I talked with Rowena Farnham, the Rector of St. Jude's. She will give us cover," he said. "We are flogging their battered women's shelter, called Haven House."

She shrugged.

"This is what I get for associating with Anglos," she said, getting up from the bench.

"Is that how a beautiful *mestizo* says yes?" he asked, going for broke.

The long, wearisome hours of work and the confinement were wearing down Rigoberta's resistance. With the possible exception of Hazel, whose cold detachment and rawhide toughness

kept her going, Rigoberta's life of constant work and depriva-
tion had prepared her better than any of the other women to
endure the rigors of their situation.

It was being cut off from her children that was undermining
her resistance. Her weeks on the road and her time with her
uncle and aunt had been endurable because she was confident
that she would soon be working and earning money to bring
them together. Increasingly, despite her uncle's promise to stay
in touch with her and his assurance that if she worked hard
things would go well for her, she lost the ability to believe what
she had been told.

"I am not sure he told me the truth," she confided to Hazel.

"Maybe not, but your leg has healed. You're not a crack head
like most of these women, and you've got me. When things have
cooled down out there, I'm going, and you're going with me."

Rigoberta looked around the small, stuffy room. It was nearly
time for the lights to be turned off, and several of the women
who were addicts were already unconscious. Their captors
provided the addicted prisoners with enough dope to keep them
functioning and took half their meager pay in exchange.

"Look at them," Hazel said. "Pathetic."

Rigoberta had been working hard on her English and found
that she could practice even when she was working at her
machine. The sewing they were doing, mostly sewing logos onto
T-shirts and other simple tasks, left her mind free to recite
words and compose sentences. Sometimes, she forgot and began
speaking out loud, which brought complaints from those working near her, and she would go back to whispering.

Hazel did most of her teaching in the time between when the
lights were turned out and when they had grown too sleepy to
stay awake. In order not to disturb those around them, they had
pushed their mattresses together, to enable them to whisper.
The physical intimacy had another benefit for Rigoberta. It as-

suaged somewhat the loneliness and loss of physical contact with her children.

As hard and unyielding as Hazel appeared to be, she was gentle with Rigoberta, and on those few occasions when Rigoberta had begun to speak to Hazel about her children and broken down crying, Hazel had reached out and held her hand until the tears were over.

She could also tease Rigoberta into a smile and occasionally outright laughter.

"You're doing all right for an Indian," Hazel told her one night when Rigoberta was blue and having a hard time focusing on the lesson.

For a moment Rigoberta was insulted. Then she saw the joke and said in English, "For Anglo, you are one pretty good teacher."

But moments when she was able to forget her situation were extremely rare. The atmosphere in the house swung from apathy to violence. Jane, a dark-haired Anglo with two front teeth missing, and Delores, a smaller, silent, and violent-tempered Hispanic, the two oldest and most seriously addicted women, had become too debilitated from the drugs they were taking to eat properly and were in constant trouble with Maria, who cut their heroine rations in half because they were losing weight and by afternoon were too exhausted to keep up with their work, and beating them had done no good.

In response to the reductions, they tried to take the three youngest girls' money with which they intended to buy more heroin from Gomez. The girls screamed and tried to resist, but the two women threatened to hurt them and forced them to give up their pitiful earnings. The result of that was that by morning they were too drugged to work and were beaten yet again. Maria told them if they threatened the girls again she would take their ration away permanently.

"I think there will be trouble tonight," Rigoberta told Hazel.

She was right. After she had fallen asleep, she was wakened with Jane's knee in her stomach and one of the woman's forearms pressed against her throat. Delores had pinned Rigoberta's legs by sitting on them.

"Where's your money?" she demanded in a whisper.

Jane's knee had driven the breath out of Rigoberta and the arm across her throat had shut off her breath. She couldn't breathe or speak and her convulsive movements did not throw off either woman. She had no strength and had lost nearly all of her sight. Her last thought was that she would never see her children.

Suddenly, Jane hurtled off her and banged into the wall. An instant later Delores was knocked off her. Regaining her sight with her first gasp of air, Rigoberta saw Hazel step over her, grasp Jane by the hair, and slam her head into the wall. Delores had clambered to her feet, and Hazel turned and kicked her hard in the solar plexus. She went down in a breathless heap.

The room exploded into a clamor of shouting, screaming, complaining women who had been jolted out of their sleep by the sounds of the scuffle and Hazel's steady, loud, and fiery cursing. Then the light came on followed by Gomez and Maria, both carrying pistols.

"They didn't intend for us to see those," Hazel said to Rigoberta while recovering her breath and also glancing at Jane and Delores, crumpled against the wall. "You OK?"

Rigoberta nodded, rubbing her throat, not trusting herself to speak.

The next morning after Rigoberta had been at her machine for an hour, Maria called Jane and Delores out of the workroom. An unsmiling Gomez took her place and laid his pistol on the desk. The remaining women worked in silence, and Rigoberta did not need Hazel to tell her that Jane and Delores would not be back.

"Mother of God," she prayed silently, "may I live to see my children again."

But she was no longer sure, this far from her mountain, that her prayer could be heard.

15

Harry returned home to find Katherine in the kitchen, the table set with the china she and he had chosen soon after they were married. He had put it away in the sideboard in the dining room after she left and had not used it again. The sight of it jolted him.

"I hope you don't mind," she said, taking a steaming casserole dish out of the oven.

"How did you know what I was thinking?" Harry asked, slipping off his sandals.

"I thought the same thing when I saw it while I was looking for a serving dish," she told him, placing the dish on the table and pulling off her oven mittens.

They looked at one another across the table, and Harry was struck again by the complexity of the situation.

"Did you see Tucker?" Harry asked, not ready to talk with Katherine about the feelings, painful and otherwise, that seeing her as he had seen her hundreds of times raised in him.

"You were right," she said, returning to her work. "He's failed a lot. It hurt to see how much. He looked so frail in his bed that Minna sat down beside him and cried."

"How did he take that?" Harry asked, disturbed at several levels as the scene shaped itself in his mind.

"Just as you'd expect. It's the first time she's cried since . . ." Katherine began.

"I never intended to do it," Minna said, stalking into the

room. "I shouldn't have done it."

Neither Harry nor her mother had heard her come down the stairs.

"Don't worry about it, Minna," Harry said. "It wouldn't have bothered Tucker."

"You don't know that," she snapped, her face pale with anger. "You weren't there, and you or somebody should have been. He's too sick to be left alone. Why did you let them send him home?"

Minna was striding around the table with that strong, purposeful stride Harry recognized from having seen her mother walk that way when she was preparing to take his head off.

"How bad off is he?" Harry asked, looking at Katherine.

"How many times do you need to be told?" Minna shouted. "He can hardly sit up!"

"Minna," Katherine said. "Calm down. It's not Harry's fault."

"No?" Minna said, glaring at Harry. "He was supposed to be looking after Mr. LaBeau, just the way he was supposed to be looking after me! And there's one more thing. I'm not talking to anybody about anything."

With that she ran out of the room and fled up the stairs.

"I'm sorry, Harry . . ." Katherine began, her face crumpling toward tears.

"It's all right," Harry said.

Without hesitating, he stepped forward and pulled her into his arms.

"She's upset," he said, pressing his face against her hair, speaking softly into her ear as he had done for reasons great and small so many times in the past.

Katherine leaned into his embrace, wrapping her arms around him, pressing herself against him.

"I'm so worried," she whispered, her breath catching.

"Sure you are," he told her, "but we'll get help for her, and in the end she'll do what you want her to do. She's too smart not to."

Despite his concern for her and for Minna, Harry was becoming increasingly aware of the fact that he was embracing a woman whose body he knew intimately and had once responded passionately to his. After a moment of tightening her hold on him, Katherine leaned back in his arms. Although her eyes were bright with unshed tears, Harry found himself looking at the Katherine he had once loved so intensely.

"Oh, my," she said blushing, and, giving him a quick kiss on the cheek, stepped back and turned away. "Do you have a psychiatrist's name?" she asked, fiddling with some pans on the stove.

When she turned back, her face had lost the color and animation that a moment before had brushed away the years.

"Esther Benson suggested Gloria Holinshed. Benson says she's especially good with adolescents."

"You're going to sit down and eat," Katherine said suddenly, "and Minna and I are going to eat with you. Wash up and sit down," she said decisively, pulling off her apron and starting for the stairs. "I'll be back in a minute, and I'm going to have that girl with me."

"Don't be too hard on her," Harry said, but found he was talking to the sound of her feet drumming up the stairs. Some things don't change, he thought, and was suddenly full of joy.

It did not last, but by the time he had put his things away, washed, and come back to the kitchen, Katherine and Minna were already seated. Harry did not wait for either of them to speak but went directly to Minna and kissed her on the forehead.

"I'm sorry, Harry," she said quietly.

"Me too," Harry said. "You were right. Tucker shouldn't have been left on his own."

"I've got something else to say," Minna put in quickly before her mother could speak. "If Mr. LaBeau will have me, I'm going to spend most days over there looking after him."

"Great idea," Harry said. "He'll be pleased as punch."

"When do I get to speak?" Katherine asked.

"I have a feeling you've already done some talking. It seemed to work."

Harry caught her eye.

"You two," Minna said. "You're like twins. You even have a secret language. I don't know why you ever broke up."

Harry almost said neither do I, but stopped himself.

"Let's eat," Katherine said, "before everything's cold."

The next morning just as Harry was setting off with Katherine and Minna to see Tucker and care for the animals, Jim called him to tell him that two women had been found in the Luther Faubus Canal. Both had been shot in the back of the head.

"When we have more information I'll let you know," Jim said. Before hanging up, he added, "It looks as though somebody's cleaning house."

Harry put away his cell without telling Katherine what the call was about, and it occurred to him that the murders were probably only the beginning.

Heather Parkinson had done what she could to clean up the wound in the sow's front leg and fashion a metal splint that she couldn't chew off, a development that had done nothing to improve the pig's savage disposition. The piglet, on the other hand, greeted with squealing enthusiasm anyone who appeared at its cage, including Oh, Brother!, who had taken an interest in the two animals. Sanchez refused to have anything to do with either one of them.

Later, having left Katherine and Minna with Tucker, Harry drove to police headquarters.

"Both women were easy to trace," Jim said wearily. "They

had records and had been reported missing a month ago. The autopsies showed high levels of heroine in their systems."

"Doesn't sound as if they were killed in a drug bustup," Harry said.

"No, and their being dumped in the Luther Faubus Canal is strange," Jim said, "Whoever put them in there either didn't know or didn't care that in water this warm they would float in three days."

"Were they prostitutes?"

"Suspected but not proved and no convictions," Jim said. Harry assumed he was reading, "Petty theft, possession of controlled substances, disorderly conduct, assault. County jail is as far as they got in the incarceration system."

"Have you talked to anyone about them?"

"Frank sent out some CID people," Jim replied, "but it didn't turn up much. There were unsubstantiated reports that Rhodes and Contreras had been seen hanging out with some Guatemalans and were bragging about the drugs they were getting. Then, about a month ago they vanished, and it was thought they'd gone off with their new friends."

"Soñadora and I are going back to La Ramada in a couple of days," Harry said. "We'll try to find out if anyone knows anything about them. You'd better give me their full names."

"Jane Rhodes and Dolores Contreras."

"Ages?"

"Rhodes was thirty-seven, Contreras, thirty-nine."

"OK. I'm going to see Tucker. Katherine and Minna are on their way there now."

"How is he?"

"He's pretty weak but still in good spirits."

"How's Minna?"

Harry paused before answering, not sure how to respond.

"I guess I'd say that she's strung very tight and right now is

127

dumping a lot of her anger on me and her mother. Coming to the Hammock seems to have stirred up something. We're getting her to Gloria Holinshed as soon as we can. Do you know the name?"

"Yes, she's in juvenile court a lot. I hear good things about her."

"I hope you heard right," Harry said, trying to feel encouraged.

Walking to Tucker's place with a thin mist still floating over the Puc Puggy Creek and a huge orange sun rising through palms and slash pines beyond the Creek's floodplain, Harry wondered if anything Jim had told him offered any access into why the two women had been killed and whether their deaths were connected in any way to human trafficking.

They were clearly women who had been living on the violent edge of Avola society. They might have been killed for any of a number of reasons. Without consciously willing it, Harry's thoughts drifted back to Minna and the accusation that he should have been looking after her. Telling himself it was only displaced anger talking did little to assuage either his guilt or his own anger. The anger was not directed at her but at her assailant and in a less defined way at a world that created such twisted minds with their capacity for acting out the unspeakable. Wandering in that swamp, lost to everything around him that was his refuge against such anguished thinking, he was returned to sanity by the appearance of Oh, Brother!, who came trotting down Tucker's driveway to greet him.

"How are you feeling?" Harry asked Tucker, who was propped up in bed with a mug of tea in his hand, basking in the attention Minna and Katherine had been giving him.

"I'm feeling pretty well, and you obviously fall short of deserving one, not to mention both, of these lovely women,"

Tucker replied.

"You look like hell," Harry said. "How long are you planning to linger on?"

"Harry!" Minna shouted.

She had been washing the window and spun around, wearing an outraged expression.

"Don't let him get you going," Tucker said, beaming. "He's just jealous."

Katherine was sorting out a basket of dry clothes she had brought into Tucker's bedroom and refused to take sides when her daughter appealed to her.

"You're standing up for him while pretending not to," the girl protested. "That's deceitful."

"You've forgotten, Minna," Tucker put in, "these two have known one another a long time, and they've been married, which makes them either best friends or mortal enemies. Which of the two do you think it is?"

Minna looked carefully at Tucker, who continued to smile at her.

"I'm not qualified to answer," she replied, narrowing her eyes.

"Here's the thing, Minna," Tucker said. "By the way, since you're on your feet, would you get me some more tea?"

Once she was out of the room, Tucker leaned back against his pillows, making a face as he shifted position.

"What do you say we get you some professional help in here," Harry said, trying not to sound as concerned as he felt.

"I'm way ahead of you," Tucker said. "Wetherell Clampett's wife Doreen is going to come in—something's held her up today. I'll be all right."

Harry groaned inwardly. Doreen Clampett sent Wetherell to work with holes in the knees of his overalls, shirts that had never seen an iron, a hat that a pet goat had partially eaten, and a lunch pail the size of a carry-on bag.

"But never mind that," Tucker said, glancing at the door. "In case you're worrying, it's fine with me if Minna wants to come over here and scrub and polish. The place could use some cleaning, and I don't think Doreen's skills include those activities."

Katherine, who had slipped into one of her silent spells, which told Harry that she was brooding over something, most likely Minna, finished folding the clothes and said, "You know what she's doing, don't you?"

"I suspect her wanting to look after me is a substitute for looking after herself," Tucker responded.

"Yes," Katherine said sadly, "it's called a flight into health, but at least she's talking and not hiding in her bedroom, staring at the wall."

"Just when she needs to cope with her own pain," Harry added, anguished by the picture of Minna alone in her room.

"It's not my line of work," Tucker responded, "but I don't think this has to be an either/or situation. Her working here might keep her mind from running in a circle like a squirrel in a cage, which, I suspect, it's doing now. If it's all right with you, I'd like to give her those two pigs to work with. I want to try to tame that sow."

"I don't want her in the run with that wild pig," Harry protested, his heart jumping with alarm. "Lame or not, she'd chew Minna to pieces."

"I don't think she's all that bad," Minna said to Harry, coming back with Tucker's tea. "She's just hurt and scared. And so would you be," she added with a scowl, fists on her hips, "if you'd lived all your life in the woods with family and friends and ended up in a cage with a baby and a broken leg, surrounded by scary creatures."

"That's just about how Oh, Brother! put it," Tucker agreed, having thanked Minna for the tea. "He's guardedly optimistic about the outcome. Of course, Sanchez has a different view, but you'd expect that, given what those pigs did to him."

"See?" Minna said.

Katherine looked at Harry and laughed. Harry blew out his cheeks and threw up his hands.

16

"How long have you lived in Avola?" Soñadora asked Harry after a longish silence.

They were driving on the East Trail in the direction of La Ramada.

"Almost thirty years," Harry said, surprised by her question.

It was the first time she had expressed any interest in his life, past or present.

"Have there been a lot of Spanish-speaking people here all that time?"

"Many more now than when I first came."

"Then why haven't you learned to speak Spanish?"

Harry groaned inwardly, a question that he had thought was a move toward getting to know him better had turned out to be a stick to beat him with. But he decided to try to answer it honestly.

"I never needed to."

"Didn't you wonder about the lives of all these people?"

"I think they're mostly like mine."

"Do you think *my* life has been *mostly* like yours?"

Harry had a choice. He could back out of this or find himself embroiled in another culture war with her. But she really did interest him, and he was strongly attracted to the fire in her, and if quarreling with him was her way of engaging with him and possibly connecting with him, then he would settle for it.

"I think your life has been very different from mine, but so

132

far, you've been very careful to keep it to yourself. Do you think if I spoke Spanish that would change?"

"You just changed the subject. The real reason you haven't learned Spanish is that you expect . . ."

"Wait," he said. "Listen to me. I want to tell you something."

Possibly the urgency in his voice caught her attention and surprised her into acquiescence.

"Tell me," she said. "I suppose it will be in English."

He let that crack go unanswered.

"Fifteen or sixteen years ago, a woman turned up on my doorstep, looking for her husband. She had two children with her, a boy and a little girl. They were living in her car and had not been eating very well for some time. Her husband was living a mile or so from my house. He was associating with some very bad people, so I went with her and found him shot to death in his cabin."

"This has something to do with your not needing to learn Spanish?" Soñadora asked.

Harry ignored the question. He had seldom talked with anyone about this. Now that he had begun, he was determined to finish it.

"Later on, I married Katherine and adopted the kids. Katherine had suffered a lot of neglect and abuse in her life, and she was abrasive and aggressive and riddled with anxiety. When those qualities weren't in ascendance, she was a wonderful person, but she couldn't deal with my being a private investigator."

He paused to see if she was still with him.

"Go on," she said.

"While we were together the boy was kidnapped by a man who thought he wanted to kill me. He had been threatening me for some time, and I hadn't told Katherine. In my efforts to recover the boy, I settled the problem between me and the man who had kidnapped him and brought the boy home safely. When I told her what had happened, she blamed me for having put my life and Jesse's in danger. She demanded I give up my work. I refused, and she left me."

"I still don't see . . ."

"Stay with me. I'm almost done. Minna is now thirteen."

"Your adopted daughter, this is?"

"Yes, a little while ago on her way home from school, a man dragged her into a van, banged her around, and by a miracle she managed to fight her way free before he did what he was setting out to do. The event left her emotionally in pretty bad shape. I've got both her and her mother here with me. The idea is to get her professional help and hope we can help her get her life back."

"I hope she does. I'm sure she was terrified, but just imagine if she had been locked in one of these sex houses the traffickers are operating . . ."

"What makes you think I don't grasp the horror of it? I do, and having Minna attacked has made it more real but no more monstrous, and I don't need to speak Spanish to know what pain and misery the victims of the twisted creeps who harm them suffer."

"That's it?" she demanded.

"No. The work you're doing is terrific, but it doesn't give you the right to treat me and everyone else who isn't doing what you're doing as if we're enemies of the people."

"In many places in the world, you are," she said quietly.

"In this corner of the world, most of us are part of the solution. It would help if you got that through your head."

"All right," she said spiritedly, "it's through my head, and I still think you should learn Spanish."

"In a perfect world," he answered, losing all desire to quarrel with her.

"There's no such thing," she told him. "We have to live in this one, and we have to try to make it better."

"One *gringo* at a time," he said.

To his astonishment, she turned, put both hands against his left shoulder and shoved him against the door with surprising force. The Rover swerved slightly out of its lane, and Harry snapped it back.

"Are you trying to get us killed?" he shouted in mock alarm.

"Only you," she said, giving him one of her slicing glances. "I'm wearing my seatbelt."

He glanced down and saw that he wasn't, and a light on the instrument panel was telling him so.

"Do you know you're a piece of work?" he asked, unable to keep from grinning.

"Never forget," she replied with a straight face, "*Indios* are primitive, violent people."

"OK," Harry said fifteen minutes later, "I've got the handouts Rowena Farnham gave us. You've got the cards printed with the home numbers, the 911 number, Betsy Potter's name, and the home and church numbers."

They were parked in *La Ramada,* preparing to repeat their door-to-door canvas, and had left their sniping party behind them.

"There's nothing much new we can do," Soñadora said. "I'll talk. We'll both pass out the material."

"And I am going to watch the houses very carefully. Somebody doesn't like what we're doing."

"Wearing that jacket in this heat will tell everyone you're carrying a gun."

"Maybe not. In this country, people in the God business often wear jackets even in July."

He caught her eye and said, "Take me seriously on this. If

you see me reach for my gun, you go face down onto the dirt. Don't look around, don't think, don't try for a smart remark."

"¡Macho mucho!" she responded, climbing out of the Rover.

The first door opened before they reached it. Harry recognized the woman and expected to see her smile. She did not.

"She is saying we must not stay here," Soñadora told Harry while the woman continued speaking. "She says it is dangerous for anyone now to do what we are doing. She says there's a *disputa* of a serious nature, and everyone is afraid."

She was certainly afraid, Harry thought, noting that she stood with her hands clasped tightly at her waist, probably to keep them from shaking. The two women talked for a few moments, and the door closed abruptly.

"What's the dispute about?" Harry asked.

"She wouldn't say," Soñadora answered with a troubled frown as they stepped away from the door.

"I think it might involve a shooting war," he said, looking around at the empty street and silent houses, broiling under the cloudless sky.

Just then four women in brightly colored skirts and blouses filed out of one of the houses and hurried toward them.

"¡Hola!," the youngest of the four said when the group reached them. She then said something that sounded like a name, but Harry, puzzled by this visitation, missed it.

Nevertheless, he repeated their greeting, echoing Soñadora's response. From then on the conversation switched into Quiche and proceeded at a terrific rate. Unable to understand what was being said, Harry had time to observe them, and it was clear from their gloomy expressions and the tension in their voices that they were discussing something painful and controversial.

The conversation ceased as abruptly as it had begun.

"*Vaya con dios*," the leader said finally, shaking Soñadora's hand and nodding at Harry.

Then, turning, she and her companions strode away with the speed and precision of a drill team.

"OK," Harry said, "what's the bad news?"

"We have a hole in our welcome," she said sadly.

It took Harry a moment to catch her meaning.

"Worn out our welcome?" he asked.

She nodded. "She told us to leave and not come back, that we are in danger here," Soñadora added quietly, watching the women disappear into the house.

"Why?" he asked, looking around again and feeling increasingly on edge.

"I'm really not sure. Once Evara Tum, their spokesperson, had told me that, she began talking very fast in a dialect that is new to me, but I understood most of what she said."

"They seemed frightened," Harry said.

"Frightened and angry. They want help but don't know where to turn. She asked me if our church could be trusted. I said it could, but before I could find out what kind of help they wanted, she ended the conversation,"

"Let's go back to the Rover," Harry said. "Don't hurry, but keep moving. While we're walking we'll talk of 'shoes and ships and ceiling wax, and cabbages and kings.' "

"What?" Soñadora demanded, looking at Harry as if he'd lost his mind.

"Never mind. I'll explain another time. Just keep moving."

"I don't see . . ."

He took her arm and started moving her along. She shook him off and came to a stubborn halt, glaring at him angrily.

"I'll explain it later," he told her. "Without being too obvious about it, take a look around. Make it look as if we're thinking about where to go next. There's not even a fish crow flying over this place. Didn't you notice how fast the women were walking when they came out to talk with us and when they left?"

"I don't see . . ."

"Maybe not, but Evara did. She kept looking at that pink stucco house to our left—don't look at it—as if she expected it to jump up and bite her. With luck, whoever's watching us will decide not to shoot us."

"I don't believe you," she said, but began walking again.

"What else did they tell you?" Harry asked as they crossed the road to the Rover. "I'll tell you later," she snapped. "I don't like the kind of joke you're—"

Soñadora was yanking open her door on the Rover just as the red ball on the top of the SUV's antenna exploded with a distinct pop, showering her and the windscreen with bits of plastic. The explosion was followed by the slamming report of a high-powered rifle.

Soñadora stood frozen, staring wide-eyed at the place where the ball had been.

"Get in," Harry said sharply, clambering into his seat and starting the engine. "Don't think. Just get in."

He was leaned across the seat reaching for her when she broke out of her lock and, white as milk, leaped into the cab and pulled her door shut.

As Harry turned into the street, she hopped onto her knees on the seat to peer out the rear window.

"Someone tried to shoot us," she said in an outraged voice.

"Nope," Harry told her. "They were just letting us know they could have. It looks as if our cover held."

"What do you mean?" Soñadora asked in an unsteady voice.

"If they hadn't believed we came from St. Jude's, the outcome would probably have been different."

"We might have been shot."

"Right. What else did those women tell you?"

With a groan she slumped back into her seat.

"Not much, but they mentioned three people by name:

Rigoberta, the woman who was in that white van the police found. Agata Bal, the woman's aunt, and Cavek Bal, the aunt's husband."

"They live here?" Harry said.

"Yes, and there's more. The young woman apparently jumped out of the van and tried to run into her aunt's house and was shot in the leg by the Anglo in the van. He and the driver of the van were then killed and the van and the men's bodies driven away."

"Why did they tell you this?" Harry asked, astonished by what he was hearing.

"I think because they are very frightened," Soñadora continued, regaining some color. "Evara said that since the shootings there has been only trouble in the community. One man has been killed, others wounded. Hooded men come at night. There is a lot of fighting."

"A turf war."

"Grass?" she asked with a puzzled frown.

"No. Territory. There's something they want and someone else who doesn't want them to have it. Did she say what the fighting is about?"

"No, she would not say, but I don't think it's drugs."

"Why?"

"Because these people were brought up in a world where drugs were a commonplace trade. They would not be fighting over drugs. Something would have been worked out before anyone was shot."

"And the trouble started with the shooting of this Rigoberta person?"

"Yes. Then Rigoberta disappeared," Soñadora said. "Evara claims not to know where she went, which may or may not be true."

"Maybe you can talk to her again by phone," Harry said.

Soñadora shook her head.

"They will not have land lines in their houses," she said, "only cell phones."

"Fear of being traced," Harry said sourly.

"It is an intelligent precaution," Soñadora insisted.

"But not perfect. They can be traced through their names."

Soñadora shrugged. "Names can change."

17

Two days later, Harry got a call from Jim Snyder, asking him to meet him at the Luther Faubus Canal, running through a remote eastern corner of Tequesta County.

"Frank's already out there," Jim said. "He thinks there's something you need to see."

"I take it this something is dead," Harry said.

He and Katherine had just lost another round to Minna in the dispute over whether or not she was going into counseling, and Harry's temper and his nerves were both frayed. Even though he was as concerned as ever over what had happened to her, trying to cope with her reactions had rattled him.

"She's thirteen years old and we're bigger than she is," Harry had said to Katherine after Minna had stormed out of the room. "What's wrong with this picture?"

"Nothing," Katherine said with a sigh of frustration. "It's just that she *is* a thirteen-year-old girl who wants to bite the world's head off, and is practicing with ours. Be patient."

Turning the other cheek was not what Harry wanted to do, but he couldn't think of anything short of rolling her up in a rug and carrying her to see Dr. Holinshed as an alternative.

"It's my guess," Frank told Harry and Jim as they scrambled down the weed-grown bank of the canal past the uniformed officers laying out yellow tape, "what the ME's going to find when he opens her up is that knife went straight into her heart.

She didn't bleed much and never had no time to struggle. There she is."

The young woman lay on her back up to her waist in the water with a long, thick, black braid draped over her right breast. She was naked and staring up at the sky as if she was watching the clouds; her face wore an expression of almost beatific calm. Silent plain-clothed men and women from the CID squad were stepping in and out of the water, taking pictures and measurements and putting bits of things in plastic bags. They had already made plaster molds of two sets of footprints, pressed into the soft earth.

"Anyone you know?" Hodges asked Harry.

Harry looked at the woman, at her tranquil beauty, at the trampled bank, and then at the very large alligator, floating twenty or thirty feet out from the bank, watching them with interest.

"Looks like we found her just in time," Hodges said, following Harry's gaze.

"How likely is it that Harry will recognize this woman?" Jim demanded of his sergeant, his ears getting red. "You should have cleared this with me before dragging him out here."

Harry knew Jim didn't deal well with dead bodies and when forced to confront one tended to take out on Hodges his anger, pain, and general despairing doubt that the human soul could ever be redeemed.

Hodges was philosophical on the subject.

"It was that preacher father of his who's behind the whole thing," Hodges had once told Harry, "bringing the boy up on hellfire and brotherly love kind of tangled his head."

Harry recalled that judgment briefly, assigned Hodges extra points, and then turned back to the corpse.

"Her name is Evara Tum, Jim. I think I mentioned her name earlier," he said to the glowering policeman, who was doing his best not to see what he had climbed down the bank to look at.

"She was one of the women Soñadora talked with in La Ramada two days ago," Harry added, getting no response.

Jim nodded and clambered back up the bank with Harry and Hodges following him just as Kathleen Towers, the County Medical examiner, and her team were unloading their gear from a gray van.

"Hi, Jim. Hi, Harry," the slim, brown-haired woman, dressed in a blue jumpsuit, said, returning Hodges's wave. "They ready for me down there?"

"CID is just finishing up," Jim replied. "It's bad."

He started to say something more and shook his head instead.

She and Harry exchanged glances.

"Like that woman those kids found in the mangrove swamp," she asked, "the one the crabs had been chewing on?"

"No," Harry said, "but I'd have to agree with Jim that it's bad."

"Then I'd better get at it."

She waved her team forward and plowed down the bank toward the group of men and women moving around the corpse, taking the last of their pictures.

"I figured from the face, the braid, and the clothes Deputy Robbins found in the culvert down there where Jefferson Toomey used to live, she might of come from that bunch in La Ramada," Hodges told Harry when he regained his breath from climbing the bank.

"You were right," Harry said and looked down the narrow, palm- and brush-lined road, the decaying shack where he had once found a man named Toomey sprawled in his cabin in a pool of blood and his own name scrawled in that same blood on the floor, a last, desperate appeal from the dying man.

Perhaps, he thought, Katherine had been right all those years ago when she told him to find another line of work. As it was, his memory was crowded with faces of the dead.

"I suppose we'll find she's been raped," Jim said darkly, rejoining the conversation after a period of brooding.

"She don't look bruised," Hodges said, showing interest. "Usually when that happens, which *is* usually, they'll have—"

"That's enough, Sergeant!" Jim said loudly.

"She was probably undressed after she was killed," Harry said. "It was done to insult her. I don't think she was sexually assaulted.

"I'd of thought killing her was insult enough," Hodges protested.

"Not in their culture. In their view, insults to the corpse accompany the dead person's spirit on its journey," Harry said.

"The question is why she was killed in the first place," Jim insisted, stifling Hodges's attempt to respond.

"When the women came out to meet us, Tum did most of the talking," Harry said. "Her efforts to organize an effort in the community to stop the violence probably contributed to her death."

Jim did not seem to be convinced.

"Why kill someone for wanting to keep people from dying?" he asked.

"I'd like to have Soñadora with me before I go very far with this," Harry replied. "She's the one who actually talked to Tum and the others. That said, I think Tum was trying to go to the root of the violence in La Ramada and put an end to whatever is causing all the shooting."

"And that's probably connected to the shooting of Rodriguez and Baker," Hodges put in.

"Plus the Rigoberta woman, who was wounded in that fracas," Jim added, "possibly while trying to run away from Rodriguez and Baker."

"Are you going into La Ramada in force?" Harry asked,

recalling that Soñadora had predicted it.

Jim ran his hand over the top of his head as if he was brushing off spider webs. His ears had gone very red.

"By my last count, we've got five murders on our hands, two are clearly connected. The other three may or may not be connected. Added to that, we have a missing person in this Rigoberta woman."

Jim gave his head a final rub and started to walk off, then turned and came back, his boots kicking up puffs of dust from the sandy road. Harry couldn't remember when he'd last seen his friend this agitated.

"And I have no evidence, and from Evara Tum not even a slug, just a naked body with the face of an angel."

"The investigation is just beginning," Harry said in an effort to be encouraging, finally understanding that seeing Tum had set Jim off.

"And I'm pretty sure that when we do go into La Ramada— because in the end we will have to—it's going to carry a high price," Jim said, speaking as if he had not heard Harry's comment.

"We've got a team trained for that sort of thing," Hodges said encouragingly, "and they've got fire power enough to flatten the entire place."

Harry winced, guessing that Hodges had hit a hot button.

"Wouldn't that be just grand?" Jim demanded loudly, turning on Hodges. "That place is stiff with women and children."

If there was a cow flap around, Hodges would step in it, Harry thought ruefully.

"Captain, there's always some collateral damage in that kind of operation," Hodges said.

"Collateral damage!" Jim repeated, his ears flaming. "If you just had someone in your family killed by a SWAT team, would you say, 'Oh, that's all right, it's just 'collateral damage'?"

"I've got a couple of cousins I could spare," he said, grinning at Harry.

Harry launched a rescue mission. "I think I've worn out my usefulness to you," he told Jim, "at least so far as La Ramada is concerned, but Soñadora's Quiche and her knowledge of that underworld is probably way ahead of anything the Sheriff's Department can produce. And she's eager to help."

Jim showed interest by turning away from Hodges, who still looked like the Cheshire Cat.

"No," Jim said, "we can't send you back in there, but yes, if I'm going to move this investigation forward, I'm going to need help. Do you think she'd talk with me if you were with her?"

"I'll ask, but it's got to be agreed up front that nothing will be said or asked about her immigration status," Harry said, "or of those in her organization."

"You've got my word," Jim answered.

Harry left, the thought of Jim talking with Soñadora intriguing him.

For a moment he wondered if Jim might find her attractive, then squelched his impulse to become a matchmaker. Ever since Colleen McGraw had been shot to death on the Okalatchee River, Jim had not even looked at another woman. The loss of Colleen had, Harry knew, almost brought his friend down, but he still hoped Jim might find someone who would break through the emotional wall he had erected around himself.

"I want the money you both have been hiding," Maria said.

She had kept Rigoberta and Hazel in the workroom after the others had left. Her hand rested on the heavy revolver that now was always with her and she stared down at them from the dais with a cold intensity that frightened Rigoberta.

Since the disappearance of Rhodes and Contreras, Gomez and Maria had been increasingly hard on the women, demanding longer hours of work and watching them more and more closely. Maria had also become increasingly suspicious of Hazel and Rigoberta.

"I don't think so," Hazel replied. "It's ours. We've worked for it."

Maria's brooding expression did not change, but her attention became focused on Hazel.

"Come up here," she said after a long pause, pushing her chair back from the desk.

Hazel lifted her skinny frame out of her chair and walked up to the desk. Rigoberta caught her breath. She was sure her friend had put herself in danger by rejecting Maria's demand.

"Come up here," Maria said, smiling and gesturing to her left.

"OK," Hazel said and hopped onto the dais.

With her hand still on the revolver, Maria pushed herself onto her feet. When Hazel stopped in front of her, she suddenly swung the hand that had been resting on the gun at Hazel's face. Had the blow landed, it would have knocked the smaller woman off her feet because it had all of Maria's considerable weight behind it. Rigoberta shouted a warning.

Hazel stepped back, avoiding the blow. Maria, having missed her target, lunged forward. Continuing to step back, Hazel caught Maria's wrist, pulled up her arm and then down in a flying arc, twisting it hard as she did so. With a cry of pain Maria was thrown off her feet and fell hard, her head striking the edge of the desk as she went down.

"Come on, Riggs," Hazel said with a wide grin as she stepped over Maria's sprawled body and gathered up the gun. "Let's grab our shit and get the hell out of here."

"What about her?" Rigoberta asked as she forced herself toward the desk and saw with horror the blood spreading around the woman's head.

Hazel kicked Maria in the side, but there was no response.

"Dog meat," Hazel said. "Move! Move!"

"What if Gomez is coming?"

"He'll think it was one of us screaming. Now go!"

With Rigoberta in the lead, they ran down the hall, then slowed to a fast walk as they passed the room where the other women were eating in the imposed silence that marked all of their meals. Rigoberta caught a glimpse of Gomez, standing, watching the women, holding his gun. She could not tell whether or not he had seen her and Hazel and was suddenly very frightened.

"Run!" Hazel told her once they were past the door and approaching their sleeping place. "Grab your sack."

They had no problems hurrying through the darkened house until they reached the front door, which was fastened with two locks and a heavy sliding bolt. Rigoberta slid back the bolt but had no idea what to do with the locks.

"Let me," Hazel said, pushing Rigoberta aside.

Rigoberta heard voices. "Eating is finished," she said in a nervous whisper.

Hazel finished opening the first lock and gripped the door handle.

"Shit!" she said. "It's still locked."

There was the sound of heavy footsteps coming along the hall.

"Gomez!" Rigoberta said, her heart beginning to pound harder with fear.

"Step back," Hazel said and stepping back herself, raised the pistol in both hands and blew the second lock to pieces, then pulled open the door.

Rigoberta, her head ringing from the crashing explosion of the gun, rushed out after Hazel into the twilight of late evening. In front of them a graveled drive with two SUVs parked in it led away through a tangle of bamboo, stopper bushes, oleanders, and saw palmetto.

"Run!" Hazel said and started down the driveway, followed by Rigoberta, who was sure that Gomez would step out the door and see them fleeing.

"He'll shoot us!" she said, already half out of breath from the lack of activity.

"Run!" Hazel shouted, "And don't look back."

So Rigoberta ran, but she was sure she was going to die, and her mind filled with images of her children and a terrible sense of loss. But they were nearly at the first turn in the driveway before she heard Gomez shout at them to stop.

Hazel glanced over her shoulder at Rigoberta and saw her falter.

"Goddamn it, Riggs, run!" Hazel shouted and, reaching back, grabbed Rigoberta's arm and yanked her forward.

She either had to run or fall on her face so she ran until Gomez shouted again, making her feel that flight was useless. If she was going to die, why not die standing, with dignity, not like a hunted animal.

"Riggs!" Hazel shouted, "Don't you go all Indian on me. Run!"

Ridiculously, Rigoberta found herself wanting to laugh, and the folly of it kept her running until they were around the first turn and paused to catch their breath.

"It hurts to be shot," Rigoberta gasped.

"Your leg?" Hazel asked.

"Yes. Gomez will soon be here."

"Go into the bushes, and stay away from the saw palmetto. It cuts."

"He will follow us," Rigoberta gasped, pushing into the tangle. "Why he didn't shoot us?"

"We're worth money alive. Nothing if we're dead. Hurry up!"

Once past the thick edge of the woods the trees grew larger and the undergrowth thinned. Hazel pulled Rigoberta to a stop and whispered, "Listen."

They could hear Gomez on the road crunching up and down, swearing.

"Where are you?" he shouted. "Come out. You can't get away. If you come out now, you will be safe. If you don't, I will beat you hard."

In the shadowed safety of the woods, a change came over Rigoberta. Her fear fell away. Even with Gomez shouting threats from the road, she was not afraid. She had escaped the prison house. The trees surrounded her. The damp, sweet smell of earth and growing things filled her nostrils.

Something inside her wakened and stretched. She was alive. She was no longer a captive. She had not been shot. She was not thinking of her children or of her mountain. For the moment she was totally in the present. Perhaps for the first time in her life, she felt a powerful and expanding awareness of herself, she was free.

Gomez shouted again at them, and his threats suddenly made Rigoberta angry. What right had he to threaten her? Her new self swelled with defiance and she shouted as loudly as she could in English what she had often heard Hazel say quietly, "Fuck you, Gomez!"

"Oh, shit!" Hazel said. "Why did you do that?"

"I wanted to," Rigoberta answered defiantly. "I have not done many things I wanted to do in my life, only things I had to do. It is something you would do, but it is new for me."

"That's probably true enough," Hazel said with a short laugh, "and look where it's gotten me."

Gomez was crashing toward them through the thickest part of the brush.

"Get behind that saw palmetto," Hazel told her. "Get as low

as you can."

"If you can," Rigoberta said quietly when she and Hazel were huddled together, peering back through the dense, pointed tops of the palmetto fronds, "shoot him in the leg. It hurts much."

Before Hazel could answer, Gomez stepped out of the heavy growth into the more open space where Hazel and Rigoberta had been standing. He was holding his gun in front of him with both hands, turning it in a slow arc as he searched the space in front of him. But in the dim and broken light, objects had lost their edges.

"Come out," he shouted, frightening a pair of fish crows that, cawing loudly, clattered out of a slash pine to Gomez's right.

He swung toward their racket, and Hazel said, "Don't move, Gomez, or I'll blow your head off."

"*Puta!*" he shouted, firing in the direction of her voice.

They were not more than twenty feet apart, but he had no target. He swung past the palmetto and fired again. Hazel stood up and shot him in his right thigh. With a howl of pain, he collapsed and thrashed around in the ferns and low brush, swearing and groaning.

Rigoberta peered over the palmetto. Hazel was still pointing her gun at the fallen Gomez.

"Perhaps you should shoot him again," Rigoberta said loudly in Spanish.

Just then the sound of a car grinding toward them over the crushed rock road cut off Hazel's response. Gomez began shouting. Hazel ran forward and smashed the barrel of her pistol against his head. He collapsed, plowing his face into the dirt and leaves, and did not move.

"Help me find his gun," Hazel said anxiously.

"I have it already," Rigoberta replied.

The car, spewing rocks into the woods, raced past them, its lights swerving like a shattered searchlight through the trees as it swung around the corner and raced toward the house.

"Let's go. They'll be back," Hazel said.

"Which direction?"

"The road. Damn, where is it? I'm turned around."

"Follow me," Rigoberta said. "We still have some light left."

The change that had come over her in the opening was still with her. She felt confident and strong.

"How do you know where the road is?" Hazel demanded.

"Indian," Rigoberta said with a grin.

"Let me see that pistol," Hazel said.

"Why? I can carry it. Also, I can shoot it."

"I'll give it back. I want to be sure the safety's on."

"Safety?"

"This gizmo here. Shove it this way and you can fire the gun. Shove it this way and you can't."

The light was nearly gone, and their two heads, pressed together, one black and one yellow, bent closely over the pistol, were indistinguishable.

"*Muy bien,*" Rigoberta said, "If I wish to shoot someone, I will remember the safety first."

She shoved the gun into her bag and strode off purposefully.

"No shooting unless I say so," Hazel said in an alarmed voice, "and you'd better know what you're doing or the pigs will eat us."

"Better the pigs than these *mosquiteros* fucking," Rigoberta replied, slapping futilely at the air while Hazel exploded in a snort of half-muffled laughter.

18

For the first time in days, Harry woke to find he had the house to himself. He had overslept and came downstairs to find a note on the kitchen table.

"I'm going to Tucker's with Minna. She's upset about Doreen Clampett, who's supposed to be cleaning and cooking for Tucker. Minna claims she never even sweeps the floor and is filling the house with cigarette smoke. You never used to sleep this late."

The note was unsigned, and he remembered with a tinge of something very like sorrow that she had never signed her notes. He stood, folding the note and looking out the window over the sink, remembering that he had once asked her about it and she turned away the question by saying stiffly, "Who else but me is going to leave you notes?"

"My outside woman might have dropped by," he had said, thinking he was being funny, and the look she gave him was so filled with pain that he never asked her again why she left her notes unsigned and never ever again mentioned outside women. There had been none until the marriage was being measured for a box.

Recalling those unpleasant days, his mind made an uneasy transition to Cora and their still unresolved relationship. Harry missed her, and the way things were going between them, he thought there was a good chance he would never see her again. He was close to feeling sorry for himself when his more sensible self suggested that unless he unbent and called her, there was a good chance he would never talk with her again either.

He called, and when her answering system responded, he left a message. Putting down the phone, he was surprised by how disappointed he was and decided to join Katherine and Minna at Tucker's.

Oh, Brother! and Sanchez met him at the end of the driveway leading into the farm yard. Oh, Brother! looked much as he ever did and pushed his nose into Harry's chest by way of welcome. Harry stroked and patted the big mule's sleek, black neck, but Sanchez, even with his bandages off and walking without pain, looked seriously wasted. His blue and brindled coat was dull. There was more white around his muzzle, and his welcoming grin had very little energy.

"Are you two taking care of the pigs?" Harry asked, after he had knelt down to stroke Sanchez and examine the long scar across his side, which Harry saw was healing well but still looking painfully raw.

Oh, Brother! showed interest in the question by waggling his ears, but Sanchez turned his head away and stopped wagging his tail.

Harry wondered if the two animals really had understood his question and let him know how they felt about it, or was it all his imagination. Then he wondered if it mattered, which, he suspected, was a question that, left unanswered, allowed him to go on talking to them without feeling self-conscious.

"Sloth has wrecked more promising lives than rum and wild living," Tucker said when Harry entered his bedroom.

Tucker was sitting up in bed, wearing a complacent smile while Katherine was ironing and Minna was putting furniture polish on the ancient set of drawers on the inside wall.

"I met Doreen," Harry said.

A generously built woman in her forties with bleached hair

piled high on her head, tight dungarees, and a dark blue A-shirt that left no work for the imagination, she had waved Harry into the kitchen with a cheerful grin while leaning against the wall, talking on the telephone, and smoking a cigarette.

"She's not what you'd call a woman of infinite variety," Tucker said, "but she's calm as an evening lake, and her heart's almost as big as . . ." He caught himself, glanced at the two women in the room and after an almost imperceptible pause ". . . as her hairdo," he finished.

Katherine snorted, but Minna, her mind totally elsewhere gave no heed to the others. She had not even greeted Harry when he came into the room and looked thoroughly miserable. The sight of her face wrung Harry's heart.

"Tell you what," Tucker said, having caught Harry's look, "I've done more dangling than a fish line. It's time I tried a walk. I want to see those pigs."

With that he threw back the covers and eased himself onto his feet. After asking Harry to fill a basin with odds and ends for the pigs, he turned to Minna.

"Minna," he said cheerfully, "there's a robe in that closet. I wonder if you'd get it for me. I don't want those two pigs to see me in my pajamas."

Despite her distraction, Tucker's last comment had caught her attention.

"Why not?" she asked, holding his robe while he slipped his arms into the sleeves and his feet into his slippers.

"First impressions are important," he told her, letting her take his arm as he shuffled toward the door.

"Those pigs aren't going to care how you're dressed," Minna protested.

They entered the kitchen from the hall with Tucker and Minna leading, followed by Harry and Katherine. Doreen was just dropping a cigarette butt in the wood stove and complaining to Harry, still scrounging in the refrigerator, about wasting good food on pigs. She turned and broke into an uncensored laugh.

"If this doesn't look like a funeral procession with the main feature walking. Tucker, where the hell are you going?"

"To introduce myself to the pigs, do you want to come?"

This was greeted by another blat of laughter.

When she had recovered, she said, "Hell no. The only pig I want to meet is one coming off a spit."

She turned her attention to Katherine and pointed at Tucker.

"You watch him. If he looks like he's going to fall down, one of you catch him. I'll go back to doing the laundry."

"That will be a help, Doreen," Tucker said, giving her an encouraging smile, and went out the door, talking to Minna and pausing to pat Oh, Brother! who was waiting for them in front of the stoop. "Animals pay more attention to appearances than people do," he told her. "They have to, because their lives often depend on it."

Katherine waited for Harry to catch up and said, "You better watch yourself with that Doreen. She's got her eye on you."

"She's way out of my class," Harry said, red-faced, afraid she might have seen him staring at Doreen's décolletage, which reminded him rather painfully of his celibate state.

"Are you seeing anybody?" Katherine asked him.

"It's more I'm not seeing somebody," he said before thinking and mentally kicked himself.

He had been all through that and made up his mind not to talk to Katherine about Cora. He had been less definite with himself as to why he did not want her to know he was/had been sleeping with another woman.

"It's probably none of my business," Katherine said stiffly.

Harry wanted to say it wasn't a secret, but no words came.

Katherine and Harry caught up with Minna and Tucker, who

had stopped to catch his breath and take in the beauty of the day. The temperature was still not above the low eighties with a soft breeze lifting Tucker's fringe of white hair and the sun shining through it like a halo. Noticing that Sanchez had trailed behind and now stood with his back to the group, he turned to speak with Oh, Brother!

"I know you've been talking with Sanchez, and I know he's stubborn," he said quietly to the mule, "but give it another try. Being left out like this is bad for him."

Oh, Brother! gave Tucker a gentle push with his nose and turned to look at Sanchez, who had been taking quick glances over his shoulder but now looked stolidly away from the group staring at him.

"Let's have a look at those pigs," Tucker said, moving everyone along.

"If that's not a sight," he said as they reached the fenced run.

The sow, still limping but able now to walk on all four feet, trotted to the rear of the cage and turned with a defiant popping of her jaws to confront her visitors. Her baby reacted differently; the young boar came running toward them, its curly tail whirling like a miniature helicopter blade, squealing with delight.

"Bring on the feast," Tucker said to Harry with a laugh. "We've got one hungry youngster. I suspect the sow's milk has about dried up."

"Here," Harry said, passing the basin to Minna.

He and Katherine watched while the girl and Tucker talked to the piglet as she fed him. He kept shoving his nose through the spaces in the mesh in his eagerness to be fed. Tucker took those moments to scratch his head gently.

"I'm going to take something over to the mother," Minna said, taking a handful of apple peelings out of the basin.

157

"Watch your fingers if she comes up to the wire," Tucker said.

Oh, Brother! followed Minna and stood over her when she crouched down near the sow and began pushing the peelings through the fence.

"He's protecting her," Katherine said in surprise.

"That's right," Tucker said, pushing himself to his feet with difficulty but declining Harry's offer to help. "He and Sanchez learned what wild pigs are capable of when they tried to drive them out of the garden. Look over there."

Sanchez had quietly come to stand beside the mule. When the sow began to edge toward the peelings, the hair stood up on the big hound's shoulders and a low growl rumbled in his chest. Oh, Brother! put his head down and pressed his nose against Sanchez. The growl subsided.

"Come pig, come," Minna called softly to the sow, encouraging her.

The heavy brown and black animal hobbled closer and a moment later began eating the peelings Minna fed her until they were all gone. Sanchez watched her, the hair on his back gradually flattening.

Then the sow lifted her head, ears cocked, to where her baby was still feasting. A moment later the piglet crossed the cage and began eating.

"They need names," Tucker said.

"Ask Minna to name them," Katherine said.

"Good idea," Tucker said. "It might help."

They all watched the girl, sitting on her heels, talking quietly to the two pigs. Harry wished fervently that she could communicate with Katherine and him as comfortably as she was connecting to the two animals. Perhaps naming them might build a bridge. He was getting fairly desperate in their search for something that would unlock the door she had closed against them.

Harry drove Katherine back to the house.

"I'm going into Avola and talk with Soñadora Asturias," he told her.

They had tried to talk about Minna but found there was nothing to say they hadn't already told one another a dozen times. The only good part of their talk was that it hadn't gone back to his relationship with Cora.

"Well, it's just as well," she said with a rueful smile. "You were my last excuse not to make some work calls I've been putting off."

"Problems?" he asked.

"Just staying in touch and up to date."

He had stopped in the heavy shade of the live oak at the front corner of his lawn. Katherine was out of the Rover, holding open her door as they talked. She paused to look around at the house, its veranda half buried under the wisteria vine, then across the white sand road to the Puc Puggy Creek glinting through the low thick growth at the edge of the road. Over their heads cicadas were fiddling in the heat.

"I'd forgotten how magical this place is, Harry," she said with another sad smile.

"I won't go," he said quickly, pushing open his door.

"Stop!" she said. "I really have work to do. If you stay, I'll just trail around after you being a nuisance. Please! Go!"

Harry laughed. She still had the gift of delighting him.

"Two things, Katherine," he said. "One: You never trailed after anyone in your life. Two: You are incapable of being a nuisance. Do your work. I'll be back soon, and if I'm held up, I'll call."

"Just don't get shot," she said in her regular voice and

slammed the door.

He sat for a moment and watched her walk toward the house, the sun gleaming on her hair, her skirt swaying gracefully as she moved away from him. A beautiful, exciting woman, he thought, then backed the Rover into the road and drove away, trying not to think just how beautiful.

Whatever his thoughts had been about Katherine as he drove into Avola, they were scattered by the smoking ruins of the *Salvamento* building. Finding a place to put the Rover among the crowd of police and fire vehicles had him swearing before he was finally able to make his way to the scene of devastation.

The possibility that Soñadora might have been caught inside made him sick. But he pushed forward through the crowd of onlookers until he reached Frank Hodges, who, along with a bevy of deputies, was trying to push back the crowd and establish a perimeter.

"When did it happen? What happened?" Harry asked, trying to make sense of the blackened wreckage of the building.

"Give me a hand here," Hodges said in a loud, exasperated voice, trying to make himself heard over the babble of voices and the occasional blast from firemen using bullhorns. "It's like trying to push a chain."

Harry joined in the effort, and after a few minutes, they had the crowd eased back to the road. Deputies then quickly set up a yellow tape line, establishing everything inside it a crime scene.

"Were they in there?" Harry demanded.

The onlookers, their curiosity sated, slowly began to drift away. Hodges, streaming with sweat, pulled out a huge red bandanna and mopped his face. Harry waited impatiently.

"I don't know," he said, still puffing, "What I do know is that somebody fire-bombed the place about forty-five minutes ago. We got the call at the station maybe ten minutes later and got

160

out here to find the place crawling with neighbors and fire truck chasers."

Harry's cell vibrated.

"Something terrible has happened," a woman said, tremulous with emotion.

"Soñadora!" Harry shouted in relief. "God, I'm glad to hear your voice!"

"This is not the time for joking!" she shouted back. "I'm trying to tell you . . ."

"I know," he broke in. "I'm not joking. I'm in front of what's left of the *Salvamento*. I thought you and the others were all dead. How did you get out? Are you all right?"

"Yes, I'm all right. Someone always watches. Theresa saw the car stop and a man jump out carrying a red gasoline can with something taped to it and run toward the front door."

She stopped speaking, and Harry could tell from her breathing that she was struggling to keep from crying.

"Soñadora," he said quickly. "It's OK. You don't have to tell me now. Just tell me where you are. I'll come and . . ."

"No," she responded, "I want to tell you. Then, although it is not necessary, but if you want to . . ."

She couldn't get the words out.

"I will come and that's that," he said.

"We have practiced this many times," she said, but still unable to keep the tremor out of her voice. "Theresa blew the whistle. Two of us ran to the back and threw open the double doors. Everyone raced out and scattered toward our cars, which are never parked near the *Salvamento* building. A moment later there was a terrible explosion, and flames shot into the air."

"Where are you?" he asked quietly.

She told him.

"I'll be right there."

"Was that Asturias?" Jim Snyder asked.

161

He had joined Harry and Hodges while Harry was talking.

"Yes, they all got out," Harry said, blowing out his breath, his insides still feeling like scrambled eggs.

"How did they do it?" Hodges asked.

"They must have practiced," Jim said.

Harry nodded.

"They've been expecting something like this and were ready for it."

Jim looked back at the pile of charred wood and heat-twisted metal.

"Whoever did this must have wanted to stop them really bad," he said.

"Right in broad daylight," Hodges said, wiping his face again, "not very damned bright."

"I've got to go," Harry said. "I'll get back to you."

"I want to talk to Asturias and the rest of her women," Jim said, frowning at Harry.

"My guess is you'll have to talk with Soñadora first, to get to the rest of them, and she's going to be very camera shy."

"I figured as much," Jim said with a sigh. "I expect you to produce her and today would be none too soon."

"I'll try, but she may not cooperate," Harry answered, already turning away.

"Don't even think of trying to hide her somewhere, Harry," Jim put in quickly.

"Why would I do that?" Harry demanded.

"I don't know," Jim said, "but when there's a woman involved, there's no telling what you'll do."

Harry strode off with Hodges's laughter speeding him on.

19

"You're sure you're all right," Harry said, starting to give her a hug then thinking better of it.

"I have some scratches from running through the saw palmettos, and we've lost a lot of equipment," Soñadora replied, stiffly. "Otherwise, I am fine."

They were at Oppenheimer's, sitting at an outside table shaded by two huge fig trees, occupied by half a dozen pairs of ring doves, bubbling lugubriously in their branches, and Harry did not think she looked fine. Harry had picked her up at a filling station on the East Trail a little after noon, and insisted they go to a restaurant. She had protested, but Harry persisted, telling her that if she didn't want to eat, she could drink, an idea she apparently found so shocking that she stopped resisting his efforts to feed her.

"How about all your records?" he asked, surprised she hadn't mentioned them.

"We have everything backed up on small external drives, and everyone grabs her own in an emergency. In addition, we periodically back up the backups and keep those drives stored away from the center."

A tall Haitian waitress wearing an orange headscarf and a blue dress came to their table and gave them a slow smile.

"You hungry, Master Harry?" she asked, resting one hand on her hip, and waiting in perfect ironic ease.

"We are, Mirabelle," Harry said. "Who's in the kitchen?"

"Felix," she told him with a light laugh. "You always ask me that."

"Then it's the day for the Thai salad. Mine with chicken. Soñadora?"

She looked at Mirabelle, who gave her an encouraging smile. She looked at Harry, her eyes dark as onyx. Harry held his breath.

"Shrimp," she said.

"That's right," Mirabelle said. "We don't need more chicken. I've eaten so much chicken I cluck in my sleep."

To Harry's surprise, Soñadora laughed and then spoke to Mirabelle in rapid French. Mirabelle grinned broadly and slid her eyes at Harry.

"You got your hands full here, Harry," she told him, winked at Soñadora, and glided gracefully away like a slim pirogue.

"Have you any idea who did it?" Harry asked, not really comfortable with the way Soñadora was looking at him.

"Are you on a first name basis with all the waitresses in Avola?" she asked.

"There may be some, recently hired, I don't know yet," he said, inching the bread and herbed butter toward her.

She pushed it back and asked, "How many times have you been married?"

"Twice, and you?"

"I have never married. How many children do you have?"

"Why are we talking about my marriages when you've just narrowly escaped being incinerated?"

"How many?" she repeated.

Their food came.

"Time to eat," Harry said with a pathetic try at being jovial.

"How many?"

"One mouthful and maybe I'll tell you."

She took a bite of her salad and put down her fork. As she

chewed, her eyes slowly filled with tears and spilled down her cheeks.

Harry, alarmed but determined to be helpful, snatched a napkin from the empty table beside them, intending to put his arm around her shoulders, dab her tears, and say something comforting. He was on his feet when she held out hands and said in a cracked whisper, "Don't touch me." "If I could stop the tears, I would, but I can't. My mother could."

"I have five children," Harry said lamely.

"Thank you," she said, wiping her eyes and struggling to control herself. Still struggling, she said, "I have no children. It has always seemed to me that it would be a criminal act to bring children into my world. Perhaps there is less pain in yours."

Harry thought of Minna as he sat down.

"Possibly," he said, "but there's suffering everywhere. How old are you?"

"That is a rude question," she said.

Her tears had stopped and she took a second bite of her salad.

"Thirty-five," he said, picking up his own fork.

She shot him a look, and he gave himself two points for having nailed it.

"I have a daughter your age," he said. "I married very young."

He did not get the smile he had hoped for.

"What's her name?"

"Sarah."

"Does she have children?"

Harry paused, put down his fork. Pain from a new direction.

"No," he said. "Not yet."

She looked at him for a long time without speaking and finally nodded. Harry wondered if all these questions were an attempt on her part to create a temporary sanctuary into which she could retreat from the violence and threat that had engulfed her life.

"Are you intending to stay in Avola?" he asked.

She had managed to eat some of her salad, but Harry saw that it was an effort, and he guessed she had tasted none of it. His effort to get her to drink some wine failed.

"It is not wise," she said flatly.

It took him a minute. Then he caught on. Sometimes, his failures of perception awed him.

"I am not sure I should make long-range plans," Soñadora responded with a flicker of a smile.

The courage as well as the sadness in her remark touched Harry.

"If I go with you, will you talk to Jim Snyder about what's happened?"

There was a long silence, and Harry thought she would refuse, but she braced her shoulders and said, "Yes, although it is against my better judgment."

"He will help. He's a good man. His department helps people."

"If you say so, it may even be true."

"It is true. Are you feeling any better?" he asked and, unable to stop himself, reached across the table and placed a hand over hers.

"Please don't, Harry," she said quietly, tears filling her eyes again. "I am not used to sympathy."

"I plan to change that," he told her, reluctantly withdrawing his hand, painfully aware that he had no right to make this beautiful, brave, but in certain ways very fragile woman promises he could not keep.

20

Harry found Katherine sitting on the lanai, reading his copy of *River of Grass*. She was wearing shorts and sandals and one of his blue, long-sleeved shirts with the cuffs rolled back to the wrists and tails tied at her waist. He thought she looked about twenty-five, despite the white in her hair, which he chose to ignore.

"You've changed," he told her as he pushed open the screen door. "In all the years we lived together, I don't think I ever saw you with your feet up, reading. You were always working."

She closed the book and smiled up at him.

"The years have slowed me down," she said.

"I don't believe a word of it. Where's Minna?"

"At Tucker's, and she'll be there until supper time."

"Good," Harry said, holding out his hand to her. "Let's take a walk."

"I'd like that," she said and let him pull her up from the chair.

"That's something else you would never have done."

"What?"

"Let me help you out of a chair."

They were almost exactly the same height, and for a moment they stood about a foot and a half apart, looking at one another.

"Perhaps I've grown smarter as well as older," she said, a smile tugging at her mouth.

"You've grown more beautiful," he said, feeling his heart

beginning to pick up speed.

"Oh! What a liar!" she cried, putting her hands against his chest as if to push him away but only increasing the pressure enough to maintain contact.

"You never were any good at taking compliments," he said, taking her upper arms in his hands.

They stood for a long moment on the verge of something. Harry thought he knew what it was, but he did not allow himself to seize it. Neither did Katherine, who said, "I'd better get my hat. I'd forgotten how ferocious the sun is here."

They stepped apart, although still clinging to one another until the very last moment.

"Shall we walk to the cabin?" she asked when she came back wearing her straw hat with a wide brim and a trailing blue ribbon tied around the crown.

Her suggestion startled Harry. The cabin was where she and Minna and Jesse lived after Willard Trachey's death, and Harry knew the place was stiff with painful memories. She had come to the Hammock searching for Willard, penniless, homeless, with two hungry children, chin-deep in despair, only to find her husband dead in that cabin, brutally murdered.

"There's not much left," Harry told her. "That big old fig tree has just about swallowed it."

They had reached the white sand road and started in the direction of the cabin despite Harry's comment.

"Lord, it feels as if I'd never left," she said softly, taking a deep breath redolent with the odors of ferns, leaves, damp forest earth, the sun-baked smell of the road, and the more pungent smell of Puc Puggy Creek, sliding dark and silently toward the Gulf.

Standing in the road's mottled sun and shadow, they were surrounded by the strident sawing of the locusts and the cicadas in the branches of the oaks and gums and slash pines edging the road. Harry followed her gaze and saw the familiar world as she was seeing it and, hoping that she was having a rare moment free from her concern about Minna, told her, "You're welcome to stay as long as you want. Bring Thornton."

She caught his hand and walked with him for several minutes in silence.

"Who said, 'You can't go home'?"

"Thomas Wolfe wrote a book called *You Can't Go Home Again.* But you *did* go home."

"No, I think the Hammock was the closest thing to a real home I ever had, first the cabin, where I began to feel safe, then with you where I began to be happy and where I learned for the first time what love was."

"I'm going to take that as a compliment," Harry said, not knowing what else to do with it.

He almost added *it's too bad it didn't last* but stifled that impulse.

"I intended it as that and much more, Harry. You saved my life," she said seriously.

"What about you now?" he asked, anxious to find a way to suppress the bitterness that was beginning to well up in him.

The strength of it startled him. He thought he had buried that demon long ago. Apparently, the stake had worked itself loose. Perhaps asking her about her emotional life might remind her that she had left him.

"Aside from this trouble with Minna, I'm all right. My sister and I rub one another the wrong way more than I'd like, but that's pretty much the story of our lives."

She stopped and looked at him, color rising in her face.

"That's not what you mean, is it?"

"No, but if you feel uncomfortable talking about that, let's just forget I asked," he said quickly, already sorry that he'd let his self-righteousness out of its cage.

"It's all right. There's not much to tell. Thornton came along and took care of the first couple of years. Then a year later I met someone at a Christmas party one of the neighbors gave. He was just coming out of a divorce and five or six years younger than me. It ended five months ago."

"Well, I'm sorry," Harry said, assailed by guilt for having asked.

She gave a rueful laugh and said, "There's nothing to be sorry for. He told me he wanted to get married again and raise a family of his own, and to do that he needed a younger woman."

"He made a hell of a bad mistake."

Katherine dropped his hand.

"No, he didn't," she said, averting her face. "I'm too old to have more children and too old for the market, Harry."

Harry found that instead of feeling bitter, he was now furious and wanted to track down the son-of-a-bitch who had dropped her and tear his heart out. He grabbed her hand and held it so tight she flinched.

"Sorry," he said. "Katherine, look at me."

He had stopped and pulled her around so that they were standing in one of the white sand tracks, facing one another. He had acted so forcefully and abruptly that her hangdog look had vanished into an expression of alarm.

"Ever since I first met you, I've been telling you that you are a beautiful, desirable woman. I'm going to tell you again, and this time you're going to believe me. Katherine, you are a beautiful woman. You could still have children. And any man who marries you should have a gold star pasted on his forehead."

Katherine began to giggle.

"What's funny?"

"You are. I'd forgotten."

With that she threw her arms around his neck, pulled him against her and kissed him hard on the mouth. Harry grabbed her to keep from falling and began kissing her back.

"You don't really want to see that cabin, do you?" he gasped when they paused to breathe.

"No," she said, and he was kissing her before the word was out of her mouth.

"What are we going to do?" Harry asked when they stopped, looking around desperately.

"The house, Harry," she said, "The house. Remember the time I got poison ivy on my ass? Once was enough."

They ran back to the house laughing and trying to talk and reached the lanai door gasping.

"Upstairs?" Harry asked.

"Let's try," she said, pulling up his T-shirt. "I'm too old for the floor."

Quite a bit later, Katherine, lying sprawled on the bed where she had fallen off him, lifted her face out of the tangled sheets, and looked at Harry, who, supported on one elbow, resembled the dying Gaul, and said, without conviction, "Now look what we've done."

"Twice," Harry croaked and collapsed again.

The screen door on the lanai slammed and both of them said, "Minna!" before launching themselves off the bed. In the ensuing scramble for scattered pieces of clothing, they kept bumping into one another and bursting into half-smothered laughter, further hindering their struggle into their clothes.

"I've lost one of my sneakers," Katherine whispered desperately.

"Kick that one off. Go down barefoot," Harry said.

"OK," Katherine said. "Let's go. And don't make me laugh."

Minna was waiting for them at the foot of the stairs, looking grim.

"So," she said, accusingly, "You guys have been making out."

171

"Minna!" Katherine cried, her face flaming.

"Don't talk to me!" the girl shouted and raced up the stairs and down the hall toward her room.

Then she reappeared at the top of the stairs and threw something in their general direction. It caromed off a banister and thumped onto the floor at Katherine's feet.

"My sneaker," she said, and clapped her hand over her mouth.

Harry picked up the damaging evidence and, putting his arm around Katherine's shoulders, walked her to the kitchen.

"You said she wasn't coming home until dinner time."

"It *is* dinner time," she said, and they both broke out laughing.

Then they stopped laughing.

"What are we going to do about her?" Katherine asked, slumping onto a kitchen chair.

"Talk to her. Get her into Holinshed's office."

"Fat chance."

"Maybe no chance. What if you start dinner and I go upstairs and try to make contact?"

"What are you going to say to her?" Katherine asked suspiciously.

"It will depend on what, if anything, she says to me. Don't worry. I won't upset her or make her do anything she doesn't want to do."

"I'm so frightened, Harry," Katherine said, getting up from her chair.

"So am I," he admitted, "but we have to go on trying."

"Then there's us," she said as if it were an afterthought.

"I'd almost forgotten," he replied, pretending surprise. "Yes, that's going to take some working on."

"Go!" she told him, pointing at the stairs.

Harry had to knock on her door three times before Minna said, "Come in."

172

She had pulled a chair up to the open window and was sitting staring out into the middle story of the live oaks, flanking the house. The locusts and the cicadas were sawing away loudly.

"See anything special?" Harry asked.

She shook her head.

"OK if I sit down?" he asked.

She nodded and he eased himself onto the side of the bed beside her.

"Are you upset about your mother and me?" he asked quietly.

"It's none of my business," she snapped.

"Yes, it is. You're our daughter."

"I just don't see how you can . . ." she said, her voice rising.

That left Harry with alternatives when what he wanted was a single, clear direction. He gambled.

"Make love together?"

She went on staring out the window but gave the slightest nod, as if she found even mentioning the act repulsive.

"Katherine and I still love each other," he said quietly. "We made our peace quite a while ago and have managed to stay friends, despite all the unpleasantness. Does that help?"

"I'll never do it," she said in low, tight, cracked voice.

"I hope that later you'll change your mind."

That was a mistake, because she turned toward him, white-faced, and shouted, "I won't. I'll never change my mind."

"And neither your mother nor I will ever try to make you. Do you believe that?"

Her face softened a little and her back lost some of its rigidity.

"Yes," she said in a whisper so full of pain that Harry had to force himself to stay seated on the bed and not reach out to embrace her.

"Would you come downstairs and help me make the salad?" he asked.

She shrugged, jumped up, and left the room ahead of him.

When she reached the kitchen, she said in a flat voice, "I'm sorry about throwing the sneaker."

21

Rigoberta woke and for a wild instant could not remember where she was. Then in the gray first light she recognized the broken plank walls of the old shed they had stumbled into in last night's darkness. Hazel lay curled beside her, still asleep.

"*Madre de Dios,*" she said silently then, sliding into Quiche. She completed her prayer for her children, invoking the *Madre*'s and several other deities' protection for them.

"You praying again?" Hazel asked, pushing up onto her elbows and regarding Rigoberta with a sleepy frown.

"Yes, and especially for you," Rigoberta replied.

"You're wasting your time with me," Hazel said with a short bark of harsh laughter, struggling to her feet.

"It's good to make the try," Rigoberta replied, getting up and brushing off the bits of weeds and straw clinging to her skirt.

"Effort," Hazel said.

"What?"

" 'It's worth making the effort,' is what you were trying to say. God, I'm hungry."

"Even you make the effort to call on *el padre* when you are hungry enough."

For some reason Rigoberta felt very light-hearted. She stepped out from under the rotting, warped roof boards and looked across the remains of the old pasture, softened with trailing wisps of ground fog, toward the brightening point in the eastern sky. She took a deep, satisfying breath. The sense of being free had survived the night and she was thankful.

"I gave up saying my prayers when I was six," Hazel said in a hard voice. "I wanted no part of a god who would let that bastard who was living with my mother and feeding her dope do what he was doing to me."

"Did you tell your mother?" Rigoberta asked, shocked by what Hazel had said.

"She knew."

Hazel shivered and rubbed her arms. "Let's get out of here. Maybe we can find something to eat. Rigoberta put her bag strap over her head and adjusted the weight of it on her hip so that she could quickly reach the gun. Knowing the gun was there gave her courage to face what she guessed was coming.

"The dope makes people become animals—no, worse," she said, putting a hand on Hazel's shoulder. "Mother animals try to protect their young. I am sorry that something so bad happened."

"Thanks. I survived. Which way shall we go? I'm damned if I know where we are," Hazel responded, looking around with an expression of distaste for what she saw.

"We have come west since we left the house," Rigoberta said.

"How do you know that?"

"The stars. We learn as children."

"Huh," Hazel said. "You are full of surprises, Riggs. If we keep going west, we're bound to hit a road before we reach the Gulf. Let's go."

They set off across the field with the sun at their backs.

"What is the Gulf?"

"The Gulf of Mexico. You flew over it to get here."

"It was night. I saw nothing but people being sick."

Remembering the shock and fear she had felt that night and the next two days and nights before reaching her aunt's house filled her with anger.

"It was bad in the plane and then afterward. I want to tell you, but I don't have the words in English," she told Hazel.

"Tell me in Spanish."

"No, this must be said in English."

"You're weird, Riggs. You know that?"

"What is *weird?*"

Hazel caught up with Rigoberta, who was leading, and linked arms with her.

"*Weird* is when somebody who can't speak English well enough to say what she wants to say and refuses to say it in Spanish, which we both understand."

Rigoberta laughed and squeezed Hazel's arm against her side.

"It's Indian," she said, and they both laughed.

They walked for nearly half an hour through abandoned fields with fallen fences and pine and saw palmetto woods where the walking was dry but slow because of the frequent tangles of brush, which brought colorful cursing from Hazel.

In the midst of one of her outbursts, Rigoberta stopped, looked back at her, and said, "Listen."

The quiet sounds of wind, bird song, and insects was broken by the sound of a car engine drawing closer. Moving carefully now, they went ahead, the growl of the car's engine growing louder. Then they saw the road and stopped, peering through the thick growth of leaves and branches at the edge of the road and listening.

The old Cadillac was moving slowly, rocking like a boat as it moved into and over the dips and humps in the sandy road. A man with a gun in his hand and a bloody rag tied around his head was leaning out the window on the passenger side of the car, staring into the trees.

As the car approached, Hazel whispered to Rigoberta, "Don't move."

177

Rigoberta caught her breath as the man seemed to look straight into her eyes. Then the car passed. He had not seen her. She let go of her breath with weak knees and a racing heart.

"Fucking Gomez!" Hazel said when the car went around the next bend.

"I think I should have shot him again," Rigoberta said, becoming angry with herself for having been so frightened at that moment she had forgotten about the gun.

"Forget about shooting anybody," Hazel said with a grin. "Before they come back, we've got to be somewhere else."

"How did they know where to look?"

"They guessed we had to come this way, and we'd have to cross this road."

"What is the other way?"

"Alligators. Point west."

Rigoberta pointed across the road.

"Break off some branches. We're going to make a broom."

"What?"

"Escoba, escoba!" Hazel said, snapping off small branches from the bushes surrounding them.

Rigoberta, still puzzled, stopped when Hazel did.

"Now," Hazel said, moving toward the road, "we back across this road and sweep out our tracks as we go. Then we carry the branches into the woods for a ways before we drop them."

Rigoberta said something.

"What?"

"Listo, listo!" Rigoberta snapped, imitating Hazel's tone of voice.

"Very funny and, if I was smart, would I be out here in the woods with you, trying not to get shot?" Hazel asked with a grin.

Rigoberta smiled back.

An hour later, very hot, very tired, scratched, and bitten, they ran into the fence separating them from the interstate.

"What to do?" Rigoberta asked, staring up at the top of the fence, well out of their reach.

"Find a place to crawl under."

From where they were standing, Rigoberta could see only the northbound lanes.

"*El camino* one way?" she asked in surprise as they moved along the fence.

"One goes north. The other goes south. You can't see the other part from here."

They found a sag in the ground giving them space enough to crawl under the wire. The ground was wet and so were they when they scrambled to their feet.

"Shit!" Rigoberta said, trying to wipe the mud off her skirt and arms.

She found saying the word when she was angry or disgusted made her feel better, and felt the little self inside her grow bigger. They clambered up the bank to a place where the southbound lane came into view.

"What time is it, Riggs?"

Rigoberta glanced at the sun and said, "About nine hours."

"You count the trucks going this way," Hazel said, pointing north. "I'll count those going the other way."

"*Porqué?*"

"We need to get to Avola. We can hide there. At this time of day most of the trucks are going north away from the city. By afternoon, most will be going toward it."

For three or four minutes they counted, and Hazel's count was much higher.

"OK, Riggs." The blonde woman said with a grimace. "We go south, and let's try very hard not to get killed crossing the roads."

"I know south without counting," Rigoberta said, pointing

toward Avola, "and before I was shot, I could run . . . *rápido,*" she added proudly.

She still could. The effort left Hazel winded.

"*Los cigarillos,*" Rigoberta said, rubbing her wounded leg, which had decided to protest what it had been made to do.

Half an hour later a derelict Ford truck, loaded with watermelons, stopped for them. An old man with a huge handlebar mustache leaped out and ran around the truck, sweeping off his wide-brimmed straw hat before he opened the door, and with a huge, gap-toothed smile said, "I am Juan Hernandez, and it is my lucky day. Two *senoritas muy hermosas* will ride with me to the city."

It had been spoken too fast and in too fractured English and Spanish for Rigoberta to know what had been said. She looked at Hazel.

"His lucky day," she said, making a sour face.

Rigoberta, who was sitting in the middle, turned to Juan and said something incomprehensible to Hazel's ears. The old man's mahogany-colored face lit up in a wide smile. The two began a rapid-fire conversation. Hazel groaned, slumped down in the cracked plastic seat, and instantly fell asleep.

A few minutes later, the old Cadillac with Gomez still in the passenger seat started to pass them, then braked and allowed them to pull ahead. The old man paid no attention to the car, but Rigoberta did. She jiggled Hazel with her elbow. Hazel grunted and reluctantly pushed herself up in the seat.

"Gomez," Rigoberta said. Neither woman looked back, although both of them wanted to.

The next morning, Minna rose early and went to Tucker's house. An hour later she marched into the kitchen before the screen door on the lanai had slammed shut behind her. Katherine and Harry were having breakfast.

"She's got to go," Minna said loudly.

"Who?" Katherine demanded.

"That woman," Minna burst out.

"Doreen Clampett," Harry said, buttering a piece of toast.

"Yes."

"What has she done?" Katherine asked.

"Nothing, except smoke and talk on the telephone. That's the problem."

"Has Tucker said anything about it?"

"He doesn't have to," Minna replied, apparently less angry now that someone was listening to her. "He hates the smell of cigarettes. The kitchen is a mess. He's up and dressed for most of the day, but he's still too weak to do any work, and seeing his place all knocked around troubles him. I hate to see him upset when he doesn't need to be."

"It's too bad," Harry said, "but you said yourself he's too weak to do the work himself."

"What would you do about it?" Katherine asked.

"Get her out of there," Minna shot back.

"Then what?"

Harry was about to say something less indulgent then decided to listen.

"I can clean, I can cook. He doesn't need help dressing and undressing and . . . those kinds of things," she said defiantly, glancing at her father, probably expecting trouble from that quarter.

"What happens when you leave?" Harry asked, having failed to think before opening his mouth.

A blanched look spread across Minna's face as she turned to her mother.

"Are we leaving?" she asked in a troubled voice.

"You'd better ask . . ." Katherine began stiffly.

"No, of course you're not leaving," Harry said too loudly. "I

181

just meant there's a limit to how long you can," he almost said *play housekeeper,* then saved himself, "work as his housekeeper."

"Harry's right," Katherine added, making her own rapid adjustment, "We can't stay here indefinitely, and there's no telling how long Tucker's going to need looking after.

"Is he that sick?" Minna asked, appealing to her father.

"I guess I think he'll be his old self long before you and your mother even think about leaving here. I guess I made that negative remark, having forgotten how grown up you are."

It was a good try that might fool Minna, but it was not going to deceive Katherine, and Harry turned to her and said, "When I said come for as long as you want, I meant it," deliberately leaving out the issue of Minna and her emotional health.

"I heard what you said, Harry," Katherine told him.

"Is this my fault?" Minna asked with a worried expression.

"No," Harry said. "It's my fault. Right, Katherine?"

"Are you making a difference being with Tucker?" Katherine asked, ignoring Harry's question.

"I think so. He seems to enjoy talking to me."

"Then go back and do whatever you've been doing. Let *him* take care of Doreen Clampett. When *he's* ready, she'll leave."

"Parents," Minna muttered and ran out, letting the lanai door slam a second time.

When she was gone, Harry carried his toast to the toaster and pushed down the spring.

"There was no reminder in my remark that you weren't staying here permanently," he said.

He turned around and faced Katherine, who was still sitting at the table, pushing the cold scrambled eggs around on her plate.

"As a matter of fact, I hope you stay here a long time."

"I know you do," she said, not looking at him, "and staying here is the easiest thing I've done in a long time. That's why I spoke so sharply. You brought me back to reality."

"The reality is, Katherine," he said, "that I still love you, and as far as I'm concerned, you could stay here permanently."

"And I love you," she told him with a rueful smile, "but how far does that get us? You know we can't live together."

"We're older, and, as you said, maybe wiser."

She made a snorting noise that could have been a laugh.

"Don't you have a girlfriend or whatever it's called now? I've found a few things in drawers that I'd be very surprised to see you wearing," she said a little sourly.

Harry groaned just as his toast popped up. He put it on his plate and carried it to the table, searching in vain for a bolt hole.

"Yes," he admitted, trying for a cosmopolitan tone, "I was seeing someone, but she left the country about six months ago, and I'd be very surprised if she returned."

"Are you in love with her?"

"Were you in love with your friend?"

"Probably, but it doesn't seem to have stuck."

"No, me either. Let's talk about Minna."

"OK, what do you want to say?"

Katherine seemed as ready to change the subject as he was.

"When she's occupied with Tucker and his doings, you'd never know there was anything wrong with her," Harry said,

"Until you try to put your arm around her or find her sitting up in her bed in the dark, staring at God knows what because she either can't or won't tell you."

He thought for a moment about the revulsion and pain in her voice when she said she would never have sex.

"We're not giving up on this," he said. "She's going to see Holinshed."

"Go tell it on the mountain," Katherine replied.

22

Harry's cell phone rang.

"If we can go now, I will talk to Captain Snyder," Soñadora said in response to his greeting.

"Hold on."

He turned to Katherine, reluctant to interrupt their talk but seeing no good alternative.

"Business," he said. "I've been trying to get Soñadora Asturias to talk with Jim. She wants to do it now. I'd better go before she changes her mind."

"Go," Katherine said. "I've got plenty to do."

He picked Soñadora up at a Jiffy Lube on Dooley Road, a rough section of East Naples, a kind of dying businesses' graveyard of dusty, potholed streets and air heavy with the pervasive smell of oil and smoke, and rotting things. It was also where a man named Freeman Todd had once tried to kill him. It was a part of town Harry avoided.

"What are you doing in a Jiffy Lube on Dooley Road?" Harry demanded when he picked her up, half angry with her for being in East Avola at all.

"They are low priced," she said with a touch of mischief in her voice.

"You don't have a car," Harry said, not mollified. He rolled down his window and pointed to a collapsed building across from the Jiffy Lube. "Do you see that place? A few years ago that was a chop shop and when I went in there a man tried to

184

beat my head in with a wrench."

"It looks safe now. What is a chop shop?"

"First tell me why you're here."

"Someone I know owns the place. Another friend brought me here."

Cooling down a bit, Harry took his first good look at her. He saw with a shock of recognition that she had wound her braid around her head in an elaborate, black coronet. She was wearing a dark purple blouse and a black skirt and sandals. Katherine used to wear her hair the same way when he first knew her. The memory caused him a surprisingly sharp sense of loss.

"Why are you looking at me so hard?" she asked in a concerned voice.

"The way you are wearing your hair reminded me of someone from a long time ago."

"Is it a painful memory?"

"Not really. Like you, she was very beautiful and don't you dare make some crack about my hitting on you."

"Was her hair dark like mine?" Soñadora asked.

"No, it was the color of honey, but it was long and heavy like yours."

He was turning the Rover as he spoke, thinking he should have stuck with giving her hell for being here.

"Were you in love with her?"

"Why do you want to know?"

The road had so many holes in it that the Rover was bouncing in and out of them, and Soñadora had put one hand on the dash to steady herself.

"I am trying to be more . . . ordinary."

He laughed. "That's something you will never be," he said.

"Why not?" she asked with a slight frown.

"Because you are extraordinary."

She blushed.

"You are a flatterer," she said, trying to sound dismissive.

Harry made no response, and as the silence extended itself, it occurred to him that he might have found a vocation: dedicating his life to the thankless task of trying to make women feel good about themselves.

Then Soñadora shattered his fantasy by saying, "Thank you for saying I am beautiful. It was a ridiculous thing to say, but I know you are trying to make me feel better because of what has happened. Now tell me what a chop shop is."

Frank Hodges ushered Soñadora into Jim Snyder's office as if she was a mountain queen. Beaming like the sun, he pulled out a blue and white bandana handkerchief and dusted off the creaky metal chair with the cracked green vinyl seat—the best chair in the room—before he let her sit down.

"Miss Asturias," he said, squaring his shoulders, "this is Captain Jim Snyder." Then he turned to the Captain, who was already on his feet, "Captain, this here is Soñadora Asturias, and she's damned lucky not to be looking like a charcoal briquette."

Harry watched with delight as Jim's long face slowly passed through the phases of astonishment and delight to red-eared remembrance of his manners.

"I'm very sorry about what happened to the *Salvamento* offices, Ms. Asturias," he said, leaning across the desk and extending a long arm to offer her his hand. Then his face grew redder as he added, "It's a pleasure to meet you."

"Thank you, Captain," she said with a quiet smile, looking around the room. "This is not what I expected."

"You probably thought we had them high-end rugs on the floor and bank-quality paintings on the walls," Hodges said with a loud laugh.

She glanced at Harry, looking a little frightened. Jim was

glowering at Hodges like a thunderstorm.

"The Sergeant is making a joke," he told her, giving her an encouraging smile before turning to Jim.

"She hasn't had much experience with American police and is slightly apprehensive," Harry said, "Having her tell you how she and the others escaped might be a good way to begin."

"We would like to hear that story, Miss Asturias," Jim said with obvious relief. "Then, if you don't mind, I'd like to ask you some questions."

After another moment or two of uneasiness, Soñadora settled into her account and gave it clearly and with confidence. When she was finished, Hodges, who had been listening with rapt attention, asked, "Are all them women working for you illegals?"

"Don't answer," Harry said instantly, putting a restraining hand on her arm. "Jim, we had an agreement!"

"Yes, we did," Jim said, glaring at Hodges. "Ms. Asturias, ignore the question. What are you playing at, Sergeant?"

"I got so wrapped up in the story and interested in all them women," Hodges said in his usual foghorn voice, "I plum forgot. Miss Asturias, you tell a good story, even if your English ain't a hundred percent."

"Thank you, Sergeant," she said. "It is not even fifty percent."

Harry gave a silent cheer as he watched Hodges preen himself in the warmth of her smile. All signs of her earlier fear had evaporated.

A very quick learner, he thought.

Jim began asking her questions about the work of the organization and about her contacts in the Guatemalan community; and her answers, efficient but general, quickly led him to the murders.

"Is there anything you can tell us that would help us understand what's going on in that community?" he asked, leaning across the desk in his serious desire to have her say something revealing.

Harry wondered if Jim was also trying to get past the polite and respectful wall she had left standing between them.

Throughout the session, Soñadora had sat with both her feet on the floor, her hands folded in her lap, answering the questions asked her but offering nothing more.

"No," she said.

Harry was surprised when Hodges said what Harry had expected Jim to say.

"Nice as you are, you don't really trust us, do you, Miss Asturias?"

Soñadora turned to Harry with a questioning expression.

"These two men are not going to harm you," Harry told her. "You can tell them the truth."

She continued to stare at Harry, her dark eyes searching his.

"No, I do not," she said, turning to Hodges. "Nothing in my life has led me to trust those in power, especially not the . . . *fuerza publica.*"

She glanced at Harry.

"Police force," he said.

Jim pushed himself back with a sigh of resignation.

"Whatever run-ins you've had up to now with those bad apples in Guatemala or Mexico," Hodges told her in his quietest voice, "our job is to protect you."

"Harry's right," Jim put in. "The Sergeant and I won't hurt you."

"I am sure you mean well," she replied, then added, "Everything Harry and I learned in our visits with the women of La Ramada," she said, looking from Jim to Hodges and back again, "we have told you. Beyond that, my work has been trying to find and release women who are, even as we sit here speaking, living as slaves in unspeakable conditions. And not in some foreign country but right here in Tequesta County, within miles, even yards, perhaps, of this building."

She paused, and Harry noticed that her hands were clenched so tightly, their knuckles were white, whether in anger or fear, Harry couldn't say, but he thought this meeting had gone on long enough.

"We ought to wrap this up," he said, starting to get up, but Soñadora grasped his arm and pressed him back into the chair.

"No," she said vehemently. "There is more to be said. The work of *Salvamento* must go on, and the success of the program depends on its members not being known."

She paused. Jim started to speak, but Harry caught his eye and shook his head.

"As much as I want to help you to stop the killing, to use your resources to break up the trafficking rings, I risk everything by being associated with you, even talking to you. Look what happened to our building."

"You had a close call there," Hodges agreed.

"Are you sure it happened because of the work you did with Harry?" Jim asked.

"How can I be sure, Captain?" she demanded impatiently, "We worked in safety for four years. Then I pretend to be working for St. Jude's church and go into *La Ramada*, to ask questions about the murders, and what happens?"

"You get burned out," Hodges said earnestly.

"Yes, Sergeant," she responded, "and it is not that I think you and the Captain will hurt me deliberately, but you may get me killed, all the same. There is one more thing. If I give you names of people who might be able to help you, it is only a question of time before those names will reach the Customs and Immigration. The people I deal with are mostly illegals. Almost all of those being held in wage and other forms of slavery are illegal. If you find them and free them, what will happen to them?"

With that she stood up, and the three men rose with her.

189

"Thank you for coming in," Jim said. "I hope you will talk with us again. But even if you don't, we wish you well, and if you need my help, don't stop to think about it—call me. I mean that!"

"Same for me," Hodges said.

"Where to?" Harry asked when they were in the Rover.

She had not spoken since leaving Jim's office, and Harry thought it was best if he waited for her to decide what comments if any she wanted to make about the meeting.

"Where you picked me up," she said, avoiding looking at him.

"You did a good job," he offered as a white flag.

She made a noise that might have meant anything.

"Call me," he said as she was getting out of the SUV. "Better still, tell me where I can reach you."

She shook her head.

"I'll invite you to my funeral," she said, and managed this time to meet his eyes for a second and then was gone.

"Another unidentified body has turned up in your old stomping grounds," Tucker said, dropping the newspaper in front of Harry as he passed the kitchen table where Harry and Katherine were seated.

"Happens all the time out by our place," Doreen Clampett said, tossing her cigarette into the stove. "Most times the police don't even show. The Medical Examiner's van appears and the crew bags 'em, and hauls 'em away."

"This one was out by Findlay Jay's ranch. Do you remember him, Harry?"

"Who could forget him?" Harry asked sadly.

"I remember him," Katherine said with no trace of sadness. "You almost got yourself killed, getting involved with that feud between him and Ernshaw Welty."

"Well," Tucker said, giving Katherine a close look, "they're dead and Harry's walking."

"By the grace of God or the Devil," Katherine said, easing up enough to smile at Tucker.

"I think the Devil's got the edge these days in the Northeast Corner," Doreen said, giving the top of the stove a random swipe with the floor cloth. "There are times I think we're in a war zone."

"Do you ever see who's doing the shooting?" Harry asked.

"No, but I see a lot of propeller planes early in the morning, when I'm fixing Wetherell's breakfast."

"How's Wetherell taking his father's death?" Tucker asked. "I miss Hubbard," he added. "He was a friend of many years."

"Wetherell's all right now. Of course, he misses him. So do I. You know, I used to think if I had to listen to one more of his stories, I'd wring his neck, but now I miss them. You remember, Tucker, some of them was real funny."

"Where are those planes going?" Harry asked.

"They must be landing on Indian land. There ain't nothing else out there," she said with a loud laugh.

While Harry was thinking about what Doreen had told them, Tucker took his hat off its peg by the door and said, "Let's go see what Minna's doing with the pigs."

"I've got work to do," Doreen said, tossing the rag she'd been holding into the sink.

"Where's Sanchez and Oh, Brother!?" Katherine asked as they left the house.

"Ever since Sanchez has been able to run a little, they've been disappearing into the woods every day," Tucker said, sounding a little worried.

"Minna's not going with them, is she?" Katherine demanded.

"No," Tucker said. "Oh, Brother! wouldn't allow it. If I had to guess, I'd say they were looking for pigs."

"I would have thought they had seen all they ever wanted to see of pigs," Harry said.

"I told them to leave the pigs alone," Tucker said and then laughed. "I made the mistake of saying, 'Let sleeping dogs lie,' and Oh, Brother! laughed. Sanchez was so offended that he wouldn't talk with either of us the rest of the day."

"Wait, look," Katherine said.

Minna was sitting beside the cage, feeding carrots and dry dog food to the animals and apparently carrying on an intense conversation with them.

"I'd love to know what she is saying," Harry said.

"One way to find out," Tucker said, getting them moving again.

"Have you named these two yet?" he asked Minna cheerfully.

He had hurried a little, and Harry noted with a jangle of concern that he was pale and out of breath.

Scrambling to her feet and ignoring her mother and father, Minna finally answered Tucker, "I'm calling Old Grumpy here, Katrina after the calamity, and I'm calling her son Pearl Jam after my favorite rock group. How's that?"

"Fine," Tucker said. "I saw you talking to them. Are you making any headway with Katrina?"

"She listens, but I think she'd bite me if she could."

"Make sure she doesn't," Katherine said. "Pig bites are very poisonous."

"Just like humans," Minna shot back.

"What do you talk to them about?" Harry asked.

"That's private," Minna said, pushing another carrot through the fence.

Pearl Jam snatched it away from his mother with a squeal. No one laughed.

23

Following breakfast the next day, Harry left for a meeting with the manager of the Avola branch of the Blue Rock Insurance Company. He did not greet the morning as a strong man rejoicing to run a race. He walked to the Rover and got in with a stiff face. He and Katherine, who was already in the kitchen when he came downstairs, both having spent a miserable night worrying about Minna, found themselves no closer to agreeing on how to get the girl into Holinshed's office than they had been the night before, following a wrenching session with Minna, trying to persuade her to give therapy a chance to prove it helped.

"I'm not going!" Minna finally screamed, dissolving into a flood of tears. "Leave me alone! What happened, happened! Nothing can change that!"

Once the door to her room slammed, Harry, whose frustration and pain often led straight to anger, said, "Let's make an appointment with Holinshed, tell Minna's she's going, and put an end to this foolishness."

It was probably more an explosion of emotion than a rational plan he intended to put in motion.

"You'll take that child into Holinshed's office by force over my dead body," had been Katherine's response.

At breakfast, Harry made some progress convincing her that he had not meant literally to drag Minna through the office doors, but that he did think it might be time to become a little more forceful with the girl. He added, in a major misjudgment,

193

that he didn't think having Minna sit outside Tucker's pig cage feeding its inmates carrots and dry dog food pellets was a career choice he supported with any enthusiasm.

Katherine was not amused and said so, which accounted for Harry's stiff face and his ignoring Lady Godiva's screaming lift-off from the bank of Puc Puggy Creek with a writhing water snake in her talons, although he normally took a lively interest in the red-shouldered hawks' activities, especially Godiva's because she displayed a bravura worthy of an Amazon.

Once off the Hammock, however, he began to see the situation with Katherine in a slightly clearer light. A moment's reflection, he realized, would have reminded him that her harsh response had been prompted by her fierce defensiveness of Minna and Jesse. In those years immediately after Will Trachey abandoned her, her determination to protect her kids had provided her with the strength not to give up.

Those thoughts led him into recollections of their time together. After she left him, those memories were the source of a lot of pain and guilt, but now he recalled them with a degree of pleasure.

He slowed down for some roadwork that had been started a month ago by the County and then abandoned, leaving a twisting half-mile of potholes, washboard, and ruts. It had rained in the night, and Harry tried to find a route through the puddles and gumbo that wouldn't coat the Rover with mud, and focusing on the track, he was fully absorbed in his task when his windscreen exploded in a shower of glass pellets, followed by the savage clatter of automatic weapons rattling at full throttle.

Harry jammed down the release on his seatbelt and plunged out the door with the zing and whack of bullets zipping through the Rover urging him on. He struck the mud on his back and rolled under the SUV, holding his CZ over his head in both hands as he rolled, squeezing his eyes shut against the silt-laden water splashing into his face, praying that none of the bullets hit the gas tank.

He came to rest on his stomach in a rank-smelling puddle of brown water with a disgruntled green frog goggling at him a few inches from his nose.

"Keep your head down, friend," Harry said and squirmed forward, trying to get a look at whoever was doing serious harm to his Rover.

The barrage continued for another few seconds and trailed off, then ceased altogether. Harry waited. A man said something in Spanish that Harry did not understand, got an answer, then said in English, "Go over there and shoot him some more."

"No," the second man said. "The mud is too deep. You go."

"I'll go," a third man said and a moment later Harry heard a rich, sucking sound as the man stepped into the mud.

"I have lost my shoe," the man shouted. "The fucking mud ate it."

This was followed by laughter and more swearing.

"We can make sure from here," the first man said. "Blow it up."

Harry heard the unmistakable sound of a clip being jammed into place. An instant later the Rover was shaken by a long blast of fire. At almost the same moment, Harry smelled gasoline. The fuel tank had been punctured.

Swearing steadily and fervently, Harry propelled himself backward from under the Rover, through more mud with bullets singing over his thrashing body, and rolled down over the shoulder of the road into an overgrown, half-drowned ditch, soaking whatever part of him was not already wet. To Harry it looked and felt like paradise.

Once the spasm of relief has expended itself, he found he was not willing to just lie there quietly until the jokers on the other side of the road went away. He was very angry about what they

195

were doing to the Rover, and if he could, he intended to do some damage of his own.

He had concluded from the voices that there were three men, and they were located directly across the road from where he was lying. The problem was that the Rover was blocking his line of sight, and if he wanted a crack at them, he was going to have to move either right or left.

The shooting died down again, and one of the men said, "Try again."

"We have stayed here long enough," another complained.

Harry thought that was the one who had lost his shoe.

"Let's go. He's fucking dead," the second man said.

While he listened, Harry had been scrambling along the bank to his right, staying as low as he could and still move. Another ten feet and he crawled up the bank and peered through the weeds. There they were, shoving fresh clips into their Uzis.

Ancient weaponry, Harry was thinking just as the first man opened up on the Rover.

"Bastards!" he whispered and stood up, looking like some creature from the swamp with mud, weeds, and water running off him. He swung up his CZ, but at that instant a huge orange ball erupted from where the Rover was standing, engulfed Harry in its fire, and blew him backward into the ditch. The last thing he heard was its deafening roar.

Harry woke to see Hodges peering down at him.

"The doc figures it was the water and mud that kept you from being fried," Hodges told him with satisfaction.

Hodges's face was joined by Jim's countenance, making a circus version of the masks of tragedy and comedy.

"Katherine's on her way," Jim said in a sepulchral voice. "I've got a cruiser picking her up."

"It's a good thing you landed in that ditch on your back,"

Hodges put in, "otherwise you'd be drowned now."

Harry was gradually becoming aware of sore places that took in most of his body, and his face felt as if he was standing too close to a stove.

He must have grimaced because Jim said, "Your face looks as if it's been badly sunburned. Your eyebrows are singed, and you've got burns in other places. Nothing serious."

"You also lost some hide to the shooters," Hodges said. "They nicked you in a few places."

"Shooting at me?" Harry asked, angry at not understanding what Jim and Hodges were talking about.

"The adrenaline probably kept you from feeling it at the time, but they dinged you pretty good," Hodges told him, ignoring Jim's protests.

"Katherine," Harry croaked, "is not going to like this."

He was right. She arrived at about the same time that Harry's head cleared enough for him to tell Jim and Hodges what had happened.

She and Jim exchanged an awkward hug while Hodges placed one of the gray chairs beside the bed for her. While that was going on, the nurse, who had come in with Katherine, injected something into the drip, and left.

"You look like a fried tomato," she told him.

"Is it an improvement?" he asked, a hoarse whisper being about all he could manage.

Her stern expression slipped and, starting to smile, she leaned over the bed and kissed him on the forehead. It hurt.

"The explosion looked like an enormous, orange balloon," he told her, his eyes suddenly feeling very heavy, "and the sound was like all the jet planes you ever heard going right over your head."

That was the last thing he said for several hours.

★ ★ ★ ★ ★

Katherine sat for a few minutes holding his hand, looking concerned and sad and angry all at the same time. She was interrupted by the nurse, who told her the doctor wanted to see her.

He was tall and dark-haired and looked to Katherine at least ten years too young to be a doctor.

"I am Dr. Sanjay Ambani," he said in very careful but rapid English, shaking hands with her as he spoke. "The news is so far good. We are able to say that, as of now, all of our testing has shown your husband to be free of internal injuries. He has first- and second-degree burns on various parts of his body and several superficial wounds, inflicted, we are currently thinking, by bullets."

"Harry isn't my husband," Katherine said.

The news brought a look of consternation to his face.

"It's all right," she told him. "We were married, and I'm still the closest thing he's got for a wife. Getting shot is just one of his bad habits."

They were in a small consulting room, and Ambani looked around somewhat desperately. Katherine had not smiled, and Ambani had not been in the country long enough to recognize irony unaccompanied by unmistakable verbal and nonverbal clues. Her intensely green eyes did not seem to blink and interfered with his thinking.

"We are keeping him for further observing, but I am expecting to release him tomorrow. Does he have a place to go where someone can care for him for a few days? He is going to be very sore in sundry places. Mostly on the front of his body."

"Has something happened to his . . ."

"No! No!" He was mortified. "It is nothing of that sort. Mostly his upper torso is having been burned."

"He doesn't deserve it, but I'll look after him," Katherine

said. "Thank you, for taking the time to talk to me."

Ambani fled, gripping his clipboard.

"I'm a little muddled, probably from the medication," Harry said hoarsely.

His throat was sore, and Dr. Ambani thought he had opened his mouth and breathed in just as he was being knocked off the bank. Harry had been home two days, and he was lying on his bed because it was where he was least uncomfortable. Katherine had put up the ironing board beside the bed and was working as well as keeping him company.

"You've drifted off again," she said.

"Sorry," Harry said. "How long before Minna has her test?"

"Next Wednesday."

"And this is?"

"Friday."

Harry swung his legs off the bed and eased himself into a sitting position. His face had begun to peel, and it itched and hurt at the same time. The skin around his eyes was swollen, and he had not been able to shave, adding to his overall feeling of unattractiveness.

"Has she said anything to you about it?"

"No."

"All she talks to me about is Tucker, Doreen Clampett, and the pigs," he said.

"Katrina and Pearl Jam," Katherine corrected him, slipping one of Minna's sundresses onto a hanger. "This morning she almost bit my head off for calling them pigs."

"How are you feeling about it?"

"The test?" she asked, hanging the dress from the door.

She came back and sat down beside him, folding her hands in her lap as she so often did.

"The test," he repeated, placing a hand over hers.

She freed one of her hands and put it over his. Harry felt comforted but uneasy. He was supposed to be thinking about Minna.

"I try very hard not to think about it," she said after a long pause, gently stroking his hand.

"Sometimes, I forget it's coming, and when I remember, it scares me half to death. I don't know how she deals with it," Harry said grimly.

"I'm not sure we ever will, but this thing has aged her. She's not a girl anymore."

"No," he said, "she carries herself differently, and her eyes don't seem to have any joy in them."

"She's angry," Katherine added.

"As soon as I can move around a little better, I want us to make a major effort to get her to Holinshed."

"We'll try."

Katherine did not sound hopeful.

24

Hazel pulled Rigoberta back into the corner of the noisy cab and looked out the rear window, making sure to keep most of her face out of the glass.

"I see the bastard. The two others are still with him. We're in trouble."

Rigoberta foraged in her sack and pulled out the flier the old woman in the slave house had stuffed into her shoe.

"There's this," she said.

Hazel snatched it out of her hand and studied it briefly.

"St. Jude's Shelter," she read. "And there's half a dozen telephone numbers."

She leaned back in the seat and thought.

"Ask him if he's got a cell phone," she said finally.

Rigoberta did.

"*Si,*" the old man said with his infectious grin and passed it to Rigoberta, who gave it to Hazel.

"I have an idea," Hazel said just loud enough for Rigoberta to hear her. "I'm going to call one of these numbers and tell whoever answers that you're running from your husband who has threatened to kill you."

"They will tell the police!" Rigoberta protested.

"No, they won't. I'll tell them you're an illegal. This bunch won't turn you in."

The old man wasn't as deaf as Hazel thought.

"It is the men in the big car who started to pass us and are now following us?"

"*Si*," Rigoberta said quickly.

Hazel was shaking her head, but Rigoberta ignored her.

The old man leaned forward and looked at Hazel.

"Tell those you call to meet you where there are lots of people," he said. "Then those bad ones will be *frustrados.*"

"But where?" Rigoberta asked.

"Let me think," Hazel said, pressing a hand to her forehead.

"We leave the highway at Pine Ridge," Hernandez said. "It is *mucho animado,* and then we will cross the Forty One and turn into the Mall. Tell them to meet you at the Sack."

Rigoberta looked at Hazel to see if she had understood anything Hernandez had just said. For a moment she looked as puzzled as Rigoberta. Then she began to laugh.

"He means Saks. It's a store, Saks Fifth Avenue. Lots of people, very expensive."

Hernandez glanced at his watch. "Tell them in thirty minutes."

Hazel punched in the number. A woman answered, and Hazel began speaking so rapidly that Rigoberta could not follow her. Then she listened for a moment, said, "Yes," from time to time, then closed the phone and passed it to Rigoberta.

"This is so crazy it might work," Hazel said, leaning to the side again and peeking out the rear window. The Cadillac was still trailing them. "Unless they decide to shoot us first."

"Why have they not shot us already?" Hernandez asked.

"Because they know we will shoot back," Hazel answered.

"You have guns?"

"And we can shoot them," Rigoberta said proudly in English. "I was shot once, and now I will shoot first."

"Shoot," Hazel said sourly. "I've created an Annie Oakley."

"Was she ever shot?" Rigoberta asked.

"I don't think so," Hazel said with a half-suppressed chuckle.

Hernandez's estimation of the time was good, and probably for the first time a truck filled with watermelons came to a loud and smoky stop in front of Saks. The Cadillac had fallen behind and was now hovering in the approach road, blocking traffic and drawing a lot of attention.

"We are here," Hernandez said, "but where are your people?"

A steady flow of shoppers, mostly women, were coming and going through the store's bank of doors.

"Here they come," Hazel said, pointing to five women in flowered dresses and wide-brimmed red hats who had emerged from the store and were striding toward the truck.

"A police car is coming," Hernandez said nervously, glancing at his rearview mirror. "It is time for me to go."

"Thanks, Juan," Hazel said, climbing down from the cab.

Rigoberta said goodbye to him in Quiche, sliding across the seat with one hand inside her sack, gripping the pistol.

"Shoot straight," he said with a grin and pulled away as she slammed the door.

In the next moment she and Hazel were surrounded by five large women who hustled them into the store. Hernandez was gone and the Cadillac was trying to follow but was delayed by a new stream of shoppers crossing from the parking lot.

The following morning, Harry was easing himself down the stairs, determined to be done with bed, when he heard someone rapping on the lanai door.

"I'll get it," Katherine called from the kitchen and returned almost at once, wearing a strange expression, and nearly ran him down getting up the stairs.

"You might have warned me," she said, in her rush. "She's out there."

Harry made a poor job of getting to the lanai quickly, unable to imagine who Katherine was talking about.

"You look awful. I thought you said you were divorced."

"Thanks. I am. How did you . . ."

Soñadora, wearing black slacks and a lavender blouse, was not smiling, but Harry wondered, nonetheless, if she had wrapped her braid around her head because he had told her it made her look very regal, which it did.

"I borrowed a car," she said dismissively. "Who is this imposing person preparing your breakfast?"

They talked at cross-purposes for another few minutes, and Harry said, extending his hand, "Come, I'll introduce you."

The gesture was so surprising that she took it.

When they got there, Katherine, her makeup on, was back in the kitchen, whisking something in a bowl, having changed out of her bathrobe and into her new green dress with the string shoulder straps. And she was, to Harry's astonishment, shining like a new gold dollar.

"Katherine," he said, "this is Soñadora Asturias. She is the person who was running a recovery program called *Salvamento* until someone fire bombed it and nearly killed Soñadora and several other women."

"We are rebuilding it," Soñadora said quickly, "I am very pleased to meet you."

"Come in," Katherine said. "I'm sorry about your shelter, and what a terrible thing to have happen, but at least you're alive. Harry, pull out a chair for her. Don't just stand there. Give her some coffee, or would you rather have tea? These eggs will be ready in a minute."

They were, and when the three of them were seated, Katherine smiled at Soñadora and said, "Harry told me you were beautiful. He's right. Everybody eat, and then you and Harry can talk."

But Katherine talked and ate, and in a few minutes she had Soñadora talking about her plans for the building and the changes she wanted made in how it was to be laid out. Harry had never heard her say as much about anything. Then Minna came downstairs, and lost in an effort to get out the door without breakfast. Once she learned what Soñadora did with *Salvamento,* she sat and listened and forgot not to eat.

Later, when Minna had left to see Tucker, and Katherine had gone upstairs to make some calls, Harry took Soñadora onto the lanai, eased himself onto a lounge chair, and said, "How did you find your way out here?"

"How many humpy bridges could there be leading off County Road 19?" she replied.

"One. Are you going to tell me why you came?"

She was perched on the edge of the cushioned chair beside Harry's, hands clasped on her knees.

"No extra charge for leaning back and putting your feet up," he told her.

"Charge?" she asked, frowning.

"Try it. Slide back, swing your feet up, it's easy. You'll like it."

"I don't . . . It's not . . ." She stuttered to a stop and started again. "There are rumors of two women who escaped from a house where they were being kept to work. One of the people running the place was, perhaps, killed, another wounded. They are being hunted."

"When did you hear this?"

"Last night. None of the *Salvamento* women has been able to learn more."

"How did you hear about this?"

"From one of our sources," she said.

Harry saw that she would not be more specific and did not press her.

"Do you know where they were seen?"

"It is nothing so definite, but I think on 75."

"You could have called me," Harry said. "If you are being

205

watched, it was reckless to drive out here. You might have been followed."

She shifted uneasily on the chair and looked out toward the Creek.

"I think it is a miracle you were not killed," she said quietly.

"It has occurred to me," he told her.

She gave him one of her gentle smiles, which, Harry thought, she might give someone retarded who had made a silly joke.

"How badly are you hurt?" she asked.

"I'm going to be sore for a while. That's about it."

"You have very good care," she said a bit stiffly.

"Yes, Katherine's a very good, very competent person, and right now she's in more pain than I am."

"I am sorry. The girl looks much like her. I think she, too, will be beautiful."

She stood up.

"I must go. If you tell Captain Snyder about the women, please don't mention me."

"Give me a hand up," he said.

She helped him onto his feet, far more gently than he had expected.

"Thanks," he said. "He's going to know how I found out."

She shrugged and said in a resigned voice, "I suppose so."

Slowly and with some wincing on his part, Harry walked Soñadora to her car. "I want to know how to get in touch with you," he said as she was getting into her car.

"Why would you want to?" she asked.

"Because you're not the only one who gets information, and the kind I get might be of help to you. That's one reason. Another is I don't like not being able to talk with you."

She looked up at him, her black eyes searching his for something.

"If I give you a number, will you promise not to give it to anyone?"

"I promise."

"Thank you," he said when she gave him the number. "Be careful."

25

Jim and Harry watched in silence as the Medical Examiner's people, knee deep in the canal's muddy water, untangled a woman's body from the thick, green weeds, and pulled it dripping onto the shore. While Kathleen Towers, the ME, worked over her, the CID technicians went on taking pictures. Then she straightened up, stepped back, and let her two male assistants slide the dead woman into a blue body bag and zip it shut.

"How many does that make, Captain?" Towers asked, having scrambled up the bank and pulled off her hat and shook out her brown hair with a sigh of relief.

"Counting the two in the van, this one makes six."

"What do you make of this one?" Harry asked.

Kathleen went on pulling off her gloves and boots and jumpsuit as she answered.

"Hispanic, I'd guess Mexican, fifties, five-nine, one-eighty, contusion and extensive bruising on right temple, possibly the cause of death, no other visible trauma. I'll know more after I've had her on the table."

"Anything else?" Jim asked.

"Yes, her dress, underwear, shoes are expensive. Her fingernails were professionally done. She had rings, but they were removed. Another oddity, aside from the wound on her temple, she shows no sign of having been messed with."

She turned to Harry with a grin.

"You thought with the other one that stripping her was some

208

kind of ritual humiliation. What about this one?"

"Robbery?" Harry asked.

"Do you believe that, Harry?" Jim asked in surprise.

"No, I don't," Harry said, "but it doesn't fit in with the rest either, and if it doesn't, why is she in the Luther Faubus Canal?"

"Give me a little time, and I might shed some light on our mystery—yours, really, Jim, but you don't much like mysteries, do you?" she asked, teasing him with a very friendly smile.

Harry was pleased to see Jim's ears light up and the blush creep up his face. Kathleen Towers was a very attractive woman and Harry knew she was not at the moment involved with anyone.

"Jim," he said, "I think you and Kathleen should sit down over lunch and talk about these deaths, share what you know and see if you can come up with any new ideas."

He made a show of looking at his watch.

"I've got an appointment, but you two ought to be able to squeeze out an hour and a half, and it's just about noon."

"Hey, Jim—we can flip to see which one of us has to stick our department with the bill," she said with a good laugh.

"I can recommend Oppenheimer's," Harry said, seeing that Jim was caught in some heavy weather. "You know where it is, don't you, Kathleen?"

"Sure, it's a great place if you can get a table with an umbrella."

"Why's that?" Jim asked.

"Doves," Harry said.

"I don't see . . ." Jim said, events having clearly overtaken him, but Harry cut him off.

"Kathleen will explain it to you. The house pinot grigio is outstanding. Enjoy yourselves."

With that he made off for his new Rover, feeling really proud of himself, leaving Kathleen giving Jim directions to the restaurant.

The good feeling didn't last long. After he left Jim and Kathleen, he picked up Katherine and Minna and drove them to the hospital in Avola for Minna's second HIV test. The moment Esther Benson, small, dark, and very intense with snapping gray eyes, came into the examination room, Minna stopped being cooperative.

"I'm feeling fine," she said, jumping to her feet.

"That's good news," Benson said, ignoring Katherine and Harry, and going straight to Minna and putting out her hand.

Minna hesitated, but she took it.

"You've grown a little since the last time I saw you. Here, sit down on the edge of this examination table," Benson said, patting the table. "I want to talk to you for a minute, and while I'm doing that, I'm going to listen and look at some things. How old are you now?"

"I'm thirteen," Minna said in a high, tense voice, backing away from Benson, "and I'm not taking any more tests. The first one said I'm all right."

"And I expect this one will say the same thing," Benson said, shoving her hands into the pockets of her white coat. "So why not take it and make these two feel better?"

She turned her attention to Katherine and said, "Hello, stranger, you've put on a few pounds. You know it's just not fair, the older you get the more you look like Meryl Streep and the more I look like Marjorie Main."

Laughing and protesting, Katherine pulled Benson into her arms.

"It's good to see you, too," she said.

"God, it's like falling into a feather bed," Benson said, freeing herself after embracing Katherine for a moment, and turned to Harry.

"Hello, old timer, what's wrong with your face? You fall asleep in the sun?" she asked, peering closely at the peeling skin.

"I was standing too close to a car that blew up," Harry said, "Do you charge extra for the insults?"

"It's a package," Benson said, still staring at Harry's face. "Katherine, the best thing you ever did was dump this man. He's got about as much sense as an armadillo."

Minna had watched and listened to all the badinage with growing interest.

"Why an armadillo?" she asked with a laugh.

"Up on the table," Benson said, and when Minna hoisted herself onto the table, Benson put on her stethoscope and said, "When a car goes over an armadillo in the road, if the tires miss it, it jumps up and commits suicide on the undercarriage, because that's what armadillos do. They jump straight up when they're scared. Dumb. Take a deep breath."

She went on listening, looking, and occasionally probing Minna, questioning her about school and her interest in track and chorus, keeping the girl busy answering and talking when she wanted to.

"You'll live," Benson said when she was done. "Climb down."

Once Minna was on her feet, Benson took hold of her shoulders and said, "Look at me." Minna did. "Don't be an armadillo," Benson said. "Take the test."

"If I've got it, I've got it," Minna said, her eyes filling with tears. "Knowing won't make any difference."

"Yes it will," Benson told her, passing her a Kleenex. "First, I don't think you're HIV positive, and you need to *know* you're not. Second, if you are, there are a ton of new medications that can delay the development of the disease and even if it expresses itself, a lot more ways to suppress and lessen the symptoms.

Third, the sooner you start taking the medication, the better it will be for you."

Minna blew her nose and shook her head.

"Oh, Minna!" Katherine said, bouncing to her feet.

"Wait," Harry said. "Is this the girl who kicked a full-grown man out the back of a van?" He was speaking loudly but not harshly, and he had Minna's attention. "Is this the person who then jumped out of the cab and had the guts to pick up her backpack before sprinting into the woods? Did you do those things?"

"Yes," Minna said.

"You're not a coward, are you?"

"I guess not."

"I *know* you're not. Take the test."

Minna looked away from Harry to her mother and then at Benson.

"Please," Katherine said.

"You've heard from me," Benson told her.

"OK," Minna said in a resigned but steady voice, "I'll do it."

An hour and a half later, Benson called and told Minna that she was clean.

"In three months, take another test. You're OK, but take no chances with it."

When Minna said she would, Benson said, "One more thing, talk to Gloria Holinshed as soon as you can."

"I'm going to do it," she told Katherine and Harry, who were hovering, "but I don't want to talk with either of you about it. It's my business. I'll take care of it."

"Sound like anyone you know?" Harry asked Katherine, his heart feeling double its normal size.

"Sit down here," Tucker said, herding Harry onto the back

stoop and thrusting a mug of steaming tea into his hand.

"I'll be sweating this tea out of me for the next two hours," Harry protested.

Harry was convinced that drinking Tucker's tea would in time have him looking like Ramses II.

"Nonsense," Tucker said as he and Harry settled into the old bentwood rockers. "Even the British came to understand that hot tea is the best drink in a hot climate."

In front of them, the old growth forest with its dense understory and soaring canopy of oak, mahogany, fichus, and the occasional pine, spread out its cool shade and filled the air with its fragrance and the buzz and rising and falling burst of cicadas and locusts.

"Where's your staff?" Harry asked, referring to Sanchez and Oh, Brother!, conspicuously absent.

"Well, against my advice," Tucker said, sipping his tea, a moment Harry was postponing with reasonable dread, "they are somewhere out there on the edge of Stickpen Swamp, looking for that band of pigs that raided the garden."

Losing his argument with himself over whether or not a dog and a mule could be doing anything so redolent of purpose, he said, "What do they expect to learn from all their work?"

"They're trying to see if the pigs have some kind of route they're following that might bring them back here on a predictable schedule. That way, we could be ready for them."

"Why don't you want them doing it?" Harry asked, surrendering to his curiosity.

"Because, a herd of feral pigs is about the most dangerous thing in the woods. Look what they did to Sanchez. Oh, Brother! is big and strong enough to hold off two or three sows, but if there's a big boar in the herd, Sanchez will be killed, and Oh, Brother! won't escape without having his legs slashed."

Harry did not want to think about that and asked Tucker

about Katrina and Pearl Jam.

"Let's take a look," Tucker said, setting down his tea.

Harry put down his tea with relief and followed Tucker off the stoop.

"The young one is getting tame as a kitten," Tucker said when they reached the pen, "but that sow is red-eyed as ever."

The piglet ran up to them, squealing with pleasure, but the sow hung back by the doghouse, snuffling and popping her teeth.

"See what I mean?" Tucker said, reaching into his pocket and bringing out a fistful of dry dog food and tossing it through the wire.

With another squeal of delight, the little pig began eating, its tail twirling like a fan.

"You had some good news about Minna," Tucker said, moving slowly toward the sow.

"Yes. What do you think about her?"

"I think she needs help you and I and Katherine can't give her. If I didn't keep thinking up jobs for her around the house, she'd spend the day sitting out here with the pigs."

"She's still losing weight," Harry said.

"I can see it, and, frankly, it worries me. Didn't Dr. Benson have any suggestions?"

By this time, Tucker had worked them to within about six or eight feet of the sow, which was now stamping her feet, swinging her head, and snapping her jaws threateningly.

"She got Minna to agree to see Dr. Holinshed, but that was it. She said something about being patient and not expecting miracles. 'These things take time,' " she said.

At that moment the sow exploded from behind the hut with a squeal of rage and crashed into the fence, doing her best to reach the two men.

"She's getting worse," Harry said when he recovered from

the shock of the attack.

"I'm afraid so," Tucker agreed.

He had been as startled as Harry and jumping back from the fence had left him short of breath.

"In this world not every change is an improvement," the old farmer said, putting his hands on his knees, struggling to breathe.

Harry did not like his color and said, "Let's get out of this sun. I'm about fried."

He managed to slip a hand under Tucker's arm, expecting him to protest the effort to help.

"Good idea," Tucker said, to Harry's surprise, accepting his help without protest.

When they had regained the shade of the stoop, Tucker sat down with a sigh of relief and said, "That's better," dropping his straw hat on the floor beside his chair.

Harry didn't like the old man's color but kept that to himself.

"Shall I get you some fresh tea?" he asked.

"No," Tucker replied, resting his head on the back of the chair and closing his eyes. "Instead, tell me where you are with these murders."

"I'm inclined to say nowhere, but that may be too pessimistic," Harry said. "It looks as though La Ramada is connected in some way to the deaths, the first two for sure, the next three, possibly."

"I've been out of touch with things in town for a while, as you know," Tucker said, opening his eyes and showing a little more life, "but one or two of the people who have talked with me have mentioned that there are rumors about places in the county where people are being worked pretty much as slaves. It's hard to believe it."

"Human trafficking's more than a rumor," Harry said. "Jim Snyder is convinced that it's a hidden but spreading problem."

"That's the problem," Tucker said. "It's so far underground only a few people know anything about it."

"Illegals seem to be both the principal victims and the perpetrators."

"That's a second problem," Tucker said. "People are very slow to see what they don't want to see. Seeing them bent over in a bean field or with a leaf blower strapped to their backs is one thing. Being asked to confront the unpleasant truth that hundreds of them are enslaved is quite another."

"It's taken me a while to believe it really is happening," Harry admitted, "and if I hadn't met Soñadora Asturias and learned about her *Salvamento* mission, or seen the dead bodies being pulled out of the Luther Faubus Canal, I'm not sure I would have believed it."

Tucker started to get out of his rocker, made it halfway to his feet, then sank back with a groan.

"I think I've overdone it here a little," he gasped as Harry leaned over him.

He had gone very pale and seemed to be having trouble breathing.

"Let's get you into bed," Harry said, gently getting an arm around the old man and slowly lifting him out of the rocker.

"Can you stand?" Harry asked.

"Maybe."

But he couldn't. Harry swept him up in his arms and called for Doreen. It was Minna who rushed out the door.

"Where's Doreen?" Harry asked.

"In the bathroom, talking on her cell. What's wrong?"

"Hold the door," Harry told her, doing his best to mask his concern. "Tucker's not feeling good, and the quicker we get him into bed the better."

"Hadn't you better call the doctor?" Minna asked, putting

the pillow under Tucker's head as Harry laid him on the turned-down bed.

"You'd better get my shoes off," Tucker said in a weak voice, "or Doreen will give me a carding."

"She's not going to—" Minna began loudly, but Harry shook his head at her and she stopped.

"I'd like to take a broom handle to her," Minna burst out.

Tucker managed a frail chuckle and winked at Harry.

"I've had that thought myself. Minna, would you get me some water, and when you've done that, I don't think Longstreet and his hens have had their scratch feed today."

"I'm not too comfortable with that rooster," Minna said. "I don't think he likes me."

"Take the broom with you," Tucker said, trying to sound jovial and not making it. "If he tries any funny business, give him a whack."

Minna went for the water, and while she was gone, Harry tried to judge Tucker's condition.

"How are you feeling?" he asked.

"Better, I think. It makes me damned mad to be this peaked."

"Are you hurting anywhere?" Harry asked.

"Just in my pride."

Tucker closed his eyes and was asleep before Minna came back with the water. Harry eased himself out of the room. Doreen arrived, carrying more water.

"What's wrong with Tucker?" she demanded. "Minna was all pissed off about something and wouldn't talk to me."

"I think he's exhausted. He fell asleep while we were talking."

"He in bed?"

"Yes," Harry said and went on to explain that he hadn't been able to get out of the stoop rocker.

They went back to the kitchen, and Doreen put the glass beside the sink.

"You know, Harry," she said, turning to face him, her voice a little unsteady as if she was unsure of how what she was about to say would be taken, "I don't see much improvement in Tucker. He's up one day and slid back the next. He just don't seem to be thriving, and that medicine the doctor gave him isn't working worth a shit."

"Is he eating at all?" Harry asked, recalling how easily he had carried the old man into the bedroom.

"Not much. He and Minna between them don't eat enough to keep a sparrow going. Those pigs are getting most of what I cook."

"Maybe he should go back into the hospital for a while," Harry said, thinking out loud.

"If you ask me," Doreen said, lighting a cigarette and tossing the match into the stove, "he belongs in a nursing home. I think he's on his last legs."

26

Rowena Farnham's normally rosy, smiling face wore a frown as she regarded Rigoberta and Hazel, newly showered and rigged out in clothes the women running the shelter had provided. Rigoberta and Hazel were sitting at a small conference table to the left of Farnham's desk, and Farnham was pouring tea.

"Riggs," Hazel had said after they had showered and she was reading the labels on the underwear, slacks, blouses, and sandals they had been given, "we're going to be dressed like the high-end feeders."

She had said it in English, and Rigoberta, already dressed, regarding herself critically in the dressing room mirror, asked in a preoccupied voice, "What is high-end feeder?"

"All these women who met us and who have been tending out on us are rich people, Riggs. Those slacks you're wearing cost more than a week's wages."

"I never had a week's wages. I like these clothes. Look nice," Rigoberta replied, turning to look at herself over her shoulder, "but I am worrying about my ass. It is too much."

Hazel exploded in laughter.

"No, it's not," Hazel said. "Believe me, Riggs, you look great, and don't go around talking about your ass. Call it your rear end. On second thought, don't talk to these people about it at all. They all pretend they don't have one while making a lot of use of it."

"You two have put me in a hard place," Rowena told them,

filling her own cup and sitting down.

For the past half hour Hazel had been telling Farnham about the place where they had been imprisoned and about their escape. She had left out the parts about taking Maria down and shooting Gomez.

"I think Riggs is the real problem," Hazel said, "If the bastards who put her in that lock-down sewing mill get hold of her, they'll kill her."

"I try to shoot them first," Rigoberta told Rowena in English. "Then I will work, make money, bring my children."

Farnham stared at Rigoberta in alarm. Hazel kicked Rigoberta.

"Riggs's English isn't too good," she said. "She gets her words mixed up."

"How many children do you have?" Farnham asked, shifting to Spanish and looking relieved.

"One girl Mireya," Rigoberta replied in English with a proud smile, "and one boy Manche. I miss them both. It hurts."

"Of course it does," Farnham said in English, putting her hand over Rigoberta's.

"And don't, for Chr—" Hazel pulled herself up short. "Don't tell the police about her. They'll hand her over to Immigration, and if they don't put her in one of those detention places, they'll send her back to Guatemala."

"I must not go back," Rigoberta said flatly.

"Yes, that is part of the problem," Farnham agreed. "And what about you, Hazel?"

Hazel shrugged.

"If I can get to Jacksonville, I should be OK," she said. "I was hoping to stay out of sight for a few months, but as you know that idea kind of got shot in the head."

Farnham sighed.

"Here's our situation," she said, mustering a show of

confidence. "We've got to shut down that place you escaped from, but you tell me I can't involve the police."

"Right, no cops," Hazel said. "Maybe Riggs and I should just wait until dark and split. You've done plenty for us already."

"Out of the question," Farnham protested. "You said yourself what would happen if the traffickers found you. No. You stay with us. I may be able to solve this problem and meet all our needs."

"You do know whoever followed us to Saks may have followed us here," Hazel said.

Farnham had considered that danger before Hazel mentioned it, and, smiling despite her fears, she said, "Yes, I know. I'll pray for guidance."

"No offense," Hazel said, "but I'd rather you worked on your plan."

Harry had to turn away from Doreen, to keep her from seeing how angry he was. In fact, he was furious and wanted to strangle her for saying that Tucker was dying. He walked to the screen door and saw Oh, Brother! and Sanchez coming out of the woods. The dog was limping along with his tongue out, and the mule was walking with his head down. They were both wet and streaked with mud.

He forced himself to think about what they might have been doing, and once he felt in control of himself, he turned away from the door to confront Doreen again. She had gone on talking to him, but he'd stopped listening as soon as she said Tucker was on his last legs. He tuned in again.

"We had to go through it," she said, peering into a large pot on the stove and giving it a stir, "when Wetherell's father passed over. Wetherell took it awful hard, but I told him that Hubbard had a good, long life and died in his sleep. What more could anybody ask?"

She put the cover back on the pot, walked over to Harry, and put both hands on his shoulders. At close range she was a very impressive woman, and upset as he was, Harry still felt it.

"All the wanting in the world won't change what's happening to Tucker, Harry. You surely have to know that. I'm sorry I was the one to say it."

"I know that, Doreen," he said, oddly comforted by her words.

It seemed to him that he had known for a while that Tucker might be dying, and he was suddenly grateful to her. Before he could say so, she leaned forward and kissed him lightly on the cheek just as Minna came into the kitchen.

"What's going on here?" she demanded.

"Don't worry, Honey, I'm not jumping your father," Doreen told her, pinching her cheek on the way to the hall door. "He just got some bad news, and I was helping him through it."

She paused and studied Minna's red face.

"And I've got some bad news for you, young lady," she said, tilting her head at Harry as she walked. "You're not going to marry him when you grow up."

"I hate you!" Minna yelled at Doreen and slammed out of the house.

"Doreen . . ." Harry said, but Doreen put her hands over her head and disappeared around the corner.

Harry thought that later on he might understand what had just happened, but for right now he would just look in on Tucker again. Doreen was sitting in the chair beside the bed, thumbing through a copy of *The National Enquirer.*

"How is he?"

Doreen looked up and smiled. "Sleeping like a baby," she said. "He's old and tired is all."

Harry found Minna sitting as close as she could to the pigs.

"Come on," he said. "Let's go home and get cleaned up for

Dr. Holinshed."

"I'm not going."

"Yes, you are," he said. "Take my hand. We've got an appointment."

She did not take his hand but she scrambled to her feet, obviously angry.

"How could you let that woman kiss you?" she demanded.

"She was trying to make me feel better, Minna. She was being kind."

A moment later his cell jangled. It was Rowena Farnham.

Beyond asking if Tucker was going to die, Minna had very little to say to Harry on their walk back to the house.

"Probably not right away," he told her, "But he's not very strong, and that's worrisome."

"As long as he stays quiet, he's all right," she said sullenly. "It's that Doreen who keeps him stirred up and keeps urging him to get out of bed."

"When people are as old as Tucker," Harry said as gently as he could, "it's important that they get a lot of rest, but it's also important they stay active. If they don't they soon become bedridden."

He waited for her to answer. When she only kept scuffing her feet as she walked and staring at the road, he said, "Doreen's a good woman, Minna. I know she has bad habits and seems lazy, but she didn't have your upbringing. I think you're being too hard on her."

"I don't like her."

"Why not?"

"You know," she said, glaring at Harry.

"No, I don't," he said, surprised by her vehemence.

"There's too much of her, and she's always trying to show it to you."

Harry wished that he'd stopped while he was ahead, but he felt he had to say something. "She's trying to be admired. It may not be subtle, but she's working with what she's got."

"I guess she does that all right. I've seen you looking."

The bitterness in her voice troubled Harry. "You're right, and I admit it's hard not to, but nobody is hurt. Why does it upset you so much?"

"I don't want to think about that stuff—not ever!" she shouted and fled toward the house like a deer, long legs flashing in the dappled light.

Harry didn't have to ask anyone what she was running from.

"There's things we've got to talk about," Harry said when he got back to the house.

"Minna came running into the house as if a bear was chasing her," Katherine said, "And she wouldn't tell me what was wrong. What happened?"

"That's one of the things we've got to talk about," he told her, "but Rowena Farnham called me to say the Shelter has two women, one an Anglo and the other an Indian, who have escaped from a house where they were worked as prisoners, and I've got to talk with Soñadora as soon as possible."

"But Minna's got to see Dr. Holinshed!" Katherine said, her color rising.

"I haven't forgotten," he said quickly, glancing at his watch, "but we've got to leave as soon as we can. I'll take you to Holinshed's office and come back as soon as I can."

"Then you won't be able to talk with her," Katherine said, shoulders slumping.

Harry felt the old dragon of guilt stir from its long sleep and send a breath of flame running all through him.

"I may not," he admitted, steeling himself, "but the lives of these two women and whoever is sheltering them are at serious risk. Soñadora won't talk on the telephone about this, and she's the only one who can help."

"What about the police?" Katherine demanded angrily.

"Rowena wouldn't be specific, but she said the police had to be kept out of it in order to protect the interests of the two women."

"Illegals?"

"The Indian was probably trafficked in here. I can't say what the Anglo's problem is."

Katherine shook her head, and Harry could see that she was angry. It seemed to him that they were once again at loggerheads over where his first responsibilities lay as they had been years ago in their marriage.

"We should go," he said.

She said nothing, as though struggling with some emotion that had hobbled her.

"I'll come back to Holinshed's office as quickly as I can," he said, and knew even as he was speaking that it wasn't good enough.

"Yes," she said. "I'll get Minna."

After leaving Katherine and Minna at the doctor's office, Harry called the number Soñadora had given him. A woman answered, and he told her who he was and that he wanted to speak with Soñadora. She took his number and hung up. Three minutes later she called, to tell him that Soñadora was at the *Salvamento* site.

Harry found a crew of men and women clearing away the remains of the building. Soñadora, dressed in overalls, her hair wrapped in a red cloth, saw Harry and pulled the cloth off her head as she picked her way through the rubble to the Rover. Her face was smudged with charcoal and streaked with sweat.

He got out of the car.

"When you finish here, I've got some brush that needs cutting," he told her, thinking that she looked very tired.

Frowning, she stared at him for a moment then wiped her face with the cloth she had pulled off her head.

"A joke," she said without smiling. "Why are you here?"

Harry swallowed his impulse to say something harsh, but the sting of her rebuff stayed with him.

"Do you remember Rowena Farnham?"

"She is the rector of St. Jude's?"

"That's right, and the church operates a shelter for battered women."

"I remember."

"She called me to say that they have two women who escaped from a house where they were being held and forced to work. She also said something about their being followed."

"Then they and everyone with them is in danger," Soñadora said instantly. "Why hasn't she called the police?"

"She said something about it being out of the question. She was very rushed, and what I've just told you is all I know, except that she wants you to take them."

"How does she know about me?" Soñadora demanded angrily.

Harry put up his hands.

"Wait!" he said, "All she knows about you is that you got me into La Ramada."

He did not say that Farnham had said she had heard about Soñadora. In her present mood, he thought least said soonest mended.

"But she called you, asking me to help," Soñadora said, "without knowing anything about me. Harry, if you've . . ."

"No, I haven't told her anything about you except that you speak Quiche, but she said she had heard about *Salvamento* and a woman working with victims of human trafficking. You're not invisible, you know. Neither is *Salvamento.*"

Soñadora made a show of turning to look at the charred remains of the building and then back at Harry, her dark eyes snapping, and said, "The fire. The paper!"

"I'm glad you don't have a dog," Harry said evenly.

"Why?" she asked, not following him.

"Because I'd bite it," he said.

"I don't—" she began angrily, and then stopped, blushing. "This is not a time for joking," she said, trying not to smile.

"I'm not joking. I can't bite you, at least not with all these people watching."

She paused and with a flicker of a smile asked, "If I were to throw a stick, would you chase it?"

Harry grinned. She had made a joke.

"Probably," he said, relaxing a little. "What about the women?"

Harry wanted to get back to Holinshed's office. In addition to wanting to be there for Minna, he knew that if he didn't get there very soon, his life was going to be a misery.

"I'll have to make some calls. It will take time to make the arrangements."

"OK. When you get it worked out, call me if you need a driver."

"I *will* need a driver." She hesitated, then stepped closer to him and put a hand on his arm. "Harry," she said, "This is very dangerous. You have responsibilities . . ."

Harry did not want to hear the rest of it. It was too reminiscent of Katherine. So he forced himself to laugh.

"What's funny?"

"You make me sound like Ernesto Piedra with his *responsibilidads.*"

"*¡Incorrigible!*" she said, managing a smile.

"Just call me," he said and put his hand over hers for an

instant before clambering back into the Rover.

As it turned out, Holinshed was running late, and the session had just begun when the receptionist opened the door and ushered him into the office. Holinshed was about Harry's age, medium height, fair-skinned, blue-eyed, and wore her dark hair cropped close to her head. At his arrival she came out from behind her cherry wood desk, greeted him with a warm smile that softened the effect of her steel-gray suit, and asked Minna and Katherine to get up and pull their barrel chairs around so that they could all sit in a circle.

"I'm going to backtrack a bit," she said, settling her notebook on her lap, "and ask each of you to say something about what brought you to see me."

Then, focusing her attention on Minna, she said very quietly, "You can have the last go, Minna, and give us the real skinny. How's that?"

Harry felt his heart contract at the sight of Minna, sunk in her chair, shoulders bowed, her hands clasped tightly on her knees, staring blindly at the floor. Her nod was scarcely visible.

For the next fifty minutes Harry endured one of the most emotionally painful hours of his life. Minna wept and screamed and said things that turned Katherine's face the color of milk and made Harry groan out loud. Several times Harry started to get up in order to end the torment and spare Minna any more suffering, but every time he moved, Katherine reached out and snagged his wrist in an iron grip, nailing him to his seat.

Holinshed, serious and attentive, behaved throughout the session as if tears, screams, and expletives were the stuff of normal intercourse. She passed the Kleenex box when needed, ended the session with a satisfied smile, and, leaned back in her chair, waved her pen at Katherine and Harry and said, "Good,

Minna, I'll see you in a week, only we'll leave these two out of it. OK?"

"I don't have anything more to say," the girl said loudly.

"Yes, you do," Holinshed told her, friendly as ever, "and so do I."

At the door, she sent Minna out first and told Katherine and Harry to wait.

"Why have you waited so long to bring that girl to see me?" she asked sternly.

Harry found himself tongue-tied but Katherine was not so easily intimidated.

"Because she wouldn't come," she said defiantly, "and I told Harry that if he tried to force her, I'd feed him to the pigs. She's had enough rough stuff from a male to last her a lifetime."

Holinshed looked at Katherine with renewed interest.

"Would you like to talk about that?" she asked, then shook her head. "No, we'll postpone that. Back to Minna. At this point I'm not going to prescribe anything for her. Let's see if we can talk her through this—correction: help her to talk her way through it. I'm hopeful, but here are some dos and don'ts: Don't talk to her about what she said here today, and don't ask her about our sessions in the future. I'll tell you both when I need you to do or stop doing something. Are we agreed?"

They both said, "Yes."

Holinshed shook their hands and said, "Treat her like a normal, thirteen-year-old girl. No long faces; don't watch her, don't ask her how she's feeling, let her eat or not. The reality is she's got to do most of this herself—with help from the rest of us—so give her the space to do it in."

Katherine, still whey-faced, turned to Harry and said, when the office door closed behind them and before they could be heard by Minna, "I had no idea she knew words like that. Did you?"

229

"No."

"Did you learn anything from that session?"

"You don't have to get shot to have a near-death experience."

"I'm not talking about it," Minna said when they were going down in the elevator.

"Talk about what?" Harry asked.

"Wise ass!" Minna snarled.

"Uh, uh," Katherine told her. "If you speak to either of us like that again, you'll wish you had never learned to speak at all."

Minna brooded on her mother's warning until the elevator stopped, and then, turning to Harry, she said, to his surprise, "Sorry, Harry. I know you're trying to help."

27

Dinner, a more than ordinarily subdued meal, was over. Minna had trailed away to her room, having eaten next to nothing, and Harry and Katherine, now sitting over their coffee, had not urged her.

"I was wrong about something," Katherine said dispiritedly after a lengthy silence. "This is not going to be fixed in a few short talks with Holinshed."

"No, but that's OK," Harry responded, trying to sound hopeful. "We can see her through it. I thought that over dinner, she seemed more preoccupied than depressed."

"After what she went through, I imagine she's exhausted," Katherine said, staring at her cup for a moment then looking up. "Harry, I can't stay here indefinitely. I've got a job and a house and two other children to look after."

Harry was not sure what he was hearing. It was true that her leave, including holiday time, meant she would have to be back in Georgia before Labor Day. But he wondered if there was a question buried in her statement. Was she asking if he wanted her to stay permanently?

Was that what he wanted? The answer to that question depended, in part, on what she wanted.

The next question was, What about Cora? It was only his own stubbornness that was keeping them apart—that and his pride that wouldn't let him take from her things, such as a trip to Scandinavia, that he couldn't give her. It was clear enough. If she didn't come back to Avola, they were finished.

All this thinking required about four seconds, but Harry knew beyond question that before he could know if he wanted him and Katherine to be together again, he had to know what she wanted, and the thought of asking her scared him, but he took a deep breath and walked out on the plank.

"Katherine," he said, "are you asking me . . ."

His cell vibrated in his pocket.

Soñadora, he thought. I'll call her back.

"Just a minute," he said to Katherine, taking out the phone.

"Harry, it's Doreen. I don't like the looks of Tucker. Can you and Katherine come over?"

"Yes," he said, "we'll be right there."

"Doreen?" Katherine asked.

"Yes. Tucker's apparently taken a turn for the worse. Do you want to go or stay with Minna?"

"Give me a moment to speak with her. She might want to come with us."

When a few minutes later Katherine came down the stairs, pulling a sweater over her shoulders, she was alone.

"Is she OK?" he asked.

"She's reading," Katherine said as they hurried toward the door. "I haven't seen her reading since she was attacked."

"But she doesn't want to go with us?"

"I think she's had enough of our company for one day."

Sanchez and Oh, Brother! met them when they got out of the car and escorted them to the house.

"I'd forgotten they always seemed to know when we were coming," Katherine said, walking beside the big mule with one hand on his glossy, black shoulder.

In the early moonlight he strode along like a great protective shadow. Sanchez walked directly in front of Harry, glancing over his shoulder now and then as though checking to see if he was keeping up. Just short of the stoop, the animals stopped, allowing Katherine and Harry to go on alone.

Doreen met them just inside the door. She looked tired and worried; her usual high color had faded to a weary gray. The kitchen was heavy with cigarette smoke.

"He couldn't eat any supper to speak of and kept dropping off, but when he was awake he said he didn't have any discomfort."

"You're way past your leaving time," Harry said. "What kept you here?"

"I'm not sure exactly, but I called Wetherell around six and told him to go ahead and make his own supper."

She was moving toward the hall door, taking Harry and Katherine with her.

"Half an hour ago, I was thinking I'd go along, but I went one last time to check him, and his breathing seemed funny. He's a little feverish. After watching him for a while, I got scared and called you."

"Let's have a look," Katherine said, hurrying Doreen along.

It hurt Harry to see how small Tucker looked in his bed. He seemed hardly to make a bump in the sheet covering him.

"I agree with Doreen," Katherine told Harry. "He's feverish. His breathing is really very light, and his pulse is way too slow for my liking."

"Then he'd better be in the hospital," Harry said.

"I don't think we should try moving him," Katherine said.

"Call 911," Doreen said, "that way he'll get looked at right away."

"I'll make the call," Harry said.

When that was done, Katherine said to Doreen, "Why don't you go home? There's nothing to be done but wait, and Harry and I can do that. You look tired out."

"I suppose I may as well," Doreen said. "Wetherell and the kids will be looking for me."

Before she could leave, Katherine said, "While Tucker's in the hospital, Doreen, would you be willing to keep on coming over here? We'll pay you, of course."

"We can look after the animals," Harry said. "Doreen might want a rest from this place."

"I'm not thinking about the animals," Katherine said a little shortly. "I'm thinking about Minna."

"And the pigs," Doreen said. "I'll come."

"What's the pigs got to do with it?" Harry asked.

"Minna's going to keep on coming over here," Doreen told him, "and I'm guessing Katherine would just as soon not have her here alone with those pigs."

"That's it," Katherine said, "and I can't be here. She'd say I was spying on her or that I didn't trust her."

"Do you want to do this, Doreen?" Harry asked.

"I'll be here," she said.

She walked over to the bed and pulled the sheet a little and then touched Tucker's shoulder.

"If he's got to go, I hope he goes quickly," she said, turning back to them. "He's a good man. There's not all that many of them, present company excepted."

With that she left.

When the EMS team had Tucker safely loaded in the ambulance and his doctor notified, Harry and Katherine drove back to tell Minna what had happened. She began crying, and Katherine held her until all the pain of the day had been wrung out of her. Then Harry drove to the Avola Community Hospital. He found Tucker in a bed with the curtain drawn around it and Dr. Post and two nurses working over him.

Harry sat down near the nurses' station and waited. His mind dredged up the night Tucker blew the treads off a big Caterpillar tractor, to stop a gravel company from bulldozing a piece of land that was home to some rare butterflies he had found. The explosion had jumped Harry out of his bed and sent him running out of the house just in time to see Tucker in his buckboard, pulled by Oh, Brother! with Sanchez racing in front of the mule, flash past him in the moonlight, trailing a tunnel of silver dust.

He was enjoying the memory and thinking that it was a simpler, more innocent time when that happened. Post ended his examination, and came out of the ward, to slump down beside Harry, pushing out his feet with a grunt of weariness, and rubbing his eyes with the heels of his hands.

"Is he conscious?" Harry asked.

"In and out," Post answered.

"What's wrong with him?"

Harry was struggling to calm the anxiety welling up in him and losing.

"I don't have all the information that the bloodwork and other tests will give me, but if I had to say right now, I'd call it CHF."

"Cold hands and feet," Harry said edgily.

"Yes, that too," Post told him with sour grin. "Congestive heart failure, which is, much oversimplified, failure of the heart muscles to pump the blood where it needs to go."

"His heart has been doing its work a long time," Harry said with a sinking feeling. "It must be tired."

"Don't bury him yet," Post said, using Harry's shoulder as an aid to regaining his feet. "We'll keep an eye on him for a few days, do some more work, and make some decisions."

"About?"

"How strong his heart is because in the end, that will lead to a prognosis, one I can't make now. Go home. Leave him to us.

We'll take good care of him."

When Harry got home, the kitchen smelled of baking. Harry gave Katherine Post's report, and she smiled with relief.

"You know, I thought it was going to be a lot worse."

Harry nodded.

"So did I. It's serious, but Post really didn't seem all that worried. So I guess we don't have to be. What have you made?"

"It's a raspberry tart," Katherine told him, "and we're going to eat it. Coffee, tea, or milk?"

Harry pulled a long face.

"What's wrong?" Katherine asked, stopping halfway between the oven and the table, holding the tart in two dishtowels like an offering to the kitchen god.

"I'm disappointed," Harry said. "Isn't it supposed to be, 'Coffee, tea, or me'?"

"That dates you," she said, blushing as she set the Pyrex pie plate on the table. "Wash your hands. We'll eat this thing and watch our bums grow."

"You've spent too much time with kids," Harry told her, complying with the order.

"How so? Bring two forks when you've dried your hands."

"First, you told me to wash my hands. Now you've told me to dry them."

"You've been in a hospital. You're a walking plague."

"I'm being badly spoiled," he said when they finished eating. "That tart is way above my performance level."

"I'll take that as a compliment," Katherine said and then without a pause asked, "What was the question that was cut off by Doreen's call?"

Now Harry saw the raspberry tart in a new light. Had she been softening him up? Did she already know what he was going to ask her? What if the answer to both questions was yes?

Worse yet, what if it was no?

Harry looked at her. She was balancing her chin on her hands, elbows on the table, a quiet smile curving her lips, staring across the table at him, a teasing light in her glorious green eyes. Also, leaning forward as she was had tightened her yellow jersey across her firm and ample breasts. If this was manipulation, who was he to resist it?

"Have you thought about living here permanently?" he asked, then holding his breath, thinking he was shaken as much by the possibility she would say no as yes.

"Harry!" she cried, reaching out and catching one of his hands in hers. "Are you proposing to me? Have you lost your mind?"

"I guess I am and probably," he told her, adding his free hand to the pile.

Her eyes were wide with surprise. Then suddenly she laughed, one of her deep, good laughs.

"And I thought you were going to proposition me. I even baked the tart as an added incentive."

The next morning, still single and with his question unanswered, Harry woke smiling. The tart had done its work, and after breakfast, he drove to Avola to talk with Jim Snyder. The heat had settled in for its summer run. When he got out of the Rover in the Sheriff's parking lot, the cicadas in the pin oaks blasted him with the sound of a thousand tiny saws cutting through a tin roof, and the sun flaring off the tarmac made him squint even behind his sunglasses.

"You're looking a little worn down, Harry," Hodges said, bringing him a cup of coffee. "You still having trouble from being blown into the ditch?"

"No, I'm pretty well over that," he said without offering any other explanation.

"Just the same, it would help if you made sure you were getting your rest," Jim said, "Katherine says she thinks you're working too hard."

How much are those two talking? Harry wondered, surprised to find a small, green monster hopping around in his brain.

"I'm fine, but Tucker's not doing too well," he responded, eager to change the subject and brought them up to date on Tucker's troubles.

"This morning they're saying his condition is guarded," Harry concluded.

"Well, I hope nothing happens to that old bird," Hodges said. "Now that old man Clampett's gone, there's not another one like him in southwest Florida."

"Frank," Jim said loudly, "there's no need of talking about that. Tucker just needs some care is all. Isn't that how you see it, Harry?"

"It's what I hope," Harry admitted.

"We all do," Jim said quickly.

Hodges was nodding earnestly and added, "That's right, he's lived a long time, and he's going to take a lot of killing."

Harry laughed in spite of himself, and Jim groaned out loud.

"What?" Hodges demanded, his face getting redder.

"Never mind," Jim said. "Harry, there's another body, an aged Hispanic woman—no name, no fingerprint records, nothing."

"In the Luther Faubus Canal?" Harry asked.

"That's right," Hodges said, "all her clothes on right up to her apron. She was shot in the back of the head."

Jim was pushing folders around on his desk and came up with a sealed plastic bag with a wrinkled sheet of paper inside, half the size of a piece of typing paper. He handed it to Harry.

"We found this folded up in her apron pocket," he said. "Look familiar?"

"The first time Soñadora and I went to La Ramada, we passed these out. Looks like this one traveled."

"Maybe not so far," Jim replied. "I talked with Rowena Farnham at St. Jude's. She said that so far all the Hispanic women who had come to the shelter had come to escape abusive husbands. None, as far as she knew, had come from La Ramada."

"If this old lady was on her way there, I'd be surprised," Hodges said.

"So would I," Harry agreed.

"Then why would she be carrying this?" Jim asked.

"What are the chances she could read that flier?" Harry countered.

"Vanishing to none," Jim said, "but she could have been told what it says, which makes me think there's a chance there was someone she wanted to give this to."

"And that's why you found her in the canal?" Harry asked.

"It's possible," Jim conceded, "but I'll grant you it's a reach."

"Anything else new?" Harry asked, very aware that he was holding back information Jim needed and was in a position to lose his license if things went a little wrong.

"We shook out your friend Ernesto Piedra," Hodges said, getting up, his chair creaking with relief, to recharge his mug. "We didn't learn anything useful from him."

"One of these days, Harry," Jim said with a frown of disapproval, "we're going to catch him fencing stolen goods, and he's going on a long vacation."

"Believe me," Harry replied with a grin, "he needs one, but he's a good man and I like him."

"We hear he's got a lot of kids," Hodges said, "but I never hear about a wife."

"I've never met her," Harry replied, relieved to be able to say something truthful. "By the way, Jim, how was your date with

Kathleen Towers?"

Harry gambled that mentioning Towers in front of Hodges would get Jim's mind off Ernesto Piedra, and he was right.

"Having lunch with someone isn't a date," Jim protested, his ears getting red.

"When did you have lunch with the ME?" Hodges asked with a broad smile, being almost as fond of gossip as Wetherell Clampett.

"A few days ago. It was Harry's fault. I couldn't avoid it."

Harry and Hodges cruelly said nothing and just stared at Jim, watching his ears burn.

"Five will get you ten, Frank," Harry finally said, "that he's already had at least one dinner date with her."

Jim gave up and grinned.

"Two," he said, "now let's move on."

"Good," Harry said. "She's a nice person. I'm leaving. I've got to earn a living."

28

Harry spent the rest of the day checking the validity of clients' testimony for an Avola law firm specializing in criminal law, most of which consisted of defending clients in DUI cases, spousal battery, and minor white-collar crime. They were not the kinds of cases that found their way into law school case books, and Harry, doing the work, sometimes felt like the man at the circus running after the elephants with a shovel and a basket.

But it paid the rent. He frequently told himself that, fully aware this was not a mantra likely to lead to enlightenment.

It turned out to be a wearying day with delayed meetings, problems with dogs at houses he needed to enter, more trouble and delays with the Avola police at crime scenes decorated with yellow, and on his way home a six-car crash on Interstate 75, which kept him sitting, listening to the news for an hour. It was nearly dark when he reached the Hammock.

"Someone who spoke very little English has called twice in the last hour," Katherine said. "Is something wrong with your cell?"

"Yes, I turned it off and forgot I'd done it," he said. "What did they want?"

"I think it was a woman," Katherine said. "She wouldn't leave a number, but I think she said she would call again."

"Soñadora's security system," Harry said with a chuckle. "Have you called the hospital?"

"Yes, and there's been no change. He's resting comfortably, and Dr. Post has seen Tucker twice since he was admitted. They're waiting for lab reports."

She made a face.

"I haven't made dinner. Are you hungry?"

"I'm going to be."

He put his gear away in the office and, coming back into the kitchen, he asked, "Where's Minna?"

"Upstairs. Harry, I'm worried about her. She seems to be drifting farther and farther away. Even Doreen mentioned it."

"It's two more days before she sees Holinshed. Is there anything we can do?"

"I don't know if there's anything we can do except follow her advice to be supportive and not try to force anything."

Harry's cell sounded. This time it was Soñadora.

"How soon can you get here?" she said without preamble.

"Where's here?"

She told him.

"I suppose this can't be done tomorrow morning."

"Only if you want two dead women on your conscience. I'm pretty sure whoever's chasing them knows where they are. Do you?"

"Yes, I'll pick you up in twenty minutes, and we'll be at Haven House in another fifteen."

"Soñadora's found a place to take the two women I told you about and has to do it now," he told Katherine, which was true, but it was only half the truth.

"Will it take long?" she asked as he went into his office for his keys and the CZ.

"I don't know. You'd better eat. I'll call as soon as I'm on my way home."

"Why do you need your gun to drive two women from one place to another?" Katherine asked.

"Things have gotten a little sticky," he said, pausing on the way to the door to give her a quick kiss. "Don't worry. It's mostly for show. I'll explain it all later."

Everything was beginning to feel very familiar—not telling her things that might upset her. Lying about other things. He ran out of the house, the fantasy of him and Katherine together in some perfect world evaporating in the hot night air.

Once on the road, Harry called Farnham, shared what he had been told with her, and told her she should, if possible, get everyone except the two women out of Haven House.

"We have five other women in there," Farnham told him. "It won't be easy. Three of them are terrified of their husbands and may refuse to budge."

"Do your best," Harry told her and hung up.

A few minutes later he picked up Soñadora at a 7-11 on Pine Ridge Road. They drove east toward the coast and then south into a densely built-up and conspicuously wealthy section of Avola where St. Jude's and the Sanctuary were located. Soñadora broke a long silence and said, "What I've heard is that a group of four Guatemalan men have been pursuing these two women since the night before last and that tonight they plan to recapture them or, if that fails, kill them."

"How could they have found out they were in St. Jude's Haven House?" Harry asked.

"I'm not sure, and my sources are usually reliable, but nothing is certain."

"Few things are," Harry said bleakly.

Soñadora was sitting forward tensely, looking as if only her seatbelt was keeping her from leaping out of the car and racing down the road.

"Not even that many," she said, glancing at him. "Is something wrong?"

"A friend of mine is very ill," he said. "It's been on my mind."

"Have you told me about this?" she asked.

"No."

"Why not?"

"Well, I didn't think—"

"That you didn't know me well enough? That I wouldn't be sympathetic? That you didn't want to share your concern with me?"

She sounded angry.

"I tend to compartmentalize," Harry said, trying to mollify her and at the same time wondering why he *hadn't* mentioned Tucker to her.

"That means you put your relationships in separate boxes and the boxes do not communicate?"

"The man who is sick is an old man, a farmer. He befriended me many years ago at a time when I needed help. Now, when he needs it, I can't help him back."

"You have told him you love him?"

He could tell from her voice that she knew he hadn't.

"We're good friends," he said defensively.

"Not the same thing," she said definitively. "We will talk about this later."

"Are you doing some compartmentalizing?"

"Possibly. I'm very concerned that if things go as I think they might, those women are going to be killed."

"Are the men armed?"

"Find the box with your brains in it," she snapped.

"It's the smallest box in the bunch," he said.

She smothered a sputtering laugh and, straightening her back, said, "I think the most dangerous moment will come when we have the women in the car and are alone with them on the road."

"Five will get you ten that they'll go for the house."

"Why would they do that?" she asked.

"Because they probably don't know we're coming, or if they do they'll want it finished before we get there."

"I hope you are wrong."

"Well, picture them driving up beside the car and opening up with automatic weapons."

"I have brought my gun," she said. "I can use it."

Haven House was a tall, white stucco house set back from the dark road behind a wide lawn. Slivers of yellow light from the second-floor windows escaped through the Bermuda shutters. The first floor was dark and no outside lights were burning.

"I don't see any car," Harry said as he turned into the driveway.

"If it is here," she said, "we will not see it."

"About that gun," he said, "if things go bad, and there is shooting, and if the police come and find you with it, you will be in very serious trouble. You will probably be put in prison for a long time. Why not give it to me?"

"I would rather be alive and in prison than dead because you had my gun," she said flatly.

He couldn't fault the logic, so he said, "I'm going to park as close to that front door as I can," and turned off the driveway onto the grass. "Where's your gun?"

"In a back holster under my *chaleco*."

"Vest," Harry said.

He had noticed her embroidered vest. She was wearing black slacks and shoes, a black, long-sleeved shirt, and a black cloth, tying up her hair. Only the vest's red needlework had any color.

"We are going to have an English lesson?" she asked as he motioned her out of the car.

"Good a time as any," he told her, the energy that always rippled through him when he sensed danger was lifting his spirits. "Move it."

She slid out the door, keeping her head below the roof of the car. Harry, slithering out her door, saw that she was holding her gun in both hands, muzzle pointing at the ground. Not bad, he thought.

He paused to let his eyes adjust to the darkness, then said, "I'll go for the door first. If it's locked, I won't knock."

"Idiot," she said.

The car was almost directly in front of the door, and Harry went across the intervening distance as fast as he could run, not, he thought, nearly fast enough, but no one shot him, and he found the door off the latch and bounded through it, turning and dropping instantly to one knee, partially hidden by the door frame.

An instant later a slim black figure flew through the door and repeated his drop and turn across from him. The world remained undisturbed except for the chiming of tree frogs. She eased the door shut.

"Now we go upstairs," he said.

"*Now* you stay where you are and slowly place your guns on the floor," a woman's voice said first in Spanish and then in English in a back country voice.

Soñadora muttered something Harry missed just as the foyer exploded in light. For a long moment Harry was effectively blinded, and because there was no shooting, he guessed Soñadora was in the same plight.

"You were right," he said to her. "I am an idiot."

"Forgot to close your eyes, didn't you?" a woman's voice said. "You the two taking us to a safehouse?"

Easing the door shut and still squinting, Harry saw a lean, blonde-haired woman in a red dress, sitting on the stairs, knees apart, pointing a Colt .45 at them, a pair of night goggles pushed up onto her head. A second woman, holding a Glock 17, stood beside the light switch on the wall. This woman had eyes and hair as black as Soñadora's. She and the blonde, Harry noted, were dressed in very expensive clothes.

"That's us," Harry said. "Where'd you get the night vision glasses?"

"Rector gave them to me. I don't know where she got them."

The dark woman was staring at Soñadora and burst into a clatter of speech, to which Soñadora responded. Harry understood three words—*Harry Brock* and *Soñadora.*

"Is OK," the dark woman said. "I am Rigoberta Quirarte. This one," she said, pointing the gun at the blonde woman, "is Hazel only."

"Riggs!" Hazel shouted, "What did I tell you about that fucking gun?"

"*¡Discúlpeme!*" the dark woman said with a sardonic smile, lowering the pistol. "I forget. You told me I am pointing it only at some fucking body I am think to shoot."

"Saying you're fucking sorry after you've shot somebody, me, for example, won't fucking cut it," Hazel snapped.

Rigoberta looked at Harry and said, with no trace of contrition, "I'm fucking sorry."

"You're forgiven," Harry said with a relieved laugh, but keeping his eye on Rigoberta's gun, holstered his CZ. Soñadora, who was not laughing, did the same with her weapon.

"Are you here alone?" he asked Hazel.

Soñadora had crossed the foyer to talk with Rigoberta.

"We're hoping so," Hazel said, levering herself to her feet. "I was expecting some other visitors. I damn near took us out of here on our own, but before she and the others left, that Farnham woman convinced me we should wait for you two."

"I'm glad you did, but I also think they're coming," Harry said.

"One way or another," she said darkly, "they've always been coming."

"Where did you get the guns?"

"It's a long story," Hazel told him.

"Is your last name *Only?* I didn't quite get what your friend said."

Hazel gave a snorting laugh. "She meant I'm not saying my last name. If you study on it, you might be able to figure out why."

"Got you. Are you ready to go?"

"There's a couple of sacks upstairs. Where are we going?"

"Soñadora knows. All this has happened really quickly."

"Those two look enough alike to be cousins," Hazel said, looking at Soñadora and Rigoberta. "Unlike you and me, they're a pair of beauties."

"She came up here all alone, didn't she?" Harry said, silently agreeing with Hazel.

"Came up here broke, was shot in the leg by one of the fucking coyotes that brought her," Hazel said, her voice rich with admiration and something more, Harry thought, "then got sold into bondage by her aunt's husband. Except to say she misses her kids, I never heard a word of complaint out of her, and she's got more guts than a truck full of hogs."

"How did they snare you?"

He expected her to say drugs, although he saw no signs of the habitual user.

"You could say I needed to get out of sight in a fucking hurry."

"Your friend learned her English from you," Harry said.

"How'd you know?" Hazel demanded, looking surprised.

"It was just a guess," he said, struggling to keep a straight face. "We'd better go. Can you shut off those upstairs lights?"

"Yup. Come on, Riggs," Hazel said, running up the stairs.

Rigoberta ran after her. Harry watched them go, thinking the

Indian woman was certainly a beauty, and there was something strangely attractive about that thin woman with the wild yellow hair.

"They were working as wage slaves in a sewing operation," Soñadora told Harry as they waited. "I don't know the details, but there was a fight and they ran and were chased by someone named Gomez. Hazel shot him in the leg."

"Hazel said you and Rigoberta were a pair of beauties," Harry said.

"She needs glasses."

"She's got a pair. Don't you think Rigoberta is good-looking?" he asked, teasing.

"I didn't notice. Why are you asking me these ridiculous questions? We are in great danger."

"Yes, you're probably right, but at such times everything becomes very vivid for me, and I always have a great need not to leave things unsaid."

Hazel and Rigoberta came hurrying down the stairs, their bags slung over their shoulders.

"How are we going to do this?" Hazel asked.

"Put out these lights," Harry told them, "give our eyes time to adjust, then we ease out that door one at a time. The car's just to the left."

Soñadora translated for Rigoberta.

"Me first," he said, "then Soñadora, then you two, one after the other. Stay low and no talking. Are we ready?"

The three women, holding their guns, nodded.

God help us, Harry thought, if those killers find us.

"Hit the switch, Hazel," he said. "I'll open the door. Then we go."

One after another the four sprinted from the house to the car, lining up against the side of the car, crouching to peer through the windows toward the street. Night jars were booming over the lawn. Crickets were chirping, and the moon had laid a silver wash over the lawn, the trees, and the street.

"What now?" Soñadora whispered.

"There's a canal beyond that street and the line of trees," he answered. "Why aren't we hearing the frogs?"

"Something has disturbed them," she answered.

"Right. Let's wait for a while and see what happens."

Soñadora whispered to Hazel, who spoke quietly to Rigoberta.

They did not have to wait long. At the street end of the driveway, Harry saw the glint of moonlight on metal and heard the scuff of a boot on the macadam. Soñadora nudged Harry with her elbow and pointed to the other side of the lawn. Harry looked in that direction and saw a dark shadow detach itself from the tree shadow and move toward them across the lawn. A moment later two more shadows, moving quickly, appeared on the middle section of the lawn.

"Four," he whispered to Soñadora. "Switch places with Hazel. Tell Rigoberta what to do."

"You have a plan?" she asked before moving.

"We have two choices," he said. We can crawl to the corner of the house. Then get up and make a run for it and hope we can keep ahead of them, or we can hunker down here until they get very close and then open up on them."

"I say stay," she said.

"You're sure?"

"Certain."

"Right. Stay behind the car. Wait for me to shoot. Divide the targets. Hazel and I will try for the two on the left. You and Rigoberta take the other two. God knows whether or not Rigoberta can actually fire that cannon."

It was not as ridiculous as it looked, he told himself. The gunmen were in the lightest part of the lawn. He and the women were in the shadow of the house.

"Harry," she whispered and then said something he could not understand.

"What?" he whispered back.

"It means, it's a good day to die," she said.

"You think you're funny, don't you?"

"Idiot," she said, pressed her hand against his face for an instant, and was gone.

Hazel edged closer to Harry.

"You take the one on your left," she said. "I'll get the other one then start shooting at yours, and for Christ's sake, don't forget to aim and squeeze the goddamned trigger. Don't pull it."

"I'll try to remember," Harry said, choking back a snort of laughter.

"I've got to tell you, Harry," she whispered with increased intensity, "I'm fucking worried about Riggs. There's no fucking telling what she'll do. She's wilder than a goddamned barn cat."

"Soñadora is steady," was all he could think of to say.

Harry had not taken his eyes off the four shadows advancing toward them, and to remain focused, he began counting off the yards separating them from the car. When he reached twelve, he stood up and fired twice at the shadow on his left and dropped to the ground, shouting, "Get down!" as he fell.

Hazel went onto her knees. Then she stretched flat to peer under the car's chassis. Harry looked across her back and, to his relief, saw the other two women hugging the ground. An instant later there was a thunderous roar of automatic rifles, and bullets zipped and banged through the car.

"I think you got the son of a bitch on the left," Hazel said, "but I'm damned if I can see a target from down here."

The shooting stopped.

"Fresh clips," Harry said and jumped to his feet.

Across the top of the car he saw three shadows where there

had been four. He picked one of the targets and fired once. To his left, Hazel popped up and fired. Beyond her Harry thought he saw Soñadora and Rigoberta, both shorter than he and Hazel, scramble toward the front of the car then jump up to fire over the car's hood.

"Down," he shouted, grasping Hazel's arm and pulling her with him, as the two remaining attackers lifted their guns.

Hazel fell to her knees. There was another volley of firing, and Rigoberta suddenly shouted, "Fuck you!"

"Oh, shit! There she goes," Hazel said as Rigoberta bounced to her feet and ran around the front of the car, holding her gun in front of her and firing as she ran.

Soñadora, crying, "No!" tried to grasp her ankle and failed. Hazel came onto both feet and one fist like a sprinter, jumped over Soñadora, and shot around the car, running as hard as she could.

Harry, much more slowly than Hazel had moved, clambered to his feet. The attackers, apparently momentarily distracted by Rigoberta's racing into the open, shooting at them, began shouting at one another.

At that moment, Hazel caught Rigoberta in a flying tackle that brought both women to the ground with Rigoberta swearing loudly.

"*Madre de Dios!*" Soñadora said.

She had been swinging her gun but was obviously afraid to fire for fear of hitting Rigoberta or Hazel.

But in falling the two women had gone momentarily out of their attackers' sight, and they were firing at where the women had been.

"Take the one on the right," Harry said as Hazel and Rigoberta fell.

He and Soñadora fired at the muzzle blasts of the two men left standing. There was an abrupt and ringing silence.

"Hey," Hazel called, "these two are down."

"Shit!" she shouted and fired three shots into whatever had risen up in front of her.

She walked over to the fallen man and bent over him.

"Goddamn, Riggs!" she shouted, "It's Gomez."

Harry could not hear Rigoberta's answer. She was crawling around in the grass on her hands and knees. For a moment Harry thought she had been hit, but then she stood up, still talking to Hazel.

"I lose my gun," Rigoberta complained, limping back toward the car.

Then she said something to Soñadora, who laughed.

"What?" Harry asked, moving past them to look at the fallen men.

"She said, 'Now I am American, it is not appropriate to be without a gun.' "

"Why are you limping, Riggs?" Hazel demanded in Spanish, coming back to the car. "Did you get hit?"

"No. I hurt my leg when I fell."

"She was shot in the leg before," Hazel said to Harry, then turned back to Rigoberta and threw her arms around her.

"I had to take you down or you would have been killed, Riggs," Hazel told her, "but I'm sorry I hurt you."

They stood together for a moment, Rigoberta resting her forehead on Hazel's shoulder. Then she straightened up and said, "Help me find my gun."

"Wait," Harry said, "We've got about ten minutes before the police get here, less if there's a patrol car closer than the station. We've got to move."

"Do the police have your fingerprints?" Soñadora asked Hazel.

"Oh yes," she said.

"I thought so. Let's find Rigoberta's pistol and get out of

here before we all end up in jail."

Harry made a quick check to satisfy himself that they still had four inflated tires to run away on and started the car, blowing out his breath in relief when it started. He did not allow himself to think about what would happen to him if Jim or his people found him with a car full of bullet holes and three gun-toting women, one almost certainly an escapee from a prison and the other two Guatemalan illegals . . . and four dead men.

"My mother had plans for me that did not include wading through swamps in the company of wetbacks and engaging in a shootout while wearing designer-label clothes," Hazel said in a severe voice as she got into the back seat and slammed the door behind her.

The window in her door immediately fell down into the door. She burst out laughing.

"How long were you in for?" Harry asked.

"Twelve to fifteen, possession and selling," Hazel told him. "I got away by clunking a FedEx driver on the head and walking out in his uniform. Just in case you ever need to know, those FedEx trucks are damned poor getaway vehicles."

"Go, Harry," Soñadora gasped, jumping to the front seat while Rigoberta got in behind.

"Find it?" Hazel asked as the car wheeled in a circle across the lawn and bumped onto the street.

"Fucking right," Rigoberta answered.

Soñadora twisted around in her seat and began speaking swiftly and harshly to Rigoberta.

"But Hazel is good speaker of English," Rigoberta protested in English when Soñadora finished. "I learn quick. I like her also."

"Good, but swearing is bad," Soñadora said flatly. "Stop it."

Harry glanced in his mirror and saw Hazel and Rigoberta grinning at one another.

"Where are we going?" he asked.

"Get me to 41," Soñadora told him. "Then I'll know where to go."

Harry was turning onto 12th Street when he heard the first siren.

"Cross your fingers," he said. "Here they come."

Before he reached 41, six cruisers and a SWAT team had passed them.

"Well, Brock," Hazel asked as they swung onto the East Trail, the wind from the broken window tangling her hair, "This was a good start to the evening. What else have you got planned?"

"Staying out of the Luther Faubus Canal," he said.

Only Hazel laughed.

29

The house, tucked away on a tree-lined street in a quiet, middle-class neighborhood, was a sprawling, single-story, pink stucco with a low roof and a car port and stood among dense plantings of hibiscus, bamboos, and other threes that hid the house from the street. No dogs were barking. No music was blasting. Harry was impressed.

"This looks good," he said.

"Just as long as we don't find another Gomez in there," Hazel said, climbing out of the car.

"I'll shoot him," Rigoberta said.

Harry did not think she was joking.

"Nobody's going to shoot anybody," Soñadora said, grasping Rigoberta's hands as they stood clustered outside the car, looking at the dark house. "That is over. You will be safe here."

"Neither of us is going to be safe anywhere," Hazel responded, "but Riggs and me are much obliged to you both. It's been a ride."

"Take care of yourself, Hazel," Harry said, "and you too, Riggs."

"I am Rigoberta, and Hazel only calls me Riggs, but you may. Thank you."

She kissed Soñadora and shook Harry's hand.

"Now . . . my children," she said.

"So long, Harry," Hazel said, kicking one of the Rover's tires. "This business has lost you some trade-in."

"Come on," Soñadora said.

Harry stood by the car and watched them walk up the path to the house. He heard a door open. A moment later Soñadora was back.

"Will they be safe there?" Harry asked.

"I think so, but Hazel was right. They may never really be safe."

Katherine was asleep in his bed when he got home. He undressed and slipped under the covers with her and gave a quiet sigh of relief. Katherine stirred, rolled toward him, and slid a leg across his hips.

"You might have thought I'd forgotten," she said and kissed him.

What followed made sleep, when he got to that stage, sweeter.

He awoke to a room filled with dappled sunlight. As he showered and shaved, he went over the events of the previous night, astonished that they had emerged unscathed. It occurred to him that had it not been for Rigoberta's banzai attack on the gunmen, drawing their attention away from the car and giving him and Soñadora the freedom to shoot the two men left standing, they might well all be dead. Hazel had finished the job by taking out the man named Gomez.

He went downstairs to an empty kitchen and looked out the front window to see Katherine walking slowly around the Rover. She was not smiling. With an inward groan, Harry went out to join her.

"Tell me you weren't in the Rover when all this happened to it," she said with a wave of her hand that took in two missing windows and an exuberant pattern of bullet holes in the rider's side of the vehicle.

"Not when the bullets were going through it," Harry said.

She moved a little closer to him, her green eyes cold and

unwavering.

"I made love last night to a man who left the house early in the evening to drive two women from an Episcopalian Shelter for Women to another safehouse," she said with false smile. "Did you get there and back by way of Iraq?"

Harry thought a lie would not deceive her. Otherwise, he would have given it a try because he saw that Katherine was not happy, and when Katherine was unhappy in that particular tone of voice, as experience had taught him, *he* was probably not going to be happy for some extended period of time.

"There was a little trouble when Soñadora and I got to Haven House," he said. "Four men, muscle for the trafficking ring, tried to recapture the two women. There were some shots fired, but none of us was hurt, and I got the women to the safehouse as planned."

"And the men?" she asked.

"There were casualties," he told her.

"You shot four men last night and then came home and made love to me."

Harry almost said, "No, you made love to me," but stopped himself.

"Four of us and four of them were trading fire," he said in a neutral voice. "It was dark. They were armed with automatic rifles. We were in deep shadow."

"What am I supposed to understand from that?"

It's miraculous I'm actually standing in front of you was a possible answer but one he rejected.

Harry suddenly felt completely exhausted, as if the adrenaline that had carried him through the night had stopped flowing. He thought of the women and how they had fought without a whimper, of Riggs racing out onto the lawn swearing and shooting, and Hazel racing after her and tackling her just before the Guatemalans opened up on her. He thought of Soñadora, silent and calm and steady, aiming and shooting with deadly effect.

"To be honest, I'm surprised that anyone lived through it," he said, and turned aside, although no longer angry with Katherine. "I had a lot of help. The women were all using their guns. They were wonderful. Fucking bloody wonderful!"

When he finally looked back at Katherine, he saw to his dismay that although she was making no sound, tears were running down her cheeks. She seemed to be struggling with an emotion that Harry could not name but it was probably, he suspected, not a blend of warmth and admiration.

"Nothing has changed, has it Harry?" she finally asked quietly, resignation steadying her voice.

"A lot of things have changed, Katherine," he said, "for one, I've stopped blaming you for our breakup, and I've also stopped blaming myself."

"Shit happens?"

"Sometimes, and sometimes, it's just plain pigheadedness."

"So I left you out of pigheadedness?"

"No, but I'm still here, and I still love you. So you were right, I guess. Some things don't change."

She stepped around him and walked into the house. It occurred to him that the next time he saw her, she would probably be carrying her suitcase. The thought gave him no pleasure.

"We're taking you home," Harry said, trying to keep all traces of concern out of his face and his voice, but the truth was that Tucker looked as if he had shrunk to half his former size.

Half an hour earlier, Harry had talked with Dr. Post and been told that the prognosis was still guarded, but that since there was nothing to be done, short of keeping him immobile, Harry might as well take him home. The most important thing for Tucker to do was to take his medicine.

The two men shook hands, and that may have told Harry

more than anything the doctor had said.

"It's about time," Tucker replied with more verve than Harry had expected and throwing off his covers, managed to swing his legs over the edge of the bed.

Katherine was so surprised by his energy that she laughed when he brushed off her efforts to help him stand. She had not packed her bag, but things between her and Harry were still in the sere and yellow leaf stage with colder weather in the forecast. He had slept alone since their talk by the Rover, which was presenting him with a disposal problem.

He had considered the Luther Faubus Canal, but rejected that option and was procrastinating in a rental Mustang, which had prompted Minna, whom Harry thought had given up noticing anything without a curly tail, to observe, "Juvenile."

"I've never resigned myself to being wheeled out of the hospital and then dumped," Tucker complained as they were getting him into Katherine's Camry.

"There are some places in the country," she told him, "that hospitals do that to get rid of patients who can't pay their bills."

"Such practices weigh on the heart," he said with feeling as they drove away, "but I can't complain about the way they treated me, aside from shouting at me as if I was deaf and walking me to the toilet, which made me short-tempered. How's Minna?"

"Only Dr. Holinshed knows," Harry said, his impatience showing.

Katherine only nodded.

"She called me every day," Tucker told them.

"What did she talk about?" Katherine asked with increased interest.

"After asking me how I felt, the pigs," Tucker said.

"Did you try to change the subject?" Harry asked.

Tucker was quiet for a while. Then he said, "Under the

circumstances, I was uneasy doing it, but I'm obliged to say that I did, and when I did, she stopped talking."

"Oh, dear," Katherine said at the news. Then, "But I'm not surprised."

"I take it, she's not talking much to either of you?"

"No," Katherine said. "We have trouble even keeping her in the same room with us."

"I plan to work on that garden a little every day," Tucker said, "I'll see if I can persuade her to help me. If I can do that, maybe I can at least get her to talk about what we're doing."

"You go easy on the work," Harry said. "You know what the doctor said."

"Bradley Post is worse than a mother hen. 'Now remember, Mr. LaBeau, you're not a young man. Your heart is not as strong as it was. You've got to keep that in mind—and you've got to take that medicine every day. Mr. LaBeau, are you listening to me?' "

Tucker's mimicry was so accurate that both Katherine and Harry had to laugh. When they had driven into the yard with Tucker in the back seat, Sanchez and Oh, Brother! crowded so close to his door, Tucker had to squeeze himself out of the car, and it was several minutes before they would let him walk between them to the house.

"You'd have to see it to believe it," Katherine said quietly to Harry as they stood watching the reunion.

"I still don't believe it," Harry said.

Doreen had rearranged the kitchen so that Tucker could sit in his rocker and look out the door to the woods beyond the stoop, and she had sewn red-and-white striped covers for the cushions she had attached to the seat and the back of the rocker.

"You haven't got any more ass than a frog," she told him loudly, leading him to the rocker. "So you're going to set a lot easier on that cushion."

"Thank you, Doreen, thank you," he told her with a smile that wouldn't have fooled the cat. "It's good to be home and to have you here."

"Why don't we all have a glass of that plum brandy, to celebrate your return?" Doreen asked with a wide smile.

"That sounds like a . . ." Tucker began.

But Minna, who had slipped in the door without being noticed, shouted, "He shouldn't be drinking, Doreen! Even Katrina would know that!"

In the silence that fell over the room, Minna whirled around and threw herself out the door with a pitiful wail, pounded across the stoop, fleeing past Sanchez and Oh, Brother!, and disappeared around the corner of the house.

"Lord God," Doreen said, red-faced, "back to the pigs again. I wasn't going to say nothing, but I do think the child's getting worse. I haven't been able to get anything but a scowl out of her for days, and aside from pitching hay down for the mule and helping Sanchez every morning to choose his bandanna, she spends most of her days sitting beside those two pigs. If I come near, she shuts up, but I know she's talking to them because when I go onto the stoop to shake the dust mop, I can hear her."

"Just a minute," Tucker said, getting slowly out of the rocker and going to the door.

He opened it and spoke quietly to the two animals, who turned and trotted after Minna.

"It's just as well to be careful," he said.

"Thank you, but I think we'd better take her home," Katherine told Tucker.

Then she turned to Doreen and said, "Minna's not herself, and I guess you know that, but I want to apologize for what she said to you, and to thank you for looking after her since Tucker's been gone."

Doreen came forward and swept Katherine into her arms and planted a solid kiss on her cheek.

"You're the one who needs comforting," she told her, "and I hope that big lug over there is giving you plenty of loving. You need it. And don't you fret none about me. I've done more with less many a time."

"Thank you, Doreen," she said, her face flushed, when the woman released her. "You're very generous."

She and Harry said goodbye to Tucker and left.

"When Doreen hugs you, you know you've been hugged," Katherine said, still a little breathless as they walked toward the pig's run.

"That's true," Harry replied.

"Have you been hugging her?" Katherine demanded.

"She hugged me once," Harry told her, maintaining a straight face. "It was half an hour before my heart stopped pounding."

"What else happened?"

"We shook hands and agreed to remain friends."

Katherine stopped, spun around, and let him bump into her.

"What?" he said, his nose inches from hers.

"What are we going to do about Minna?" she asked, her eyes suddenly brimming with tears.

"Everything that has to be done," he said and wrapped his arms around her. "Try not to worry."

She kissed him and wiped her eyes, which, given the way they were standing, resulted in Katherine's pressing her hips harder against him. She smiled slowly.

"Why Harry," she said.

"I'm sorry," he said. "Talking about Doreen . . ."

"That will cost you," she told him, backing out of his embrace.

"It already has," he said.

"I know," she said, and caught one of his hands. "Let's go get Minna and see what we can do."

"While we're doing that," Harry said, "maybe we'll be inspired to figure out what we're going to do about us."

"Maybe," she said without enthusiasm, "but it's bloody ground, and wherever we dig, we'll hit bones."

He squeezed her hand, unable to respond.

30

By the next day, the answer remained not much, and their efforts only upset Minna, causing her to withdraw from them even further. When she wasn't with the pigs, she was behind her locked door.

"I could medicate her," Holinshed told them, "but that would only postpone her coming to terms with her anger. Once that's accomplished, I think the rest of the healing process should go quickly."

"And her fixation on the pigs?" Harry asked.

Holinshed tossed her pen onto the desk with a sigh.

"I don't have a single answer. Once her other issues are worked through, it should take care of itself. As to why she's doing it, I'm afraid that it's linked to how she feels about herself."

"You mean she thinks she's a pig?" Katherine asked, angrily.

"Not in the way you mean, but yes. She feels alienated from herself, diminished, damaged, probably cast out of her world—like those pigs are, when you think about it. Our task and hers is to find ways to bring her back."

"Is she in any risk of . . . ?"

Katherine couldn't go on.

"Committing suicide?" Holinshed asked. "No, not intentionally, but I don't think it's a time when she should be making decisions that will significantly affect her life."

Harry felt a rush of relief.

"We'll make sure that doesn't happen," he said.

After some thought and wrestling with his conscience, Harry hid his bullet-riddled Rover behind the ruins of Trachey's old cabin. He sweated and cursed for an hour until he had pulled enough brush, yards of trailing vines, and fallen branches from the giant fichus towering above the ruins, over the car, to completely conceal it. That done he fashioned a crude twig broom from the material at hand and swept away all traces of the tire tracks in the white sand that had once been a front yard.

"Stolen?" Jim asked, staring across his desk at Harry. "Why didn't you call it in?"

"Well, I guess it slipped my mind. My main concern was to get another car as soon as I could."

"That was a new one, wasn't it?" Hodges said over his coffee mug.

"Yes," Harry said glumly.

When Katherine had asked him that morning where the Rover was, he'd said, "It's been stolen."

"Why are you lying to me?"

"Because what you don't know, you won't have to testify to, should the need arise."

"I'm living with a criminal," she'd said.

For reasons unknown, Harry had recalled what Hazel had asked Rigoberta, following the shootout, and grinned.

"How do you find it as far as you've been?" he'd asked.

"As a temporary thing, I suppose it's better than nothing," Katherine had replied, Harry's grin having proved infectious.

"Why is it," Jim asked, "that I don't believe you?"

"It's the law enforcement officer problem," Hodges said, trying to look serious. "You do this a while, and pretty soon you don't believe what anybody tells you."

"That's probably it," Harry said, grasping the floating log. "I hear there's been some excitement at St. Jude's."

"Excitement!" Jim protested. "Four men dead, three Guatemalans and a Mexican, Haven House shot up, and enough empty shell casings scattered over the grass to make it look like a battlefield."

"Look at that," Harry said, feigning astonishment. "Have you talked with Rowena Farnham?"

"According to her, they had received a vague telephone threat and moved the women in the place to various homes of their parishioners. I wanted to talk with the women, but Farnsworth almost took my head off."

"No one is supposed to know the women are at the place. Is that why she didn't call the police?" Harry asked.

"You've got it. Didn't want to attract attention," Hodges said, shaking his head.

"Sounds right," Harry said. "Any idea what the shooting was about?"

Jim made his long face longer.

"Another mystery," he said, "but I'd pretty well bet the farm that these shootings were some way connected to the trafficking."

He threw up his hands in disgust and said, "But the trouble is I can't prove it."

"I'm curious," Harry said, eager to change the subject, "How did you know it was three Guatemalans and a Mexican who were killed?"

"Easy," Hodges put in. "The Mexican was a small-time crook and troublemaker. Went by the name of Gomez, claimed not to have any other name. He's been in the county jail a few times, assault once, drunk and resisting arrest once, and once for possession. Usual stuff."

"Why hasn't he been deported?" Harry asked in surprise.

"Born here," Hodges said.

"The other three had no records, no identification," Jim said, then put up a hand. "Hold it. One of them had a bogus driver's license. His name was Cavek Bal, lived in La Ramada. Wife speaks no English, and neither did any of the neighbors the detectives tried to question."

"And nobody knew anything about it," Harry put in, wondering if there was any close connection between Bal and Rigoberta—not the same name anyway. Hers was what? Quirate.

"Of course not," Jim said. "Did you and Soñadora run into any Bals while you were out there?"

Harry shook his head. "Only the names I gave you."

"If I were to bring Asturias in here, Harry," Jim asked, leaning his elbows on his desk. "What would she tell me?"

"About what?" Harry asked, fully aware that he and Soñadora had not agreed on a story in case they were questioned.

"The shootings at Haven House."

"It's my guess she knows nothing about it," Harry said, mentally crossing his fingers. "She's putting all her energies into rebuilding *Salvamento.*"

"I don't suppose there's any use asking *you* if you've heard anything useful?" Jim asked.

"I've been out of touch for a bit, what with Minna, Tucker, and the insurance companies pushing me to get some work done. Then there was the Rover."

He paused and added, trying to atone for the lies he had been telling, "Something may shake loose from this fracas. They must have been looking for someone, and someone else must have been looking for them. They can't do things like this and stay hidden long."

"From your mouth to God's ear," Hodges said.

Jim sighed and shook his head, the weariness showing

through his unsmiling expression.

"It's getting worse," he said quietly.

"What is?" Harry asked.

"Everything," the lawman answered. "The killing's getting worse. The crime rate is climbing. The department hasn't got near the number of people it needs to meet the demands being made on it. We're badly underfunded. I could go on."

"Cheer up," Harry said, getting up. "You're dating Kathleen."

Hodges laughed. "We ain't supposed to know about that."

Jim's ears lit up, and he started to protest, but Harry got his shot in first.

"Don't feel bad," he said. Your pictures haven't appeared in *The Banner*—at least not yet."

"A fine imbroglio you got me into," Rowena Farnham said, bringing Harry a cup of tea.

They were in her office, and the clutter was, Harry thought, worse than the last time he was there.

"Yes, the room's a mess," Rowena acknowledged, having seen him looking around the crowded office. "We're starting a major fund drive to build a new community outreach center. It's at this point that, as they say, one's faith is tested."

"I talked this morning with Jim Snyder," Harry said. "I think you did a masterful job of dealing with him."

"Deceiving the police, harboring escapees from jail and illegal immigrants, a fine thing for the Rector of St. Jude's to be doing. What happened out there? We're still digging slugs out of the woodwork."

"It was full dark when Soñadora and I got there. The door was ajar, and when we went in Hazel and Rigoberta were waiting for us," Harry said, omitting reference to the guns.

"Are they safe now? And don't tell me where they are."

"They are, and I won't."

"Good. Then what happened?"

"We had reached the car when four men appeared out of the darkness and began shooting. I fired back."

Rowena drank some tea, put down her cup, and said, "You weren't the only one on your team shooting. Am I right?"

"Off the record?"

"Absolutely."

"All four of us were armed and returning their fire."

"How in God's name did you walk away from that unscathed?"

"One problem with an automatic weapon is that the person firing it is inclined to point it in the general direction of the target and let fly. A second problem for them was that we were in the shadow of the house, and they weren't. They couldn't see us."

He decided to skip describing Rigoberta's charge and Hazel's flying tackle.

"But I think the real answer to your question," Harry concluded, "is luck."

"Or God's will," Rowena said quietly.

"Hard to prove either way," Harry replied.

Rowena nodded.

"What happens now?"

"I'm not sure," Harry said. "I don't see how whoever has them can keep Hazel for the reason you've given, and I don't think she has anywhere else to go. You know she and Rigoberta have, I think, become very close friends. Hazel watches over her like a mother hen."

"Hazel has had a very, very hard life," Rowena said. "I learned that much about her, and she belongs in jail about as much as I do. As for Rigoberta, that woman is a hero of the people, but how she's going to survive in the current environment, much less prosper, is more than I can tell you."

For an instant Harry saw Rigoberta racing toward the gunmen, shooting and swearing.

"Well," he said, "she's lived this long and come this far, to find a better life for herself and her children. I think she might just have what it takes to make it happen."

"She goes with my admiration," Rowena said. "I have a question. Can you put me in touch again with Soñadora Asturias?"

"What for?" Harry asked, curious but suspicious.

"I think she and I can join forces," she said. "Will you do it?"

"I'll try," Harry said, surprised to find how glad he was having found an excuse to call Soñadora.

31

Hazel sat beside Rigoberta on the back steps of their smoke-free safehouse, squinting past the end of a cigarette, watching a cardinal trying to catch a yellow butterfly. The backyard was enclosed by a high board fence almost buried in trumpet vines. Somewhere in the tangle of ferns and hibiscus shrubs a mockingbird was blasting through his routine.

"Soñadora told me last night that she will soon have jobs for us," Rigoberta said.

She was dressed in blue shorts and sandals. The shorts did not quite cover the white scar remaining from her gunshot wound. Her white blouse looked freshly ironed, and long black hair was tied back with a red ribbon, and after a week of sleeping in a bed and eating properly, she looked ten years younger.

Hazel, dressed in a pink, flowered dress and white sandals, was lean as ever, but her hair was a little less frazzled and she was wearing lipstick.

"I don't know how to tell you this, Riggs," she said, breaking a long silence, "but I can't just go out here and take a job. I wouldn't last ten days."

"Why?" Rigoberta said. "Their people will get you a . . . what is it?"

"A Social Security card. Yeah, I know, but too many people know me in Tequesta County. I've got to leave here, Riggs, and probably the state."

"I go with you," Rigoberta said, turning and grasping Hazel's arm.

Hazel threw away her cigarette and hitched herself around and, after hesitating, put her hand, somewhat awkwardly, over Rigoberta's.

"You can't, Riggs," she said, the harshness failing to mask the pain Rigoberta could see in her friend's eyes.

"I am stick with you, kid," Rigoberta said with a burst of feeling.

Hazel, managing a crooked grin, said, "You've been watching too many old movies."

"I go with you, end of fucking talking," Rigoberta said loudly, tightening her grip on Hazel's arm.

"Ouch," Hazel said, glancing over her shoulder at the screen door behind them. "that hurts, and don't say *fucking* anymore. Remember what Soñadora told you."

"You say it all the time. I like it. It sounds strong."

"Too strong, Riggs," Hazel told her, "like your grip."

"I work much. Sorry. Sometimes forget. Can't lose you, Hazel. You my only friend I ever had." Tears sprang to Rigoberta's eyes as she put her arms around Hazel and kissed her.

"Riggs! Stop!" Hazel said, wriggling in her friend's embrace.

"Why stop?" she asked in a hurt voice. "You not want me for friend?"

"Of course I do."

Hazel was not good at this, but she saw that she was going to have to try to be.

"Put your arms around me again, Riggs," she said, "and listen."

As soon as Rigoberta had embraced her again, Hazel hesitantly and awkwardly put her arms around Rigoberta and said, "Riggs, you're my friend, and I love you. I don't want to leave you, but I have to." She paused, apparently struggling with something, and suddenly planted a glancing kiss on Rigoberta's cheek then broke free.

Rigoberta looked at her for a while and then smiled, "Is OK, Hazel," she said quietly. "I know you love me."

"Good," Hazel said, fishing her cigarettes out of the pocket in her dress. "Then it's settled."

"Right," Rigoberta said. "I go with you."

Two days later, Harry said, frustrated and angry, "You're making a big mistake, and if you'd ask Oh, Brother! he'd tell you the same. It's too soon for you to be working in that garden."

"Sanchez and Oh, Brother! have already made their views known, and I've spent enough time sitting in that rocker, listening to Doreen's stories. I'm going to work, come hell or high water."

"Tucker," Katherine said, taking her turn, "aren't you taking an unnecessary chance? Wouldn't it be wiser to give yourself another week or two to get your strength back?"

"I'm as strong as I'm ever going to be," Tucker told her gently, "and Minna's agreed to help. I plan to keep her busy and while I'm doing it try to get her talking. What do you think of that plan?"

"Two things. One, I'm grateful for your help and much in need of it. Second, you're a wicked charmer."

Tucker smiled his Buddha smile, which made Katherine laugh, something she had not been doing much for a while. She and Harry were still circling one another like a pair of bantam roosters unwilling to fight and unwilling to give any ground.

Somewhat later when she and Tucker were alone, Doreen made a more direct attempt to dissuade Tucker. Having exhausted her very limited store of gentle persuasions, she suddenly grew red in the face and said in a loud voice, "You're a damned old fool, and if you want to kill yourself, go right ahead and do it."

Tucker had been sitting down in the rocking chair, and when she finished, he popped up with surprising ease and planted a kiss on her cheek.

"Thank you for being honest, Doreen," he told her. "You're a treasure, and Wetherell's lucky to have you. If he didn't I just might propose."

Doreen's face grew even redder and, bursting into delighted laughter, gave him a push that, if she hadn't caught him, would have sat him back hard in his chair.

"Well, if he should fall into the brook drunk and drown, I might take you up on the offer," she told him, giving him what she considered a gentle hug that, nevertheless, squeezed all the wind out of him.

"Get Minna for me, will you?" he asked when he got his breath back. "Here's where we see if this plan is going to work."

After failing to persuade Tucker not to begin work on the garden, Harry and Katherine walked home in the thundery heat. Harry was worried about Tucker but didn't want to burden Katherine with his concern, aware that she had Minna almost constantly on her mind. But Katherine, as it turned out, was thinking of something else.

"I've been puzzling over that shootout you got into the other night," she said as they walked with a rumbling in the distance that sounded like heavy guns firing.

"And?" Harry asked, surprised by her comment.

"If I've got it right, in addition to having put your life in danger," she continued sternly, "you were breaking the law."

"How?" Harry asked disingenuously.

"One of those women was a wanted person. You didn't turn her in. Two were illegal aliens, and all three were armed, which is probably a crime in itself, never mind that they were actually firing their weapons." She paused then added with a tight smile. "You'll tell me, of course, if I'm wrong."

" 'Wrong,' " he said, "is a tough word to define."

"Give it a shot."

This was not like Katherine, Harry thought with alarm—sarcasm, irony, bitter humor. The thunder rolled again, and he suspected another storm was even closer.

"I was doing my best to get those women away from Haven House as fast as God would let me when the shooting started." He was pleased with that and decided to go on, but Katherine protested.

"Oh no you don't," she said. "I'm not going there."

"OK," he told her, becoming a little angry himself. "What would you have done?"

She stopped and turned to face him.

"I wouldn't have been there in the first place."

"I don't believe you."

The thunder rumbled again very much closer. Neither of them seemed to notice it or that the light was failing.

"There had to have been another way," she protested, her voice rising. "Shooting people is barbaric! It drives me crazy to think of you doing it."

A single, large drop of rain struck the road between them and sent up a tiny puff of dust.

"It doesn't exactly fill me with joy," he snapped, "and you're right. It is barbaric, but everything that these women are caught up in is barbaric."

By now he was well launched on his own behalf and was not attending to the weather. Several drops of rain troubled the dust, and a few fell on them. Then the thunder broke almost over their heads, a strong gust of cold wind swept past them, and the heavens opened. The noise of it pounding the forest around them was deafening. In an instant, they were soaked.

Harry unbuttoned his shirt, stepped out of his sandals, and unzipped his shorts.

"What are you doing?" Katherine yelled, trying to wipe the water out of her eyes.

"Getting undressed," Harry shouted back. "I don't like wearing wet clothes."

He shoved his thumbs into the waistband of his shorts and, collecting his underwear on the way, shoved them down to his ankles and stepped out of them. Then he closed his eyes and turned his face up to the deluge, raised his arms level with his shoulders, palms upward, and shouted, "The rain it falleth on the just, and also on the unjust fella . . ."

The water got into his windpipe and ended his declamation. With a shout of laughter Katherine unbuttoned her blouse, and in another moment was as naked as he was. Then they gathered up their soaked clothes, stepped back into their squishing sandals, and set off down the road together, laughing and singing, and stamping in all the muddy puddles, splashing one another, and being as silly as they could.

At one point Harry pulled her into an embrace and kissed her. It was, he thought, like kissing under water. When they finally dashed into the shelter of the lanai, they were shivering with cold but still full of laughter. Turning to one another they said in unison, "This is all your fault."

The following morning, after making some phone calls, Harry drove to Soñadora's *Salvamento*. The episode in the rain had settled nothing between him and Katherine. Once they had showered and dressed, a kind of guilty restraint held them apart. The rain stopped as suddenly as it had begun, and without resuming their argument about the gun fight, they drove to Tucker's to fetch Minna, finding themselves once again in that part of their lives where there was no place for running naked in the rain.

"Rosie the Riveter," Harry said to Soñadora as she walked toward him, pulling off her gloves and wiping her forehead with them.

She was dressed in dungarees, work boots, and a man's blue shirt, its tails tied around her waist. Her head was wrapped in a red cloth.

"What?" she asked, looking at him with a slight frown.

"You're making good progress," he said, nodding toward the building site. "The slab's poured. Most of the framing's up, and you've got a slew of people working."

There were at least a dozen Hispanic men and women carrying framing material, driving nails, sawing two by fours, moving ladders, talking and laughing, and advancing the work steadily.

"Yes," she said. "Why are you here?"

He had become somewhat accustomed to her abruptness, but it still made him feel like an unwanted intruder.

"I'll get to that," he said. "What have you heard about Hazel and Rigoberta?"

"Hazel has disappeared," she said.

"What do you mean?" Harry asked. "Has there been another attack . . . ?"

"No," Soñadora said quickly, "she slipped out in the night. Rigoberta is very upset."

"She doesn't know where Hazel's gone?"

Soñadora shook her head and said, "She told me that Hazel had told her she could not stay in this part of the state and that Rigoberta could not go with her, but that she had intended to go anyway. The poor woman is heartbroken."

"I've done some research," Harry said. "Hazel's an escapee from the Atlantic Work Release Center over on the East Coast. That's why she's gone. Have you heard of the place?"

"Yes. She should not have run away."

"Some people can stand being controlled. Some can't," Harry said. "I guess she couldn't."

"I think she left here in the night for Rigoberta's sake," Soñadora said.

"Meaning?"

"I think Hazel knew that if the police caught her, they would catch Rigoberta and that would be the end of Rigoberta's hopes to stay here, work, and bring her children."

"I'm sorry she's upset," Harry said, "but going with Hazel would have been a mistake."

"She does not have many good options," Soñadora said with a sigh.

"How are you?" Harry asked, catching the weariness or despair in her voice.

"Much as always," Soñadora told him with no evident interest.

"Could you get away from here for an hour?" he asked, thinking he might be able to make her feel better.

"What for?" she asked.

"Rowena Farnham wants to talk with you," he told her. "I think she wants to propose something."

"What would that be?" Soñadora asked with a bitter smile. "I thought I told you I have had nothing to do with churches since I was a little girl."

"I think she wants to talk with you, not pray with you," Harry said. "She did some good work with Hazel and Rigoberta."

"True," Soñadora agreed. "Perhaps I should show my gratitude for that by listening to her."

She paused and looked down at her clothes.

"But I cannot meet the Rector of St. Jude's dressed like this," she said.

Harry laughed.

"Don't worry. She dresses like a street person. Tell someone you've got urgent business with me."

"I cannot be gone long," she said, looking anxiously at the men and women working.

"I'll have you back in jig time," Harry told her.

"Isn't a jig a dance of some kind?"

"Yes, let's go."

"*Loco*," she said with a fleeting grin and hurried away.

Harry called Rowena and told her they were coming.

"While we were in La Ramada," he asked her once they were under way, "did you hear any mention of a man by the name of Cavek Bal?"

"No," she said, "but Rigoberta told me her aunt, her mother's sister, was married to a man named Bal, and I think she said his first name is Cavek. Why do you ask?"

"Because one of the men who died at Haven House was carrying a counterfeit license with the name Cavek Bal on it."

"My God," Soñadora gasped. "He was coming to kill his wife's niece."

"Looks that way," Harry said quietly.

32

Despite Rowena Farnham's good sense and limitless patience and more tea than Harry could remember ever having drunk, and plied with freshly baked scones with butter and strawberry jam, it took the Rector nearly half an hour to work the stiffness out of Soñadora's neck. But once the dark young woman had relaxed enough to really listen to what Farnham was saying to her, she became first interested, then enthusiastic.

"Then, to sum up," Farnham said, dusting the crumbs of the last scone from her fingers, "*Salvamento* will be up and running within the month, and once it is, you and I are going to join forces on this thing."

"Yes," Soñadora agreed. "You and your people are going to help with funding, community outreach, organization, and building awareness of human trafficking in the Anglo community. But I must remain far in the background."

"Agreed," Farnham said with a smile, "and with our help you and your people will extend your reach into the minority communities with the goal of increasing your contacts to the point that it will be impossible for these traffickers to operate secretly anywhere in southwest Florida."

"Once you know where these criminals are operating, you will have to involve the police. Then what's going to happen?" Harry asked.

"My organization will withdraw," Soñadora said. "Only Rowena's people will have any contact with the police."

281

Farnham had gotten up to pour herself another cup of tea and wave the pot around to ask if anyone else would join her. Getting no takers, she put the pot down, walked over to Harry, and pulled his head against her very substantial side while Soñadora grinned.

"I can see it now," Harry said, freeing himself. "Three or four of your ladies in wide brimmed hats will call on Jim Snyder. His ears will turn red, and, being the son of a mountain preacher, he will leap to his feet. Hodges will knock over a chair and step on someone's foot, trying to make them welcome. When they are perched on the edges of their folding chairs, their spokesperson will say in an accent that Jim will struggle with and Hodges won't understand at all that they have located a house where women are being held in sexual slavery and would Captain Snyder please send some of his people to arrest those responsible and free the prisoners. Then she will pass him a street address with directions on how to get there."

"Hold on," Rowena said when she stopped laughing, "These women are not as silly as you make them out to be."

"I didn't say they were silly. They're intelligent, educated, and managerial wizards. They have to be. Most of them have been managing their husbands' careers for years and years. What I'm saying is that once he can speak at all, Jim Snyder will begin questioning them: 'Where did you get the information? Who are your contacts? Are these people undocumented aliens? How long have you known about this situation? How did you come to learn about it?' How are they to answer him without blowing everyone's cover?"

"Harry," Rowena said, patting his head and making Soñadora giggle, "for thirty years I've been working with God and congregations in an imperfect world. Compared with those three entities, the police are babbling infants. Leave them to me."

"Gladly," Harry said, getting to his feet. "This is going to be fun to watch."

On the ride back to *Salvamento*, Soñadora was quiet. Harry assumed she was digesting all that had happened with Rowena Farnham, but when she spoke, he found he was wrong.

"There is a situation the Rector cannot manage," she said without any lead-in. "It is what has to be done about the place where Rigoberta and Hazel were being held."

"You mean finding the place," Harry said.

"No. Rigoberta knows where it is, but she can't tell the police, and neither can I."

"How does she know?" Harry asked in surprise.

"She knows the direction she and Hazel walked and for how long before they found 75."

Harry thought about that for a little while with growing concern, and then he said, "There's no way you and I are going in there to raid the place. So don't even think about it."

"Perhaps if I gave you a hug and patted your head . . . ?" she said with laughter breaking up her question.

Harry felt his face burn because he had a vivid mental picture of her embracing him, her body pressed against his.

"Nothing would persuade me," he told her, a little more loudly than necessary, hoping to disrupt the image.

"I am not going to ask you to do that, but I want you to bring a map so that you and Rigoberta and I can locate the exact place where she and Hazel crossed the highway. If we can do that, I think we can locate the road where the house is located."

"Then you want us to drive out there and find the house," he said.

"Maybe or not. Perhaps that should be left to the police."

Harry saw the drift and said, "You want me to tell the police where to look."

283

"I think so. Will you do it?"

"Only if I get a hug and a pat on the head," he said.

It was her turn to blush. She saw him looking at her and quickly turned away.

"*Tonto*," she said, but Harry could see that she was smiling, even if she did think he was an idiot.

Rigoberta could not make sense of the map, and when Soñadora became impatient, Harry said, "Let's all take a ride on 75. Perhaps that will do it."

For the first time in their conversation, Rigoberta smiled. Harry thought it was like the sun breaking through the clouds. She really was a good-looking woman. When he and Soñadora had arrived at the safehouse, she'd been very glum.

"Hazel didn't want you to be arrested, Riggs," he'd said, hoping her English was good enough for her to understand him.

"I think so," she'd replied quietly, "but hurt here."

She'd pressed her hand over her heart. He'd nodded. Soñadora put her hand briefly on Rigoberta's arm, and then said they must get to work.

"I miss sun and wind," Rigoberta said as they walked to the car. "Was outside most of all."

"Working," Harry said.

"Yes, on the mountain."

"Was it cold?"

She smiled. "Hot now then cold afterward."

"Summer and winter," Harry said.

"Yes," she said and repeated the words.

Soñadora said something to her Harry did not understand, and Rigoberta actually laughed.

"What?" Harry asked, glancing at Soñadora in the rearview mirror.

"I told her to be careful because you make love to every

woman you meet."

"Don't believe her," Harry said.

Rigoberta straightened her back, gave him an appraising glance, and smiled.

Later, when they turned onto 75, Harry asked her with some help from Soñadora how long it had taken Rigoberta and Hazel to reach Avola once they were in the truck.

She immediately said, "Half hour."

"How do you know?" he asked. "You don't wear a watch."

"In my head," she replied.

Harry drove north an extra ten minutes then turned the car onto the southbound lane. Rigoberta easily recognized the place where she and Hazel had flagged down the truck. Harry pulled off the highway. Soñadora had the map open on her lap.

"We just passed a mile marker," she said. "That should place us about here."

She passed the map into the front seat, holding her finger on the spot where she thought they were stopped. After studying the map for a moment, Harry agreed.

Then he looked at Rigoberta and said, "Tell me about the direction and length of time you walked after you and Hazel escaped."

She turned to look at Soñadora. They talked for a minute or two while Harry listened without learning anything.

"I will try explain," Rigoberta said to Harry. "If can't, Soñadora will tell it."

"Take your time, Riggs," Harry said and then thought that it would not be a good thing if a State Trooper pulled up behind them, to check if they were OK. "On second thoughts, you'd better tell me," Harry said, passing the map back to Soñadora and pulling back into the stream of traffic.

"Something is not right?" Rigoberta asked.

"Everything's fine, Riggs," Harry said. "I want to keep it that way."

Soñadora filled in the gaps, and Rigoberta said, "Assholes."

Harry broke out laughing, but Soñadora was not laughing and said something and then something else to Rigoberta, who listened with a frown on her face.

"Hazel said that word much," she insisted as if the oracle had been consulted and had answered.

"*You* don't say it," Soñadora replied, sounding very severe.

Then she turned her attention to the map, and having satisfied herself, said, "There are only two roads to the east of us that are close enough to the highway for them to have walked out to here in the time Rigoberta gave me."

"OK," Harry said. "Mark the spot on the map where we stopped, and when we get Riggs back to her safehouse, we can talk about it."

"Very wet, very fly bite," Rigoberta said to Harry, struggling for words. "Also much scratch. Hazel say many words Soñadora not like."

With that, she winked at Harry, who grinned back and thought, *Hazel was right. This is a remarkable woman, and one of these days she may find out her uncle, who probably sold her into slavery, was one of the four men who tried to kill her, but I'm not going to tell her.*

"Hazel doesn't know better, or if she does, she doesn't care," Soñadora said sharply.

"Hazel doesn't give a shit for better," Rigoberta said, defending her friend. "She say, 'Riggs, bring your kids here. Don't take crap from somebody.' "

"*Anybody*," Soñadora snapped, "and what did I say about swearing?"

"Is OK. Want to know if you listen."

When Harry, Rigoberta, and Soñadora settled on a plan, and

Harry and Soñadora were leaving, Rigoberta stopped him and said, obviously in some distress, "Many sick women there with drugs. They can be helped?"

"Yes," Harry said, not sure he was telling her the truth.

"Good," she said. "Those who are keeping them, shoot in the leg. It hurts like hell."

"Are we going to find out whether the police found the house?" Soñadora asked.

"I'll make sure you do," Harry said.

"And the police not find us," Rigoberta said.

"No," Harry assured her, "I won't tell them, and you haven't said anything about what happened when the men came to shoot you."

"No," Rigoberta said, "I never want to talk about that. Too awful."

Harry wanted to say that things too terrible to talk about seemed to be breeding under the back steps but stopped himself. Instead, he shook hands with Rigoberta, thanked her for her help, and left with Soñadora.

Driving away from the safehouse, he asked her what Rigoberta's chances were of finding a job that paid enough for her to live on.

"They found her a place in a startup shop, sewing company names onto T-shirts and jerseys at eight dollars an hour," she told him. "If she lives on that and finds some part-time work on the weekends and puts that aside to bring her children here, she's got a good chance. *Salvamento* will keep an eye on her."

"I wish her well," Harry said, his heart sinking at the thought of the penury she would be forced to live in, not to mention working at a sewing machine again.

There's something really wrong somewhere, he told himself.

33

After leaving Soñadora at her job site, Harry drove to Jim Snyder's office and found the lawman sitting at his desk behind a stack of papers.

"The bane of my existence," Jim said, collapsing back in his chair. "I swear that one of these days the boredom of it will kill me. How did you make out?"

Harry had brought his map with him and spread it out in front of Jim. While he was doing that and locating the dot marking the place where Rigoberta had said she and Hazel were picked up on 75, he asked where Frank Hodges was.

"Oh, Lord, I forgot all about him," he said, reaching for the phone and punching in a number, "A couple of hours ago there was a pile-up on the Marco/41 intersection. He got stuck directing traffic. I promised to get a trooper out there an hour ago, and it's probably getting hotter."

"You could fry eggs on the tarmac."

"Frank, are you still out at the Marco intersection? You are. Bad as that. I'll get someone to you. Missed your lunch. No water. Your nose is going to peel. I'm sorry about that, Frank. Goodbye."

Jim put down the phone.

"He said a fat woman punched him for making her wait while a goose and a dozen goslings crossed the road," Jim said. "He was kind of worked up, what with the heat and all."

"Did he ticket her?" Harry asked.

He'd been grinning all through Jim's conversation.

"I hope so. What have you brought me?"

Harry leaned over the desk and pointed at the mark on the map and began to tell Jim what he'd found out and where he thought the house was located.

"It's probably right along there on the Goodnight Road," he said. "There's nothing much but deer, bear, panthers, and wild hogs back in there," Harry said. "It shouldn't be too hard to get a warrant to look in the six or eight shacks along that track."

"I believe I'll put two teams on that road, one coming in from each end."

"Sounds good. Be sure that they don't use their radios."

"That's right," Jim agreed. "Which end do you want to go in on?"

"Me?" Harry protested.

"Not alone. I'll send Frank with you."

"And you let him talk you into that!" Katherine said.

"It's on the back edge of Tequesta County," Harry said lamely. "Not an area Jim and his people know very well."

"And you do," Katherine said.

She was kneading bread dough beside the sink, and the dough was taking a beating. She banged it down on the marble slab, kneaded it, lifted it, and slammed it down hard.

"I'm glad that's not me you're working on," Harry said, watching with admiration the way she put her whole body into the action.

"This is not funny," Katherine told him, pausing long enough to turn around and brush hair away from her face with the back of a floury hand. "You're going to go out there and put yourself in harm's way again."

"From everything Rigoberta told us," Harry said with studied calm, "there were only three people running the place. I don't think they'll add more."

"Three *armed* people," Katherine said, going back to abusing the dough.

"Two, the third is a cleaning woman, if they've replaced the one they killed. We're not going with sirens screaming," he said.

"Is that the woman who was found in the canal?"

"Probably."

"Wonderful. How many of you are going in?"

"Six, I think."

"Why doesn't Jim send in that knock-down-the-door-bunch and clean them out? Isn't that what they're for?" she asked.

"The S.W.A.T. team's too violent for the situation," he said quickly. "Remember there's about a dozen women in there, and if some of them were to get shot, the Governor would demand Sheriff Fisher's head."

"But Fisher's the sheriff."

"Right. And the governor is the governor."

Whatever had to be done to the dough was done. Katherine rubbed butter over it and set it in a bread pan, folded a dish-towel over it, and left it to rise. She washed her hands, poured herself some coffee, and sat down across the table from Harry. She did not look happy.

"I'm sorry this is so hard on you," he told her, reaching across the table to put his hand over hers.

She pulled it away.

"It's not just me, Harry," she told him with a voice full of anger and pain. "It's everyone who loves you or even cares about you. What do you think it will do to Minna and the rest of your children if you're killed?"

"We're none of us immortal, Katherine," he said, trying to keep any edge out of his voice. "What if I were an airline pilot, or the President, for that matter?"

She jumped up, took a chicken out of the refrigerator, and

set it on the cutting board. There was nothing in her expression that suggested she had found herself on the road to Damascus.

"You're neither of those. You're a private investigator who carries a gun and has, within my *recent* memory, been shot, run off the road, blown up, and nearly drowned in pursuit of your goals." She paused for breath. "And if memory serves, once, you were nearly clubbed to death in your own bed. How normal is that, Harry?"

"Well, put that way, it looks bad, but we're talking twenty years here. Those things don't happen every day."

"I rest my case," Katherine said, resuming her work.

"My options aren't all that numerous," he said. "Security guard about sums it up, and I can't retire, too young and too poor."

"Am I supposed to feel sorry for you?" she fired back. "You've been offered a job as claims adjustor in every insurance company you've ever worked for."

She looked up from dismembering a chicken and pointed her knife at him.

"I'll give you odds that if right now you were to call one of them, you'd be hired before you put the phone down."

"I'd rather rob banks. It's more honest work," he said.

"A man with a social conscience," she said and with increased ferocity went back to dismembering the chicken.

So the issue remained unresolved, lying coiled between them like a poisonous snake.

Later in the day Harry visited Tucker, and found the old farmer forking over a row of what had been a flourishing patch of corn and upending the roots. Harry had cleared the ground of the broken stalks. Minna was following Tucker, picking up the roots and throwing them into her wheelbarrow.

"Hi, Harry," she said, "Tucker's trying to make a farmer of me."

She sounded more cheerful than any time since he'd picked up her and her mother at the airport.

"We've been talking about corn borers," Tucker said, leaning on his fork, "and their life cycle."

He was panting a little, and Harry found that hurt because before Tucker's illness he could fork and talk with no trouble at all.

"They lead a really complicated life," Minna said, wiping her forehead with the back of her work glove. "From the time the eggs are laid until the last instar emerges from diapause at the end of winter and spins a cocoon in order to be changed into a moth, these insects pass through four stages: moth, eggs—laid by the moth—grub—which bores into the corn plant, and pupae, which turns into the moth."

"I guess diapauses must be something like hibernation," Harry said, delighted by her animation. "But what is the instar?"

"If a corn borer larva survives, it passes through five stages," Minna told him, "each of which is called an instar."

"She's a quick learner," Tucker said, returning to his digging.

Minna went back to loading her wheelbarrow.

"I suppose all this information has some bearing on why all this work is going forward," Harry said.

"That's right," Minna told him. "The fifth instar has to have a safe, somewhat warmer place to spend the winter if it's going to crawl out in the spring and enter the pupae stage."

"So by clearing away the roots and the stalks and any other trash, you interrupt the cycle."

"You've got it," she said with a mischievous grin.

"Wait until I tell Katherine," he said.

"Harry!" Minna said, suddenly serious, "Don't give her all

that instar, pupae, and diapause stuff. Just cut it down to the basics."

"You're not suggesting she's not bright enough to understand it, are you?"

"Nope, but my brother's been following her around ever since I can remember, trying to make her listen to this kind of stuff. She's fed up to the gills with biology. Believe me, Harry. I know."

Harry told Katherine everything he'd seen and heard, except the life cycle of the corn borer. He was saving that for last.

"How did Tucker do it?" she asked before he could get to the corn borer.

"I think," Harry said, "we can thank Holinshed for a lot of it, and then Tucker's understanding of people. He would have made a master psychiatrist."

Katherine laughed.

"Maybe the pigs deserve some of the credit."

It delighted Harry to see Katherine's mood lighten.

Not willing to leave well enough alone, he said, "Minna's got the life cycle of the corn borer down pat. It appears that . . ."

"Hold it," she said, her face getting red. "I don't want to hear it. I've climbed trees trying to escape from Jesse telling me the life cycles of all the creatures great and small, and if you try to make me listen to you talking about the love life of corn borers, I'll jump on you with both feet."

Harry smiled.

"Minna said you'd say that."

"We're going to use two unmarked cars and leave from here separately," Jim Snyder said as soon as Harry came into the office.

Jim was standing behind his desk, piled with protective vests held down by four twelve-gauge pump guns. He was grim-faced. Behind him was a large map of the area where the kidnapped women were assumed to be held. Counting Harry, three men faced him across the desk: Harry, Hodges, and Corporal Milton Johnson, a tall black man. None of the men was wearing a uniform. Harry had worked with Johnson before and liked and trusted him, but he was not happy with what he had walked into and decided now was the time to say so.

"There were supposed to be six of us, Jim. I'm counting four. Are two more coming?"

"We're it," Hodges said, obviously as concerned as Harry, but trying to put a brave face on the situation.

"I didn't sign up for a suicide mission," Harry said. "We have no idea what we're walking into."

Johnson nodded but said nothing. Jim rubbed a hand over his face, sighed, and said, "We're short-handed, and Sheriff Fisher sets the priorities. He limited me to a four-man team. Without you it will be three."

"You two had a falling out?" Harry asked in surprise.

The question broke the tension in the room and got a laugh even from Jim.

"Not that I know of," he said. "And you can be damned sure we'll have Fisher's people there in droves if this works out properly. Likely even the man himself to pose for the cameras. And if it doesn't pan out . . ." His smile, now, was empty. "Are you still in?"

"This gear ours?" Harry asked, indicating the shotguns and vests.

"Yes."

"That's the first good news I've heard," Harry said with genuine relief. "But it's still a gamble, and if it weren't for the women, I don't think I'd stick."

"Is that a yes or a no?" Hodges asked.

"Yes," Harry said, thinking of Katherine and quelling the thought before guilt could grab him.

"Then let's look at the map," Jim said.

He stepped to one side and made a half turn so that he could see the map and not block Johnson's view of it. The blow-up showed a five-mile stretch of road, marked with half a dozen rectangles representing buildings.

"The CID staff have decided this is the place right here on the west side of the road," Jim said, tapping a rectangle located about halfway between the two ends of the road. "According to the county tax records, three of the structures are derelict, and two are hunting shacks. This one has been recently bought and the back taxes paid by someone named Escobar. That's all anyone knows about him or her. A lawyer in Miami handled all of the paperwork."

"And no one ever saw him either, I bet," Johnson remarked.

"That's it," Jim replied. "One phone contact, the rest was done by fax."

Harry had been looking at the map during that exchange.

"It looks as if the place is set back from the road," he said.

"About a quarter of a mile," Hodges said. "Whoever built it wanted privacy."

"That means we walk in," Johnson said glumly.

"It should still be fairly dark when we do it," Hodges said.

"I'm feeling better already," Harry said with a grin.

"We all know what we're doing," Jim said. "Harry, you and Frank are driving in from the north end. The Corporal and I, from the south. That way we'll have both ends of the road cut off, just in case they bolt before we get there. That sound all right?"

The other three nodded.

"OK," Jim continued, "Harry and Frank, you've got about ten more miles than Milton and me to cover. So you leave now.

We'll give you a fifteen-minute head start."

"OK," Harry said. "Just remember. The roads back in there are rough."

When Harry and Hodges left the headquarters it was still dark. There was no moon, and it would be another forty-five minutes before the east would begin to brighten. They put the shotguns in the back of their car.

"You drive," Hodges said. "You know that country better than I do."

"OK," Harry said, "you can sleep, but if you snore I'm waking you."

"I never snore," Hodges protested.

"That's not what Doreen told Tucker," Harry said.

"Doreen!" Hodges said, trying to sound disgusted and failing. "I hear Minna is showing signs of improvement. I'm really sorry about what happened to her."

"Thanks. Her doctor says she's doing all right. Until a few days ago Katherine and I hadn't seen much change, but Tucker has got her working with him on the garden and that seems to be helping."

"Except for the pigs, Tucker's got everybody working on that garden. Doreen's been coming home pooped, but she likes that kind of work. She says it keeps her slim. I don't say she's wrong there."

"Wise man."

Two minutes later Hodges was asleep, quiet as a child. Harry wondered how he could sleep, knowing what was ahead of them. He thought about that and concluded it was a capacity to suppress the imagination that made it possible to live in the present and eat if you're hungry, sleep if you're tired.

The road unrolled in front of the headlights, and he checked off the markers in his mind as he passed them, recalling them from the map, until the markers ran out, and he was on the narrowing county road that was taking them back toward Goodnight Road that led to the house where, supposedly, the women were being held. At the top of the windshield, the morning star, with its two paler companions, led them eastward.

The road narrowed to a track just before the point where he could turn right onto the all but forgotten county road that had never been surfaced. Venus moved into Harry's side window, and he gave Hodges a shove.

"Wake up," he said. "We're getting close. It's still black as the inside of a boot. Let's get sharp."

Hodges did not need to stretch or yawn or groan. He simply woke up.

"Company," he said a moment after Harry saw them.

A herd of ten pigs, led by a huge black boar, materialized out of the darkness. Temporarily dazzled by the lights, they milled in the road, confused and uncertain as to what to do. Harry slowed and lowered his side window, wanting the pigs out of the way as quickly as possible. The young animals were chuffing and squealing, but the boar quickly circled them, herding them toward the east side of the road. Then in a gesture of defiance he lowered his head and made a short rush at the car, his jaws popping like a steel trap. A moment later they were gone, vanishing into the woods without a sound.

"Them young ones would make good barbeque," Hodges said. "Makes me think it's time I did some hunting. Doreen's been after me about it."

"What do you do about the boar?" Harry asked, never having hunted pigs, thinking what a formidable opponent a full-grown razorback made for even an armed man on foot.

Hodges laughed.

"You can never tell about them. Sometimes they'll run, and sometimes they won't. It's when they won't that things get interesting. They take a power of killing. But my oh my, the young ones make fine eating."

"Minna's taken a real liking to those two Tucker's got in his fenced run," Harry said.

"You might as well try to tame the wind," Hodges said. "Make sure she knows that."

"She's been told," Harry said with a brief shiver as if the shadow of something had passed over him.

He glanced at the speedometer.

"We're there," he said, pulling off the road and killing the lights.

Once out of the car with their shotguns, flashlights, and extra shells, their eyes quickly adjusted to the star shine, making it possible for them to walk without using the flashlights. They had been walking for seven or eight minutes when Harry reached over and tapped Hodges's arm. Both men stopped, staring ahead into the darkness.

"There's someone standing in the road," Harry said quietly.

Hodges nodded. Without hesitation Hodges moved to the right and Harry to the left, stepping into the deeper shadows closer to the trees. Then they went forward, walking more slowly and carefully than before. Somewhere to Harry's left, a deer blew. Both men stopped then went on.

"Milton," Harry said a few moments later, "it's Frank and me. Where's Jim?"

"Right behind you," Jim said.

"You heard the deer," Harry said, smiling to himself and thinking Jim's mountain boyhood was showing.

"I assumed it was you," Jim said, "but decided to be sure."

"Morning's coming," Johnson said in response to a sudden puff of warm air that whispered in the grass beside them.

"And we've got the driveway," Jim said. "I've walked in and back. It's about fifty yards from here to the house."

"Good," Hodges said. "That survey map had it about three

hundred yards."

"We all agreed on what's going to happen when we get there?" Harry asked.

"Harry and me go through the front door," Hodges said. "The Captain and Milton go in the back. If we're met with fire, we go to work with the shotguns. If not, we get the light switches and see what we've got."

"And we all be damned sure we don't shoot one another or any of those women," Jim said.

The four men with Jim in the lead and Harry at the tail walked quickly down the narrow, sandy track. When they reached the clearing where the house was set, the first pale light changed the tops of the trees from a black mass to vague silhouettes of leaves, branches, and palm fronds. The low white house in front of them stood silent and dark. Somewhere to their right a cardinal broke into a brief burst of song.

"Give Milton and me time to get around to the back," Jim said quietly. Then go in that front door fast. If it's locked, blow the lock out."

Harry hated waiting and found himself fighting his urge to race for the door. Hodges's problem was different.

"These damned Kevlar vests make me sweat a river," he muttered, pulling a bandanna out of his pants pocket and mopping his face. "Makes Doreen mad too. She says I stink like a skunk."

"In a minute you'll forget about being hot. Ready?"

"As I'll ever be."

They went across the open space at a run, Harry getting ahead a little and reaching the door first. It was locked.

"Both of us," he said, stepping back and raising his gun.

They fired together, blowing away the lock and sending the shattered remains of the door crashing back into the wall. Once inside, Hodges yanked out his flashlight. From somewhere deeper in the house women were screaming. They were in a short hall with a door on each side, both closed. Beyond them it branched right and left.

Harry hit a light switch just as a door on the left banged open and a man holding a gun shoved his head and arm into the corridor and began shooting. Harry and Hodges threw themselves onto the floor the instant the door opened. Harry rolled onto his stomach and elbows and fired. In the enclosed space the shotgun's roar was terrific. The man vanished.

The screaming was growing louder, and from the back of the house, Harry heard Jim shouting at someone to put down the gun.

"He's either in there or out the window," Hodges said, rising to his knees.

"Not good," Harry said. "The other door is going to be behind us when we go in."

"Let's see what we've got," Hodges said, inching down the corridor toward the open door, his gun at the ready.

Just then a pistol flew out the door and banged on the floor.

"No shoot," a choked voice said. "I come out."

And he did, springing into the hall with a loud yell, gripping an automatic rifle. It was a serious mistake.

Hodges fired, flinging the man backward like a rag doll, the charge of buckshot almost tearing him in half.

"The other door," Hodges said.

Harry, his back against the wall, reached around the door jam and tried the handle. It was locked. He nodded at Hodges, who blew the door open. Inside, a large, middle-aged woman wearing a piled-up orange wig was sitting up in bed with her right hand under the covers.

"Get up," Harry said.

He was leaned into the room, his shotgun pointing at her. When she didn't move, he gestured her out of bed with the barrel.

"She's got a gun in that right hand," Hodges said.

"Probably, but I don't want to shoot her," Harry said.

"Here comes Johnson," Hodges said as the Corporal edged into their section of the hall.

"Everybody OK here?" Johnson asked, stepping over the dead man.

"Stand off," Hodges said, tilting his head toward the door. "Try your Spanish on her, but watch yourself."

Johnson peered into the bedroom. Harry leaned his shotgun against the wall and drew his CZ, easing the safety.

"Let's see that right hand," Johnson said to the woman in Spanish.

She continued to stare stonily at the heads in the door, her black eyes narrowed to slits. Before either Hodges or Harry could stop him, Johnson stepped into the room. The hand under the cover moved. There was a loud report, and Johnson went down, writhing with pain.

The woman, still staring at Johnson, yanked the gun from under the covers, but before she could point it again, Harry fired over Johnson's falling body, hitting the woman in the right shoulder, slamming her back into the bed's headboard as she screamed in agony.

Hodges unclipped his phone and punched in a number.

"Officer down," he said and gave rapid directions.

Jim came running up the corridor. Behind him, the sound of women shouting and screaming was growing in volume.

"It's Milton," Hodges told him. "I've called it in."

While that was happening, Harry picked up the fallen pistol then snatched back the covers, to be sure there were no more weapons in the bed. The woman's screams had dropped to low moans, which grew steadily weaker.

"Frank," Jim said, kneeling beside Johnson, "There's one old woman and a man handcuffed to the stove. See that they're secure, then get to that room where the women are. Try to shut them up. Maybe you can't, but try talking to them. One of them might speak some English."

Hodges, looking as if he didn't want to leave Johnson, gave a grudging nod and left.

"Hang on, Milton," Harry said, helping Jim to ease the wounded man, who was gasping with pain, onto his back. "Help's coming."

"We're going to get a tourniquet on that leg," Jim said, "From the way you're bleeding, the bullet may have nicked an artery."

Harry scrambled to his feet and snatched a pillow off the bed and got it under Johnson's head.

Jim had yanked the top sheet off the bed and tore it into strips for a tourniquet. Harry glanced at the woman who lay sprawled with her eyes shut, her face expressionless.

"She's out, maybe dead," Jim said.

Harry glanced at the woman whose eyes were now shut. Her face was expressionless. Blood oozed slowly through her fingers and dripped onto the bed. Shock, he thought then quickly turned back to work on Milton.

For the next half hour and what seemed to Harry an eternity, he and Jim, using the emergency medical kit Jim had brought in his car, worked over Milton and the semi-conscious woman. When the medical team arrived, they stabilized Milton, sedated him, and put him in the ambulance. Then the woman was whisked away. When that was done, Jim took Harry to look at the people who had been the operation's forced labor. By now the place was thick with crime scene people, taking pictures and measuring the spaces.

Jim took two women officers away from what they were doing and told them to follow him. With the tension diminishing, Harry noticed for the first time the heavy, fetid smell of the place, an unpleasant mingling of toilets, stale air, unwashed bodies, and lingering fried fat. The halls were filthy and in places stank of rats.

"I haven't got any idea as to what we're going to do with these women," Jim said. "They're in terrible shape, a lot of them addicted, some not over fifteen or sixteen years old. The older women are just as bad, underfed, worn down from the work, sick by the looks of them. Most speak no English and are sure to be illegals."

Hodges had managed to get the seven women quieted down and seated on their mattresses. Four of the mattresses were empty.

Rigoberta, Hazel, and two more Harry thought, the significance of what he was seeing soaking into his mind, anger at what had been done to them—to all these unfortunate people—smoldering in his gut.

As soon as Jim arrived, a bony woman with white-streaked hair and a ravaged face demanded to know how long they were going to be kept sitting there.

"We're getting a bus here as fast as we can," Jim answered. "While we wait, I want you to answer some questions. Corporals Jones and Casey will speak to you one at a time," he said, waving the two police women into the room. "You can get up now if you want to, but please stay in this room until the transportation gets here."

"Where you taking us?" a small, skinny woman demanded.

"First to Headquarters, then we'll see what can be done with you."

"I ain't done nothing. I ain't going to no jail," the woman said.

"Frank," Jim said, ignoring the protest, "You watch this scene really closely. I don't want somebody in here grabbing those officers' weapons."

Meanwhile, the two women deputies were trying to get names

303

from the women, and it was proving to be slow going, most of them too terrified to speak.

"There's some very sick people in here," Hodges said with barely concealed anger. "About half of them belong in a hospital."

"We'll get to that," Jim said quietly. "You just keep the lid on until help comes, OK?"

"I'll do it," Hodges replied, "but this is one miserable place."

"The media are coming," Harry told Jim when they were back in the hall. "What's the story going to be?"

"I think it's handcuffed in the kitchen and has been read its rights," Jim said with a sigh.

Harry nodded and checked his watch. It was 8:30.

"Time I got out of here," he said.

"Go ahead. Leave the car behind Headquarters, and try to get away without talking to anybody. And another thing: Thanks."

He put out his hand and Harry shook it.

"You've done some really good work here," Harry said. "There's a chance this will unravel the whole trafficking operation in the county."

"I hope so," Jim said, not sounding as if he believed it.

Two deputies appeared and one said in an awed voice, "Captain, you've got to see this. We've found enough heroine and coke to keep the whole county stoned for the next year. You're not going to believe it."

Jim groaned.

"All we need is Narcotics breathing down our necks," he said.

"Good luck deciding what you're going to do with those women," Harry said, heading for the road.

34

As Jim had requested, Harry parked the unmarked police car behind the holding cells and drove out of the Sheriff Department's parking lot without attracting attention. As always, following hard action, he marveled that the world was so mundane. Exhausted but still too wired to relax, he drove back to the Hammock, alternating between mental scenes of violence from inside the house they had raided and the morning tranquility through which he was driving, the sun, leisurely traffic, thunderheads over the Everglades, and the endless circling of the vultures, the green earth revolving slowly under their wings.

He was nearly home before he thought of his cell phone and the fact it had been turned off ever since he and Hodges had put on their armor in Jim's office. He found a message from Katherine, which startled him because she almost never called him and did not like talking on the phone.

"Harry," she said in a voice quivering with stress, "Minna's been hurt. She was attacked by that pig. I don't know how it happened. I think Doreen saved her life. They're both in the hospital. That's where I am. Get here as soon as you can."

He pulled the Mustang into a police turn and raced toward Avola.

Katherine was sitting in the recovery room beside Minna when he found her. The girl, both arms heavily bandaged, and pale as milk, appeared to be unconscious.

"You didn't answer my call," Katherine said by way of greeting.

"The phone was off," he told her, knowing now was not the time to explain what he had been doing. "What happened to her? Is she going to be all right?"

"She's in and out. The anesthetic is still wearing off. The pig knocked her down and slashed her several times before Doreen shot the damned thing with Tucker's double-barreled shotgun. Tucker said she fired both barrels at once, and the kick dislocated her shoulder. He called the ambulance then stayed with Minna, doing what he could to staunch the bleeding and comfort her until the medics reached them. Minna and Doreen were all on their way to the hospital before he had a chance to call me."

"How badly hurt is she?"

"The surgeon said multiple cuts and bruises, mostly on her legs and arms, a cracked rib where that beast hit her; no other broken bones, and the scans show no internal injuries," Katherine said. "So I guess she's lucky."

"Did Tucker say how the pig got out of the pen?"

"No. Does it matter?"

"Probably not," Harry said, hearing the anger in her voice.

"Were you out with Jim?" she demanded.

Harry was sure that telling Katherine the details of the raid would only add to her anguish, but he did not want to lie to her.

"Just before daylight," he said. "Jim, Hodges, a Corporal Johnson, and I broke open a house where seven women were being kept as slaves. They were running sewing machines twelve or fourteen hours a day. They're in pretty bad condition, but by now they should be somewhere safe."

"Was there any shooting?"

"Not much," he said.

"How many dead and wounded?" she continued, undeterred.

"One dead, two wounded," Harry said. "Corporal Milton Johnson was shot in the leg, and the middle-aged Hispanic woman who shot him took a round in the shoulder."

"That's two shootouts in what, two weeks?"

"Katherine, it had to be done. Those women were enslaved, addicted, living worse than animals. Things down here are bad and getting worse. Violence is increasing. The murder rate is rising like a missile, and now there's this slavery thing. I can't just . . ."

"Should I be taking notes?" she asked, interrupting him.

"Would it do any good?"

"No."

Minna groaned and rolled her head on the pillow. Harry and Katherine began talking to her and rubbing her hands. In another ten minutes she had drunk some water and was fully conscious.

"How did it happen?" Harry asked her after her mother had reassured her that she was going to be all right.

"I'd been wanting to go in the cage with her for a while," the girl said, "but I hadn't dared."

"You went into that cage?" her mother demanded.

"I don't see why you're so upset," Minna said. "I've been working with Katrina and Pearl Jam for weeks. She was taking food from my hand—well, she was standing pretty much in front of me and eating it after I'd slid it through the fencing. She wasn't popping those teeth at me anymore. Pearl Jam would squeal and come running every time he saw me."

Katherine was almost steaming, she was so upset.

"Haven't you any sense at all?" she began, but Harry put his hand on her arm and asked her to wait.

"You said you were afraid, Minna," he said. "What made you decide to do it?"

"Working with Mr. LaBeau," she said without hesitation. "I don't know why, but helping him with the garden, knowing how weak he was and seeing how he wouldn't give in to it, made me feel a whole lot braver."

"Were you trying to get yourself killed?" Katherine asked, still holding the girl's hand.

She looked away from her mother. Harry started to intervene again then thought better of it.

"Minna?" Katherine asked, shaking her hand to recover her daughter's attention.

Harry thought she had probably done that a thousand times, dressing Minna, washing her, questioning, instructing, and cautioning her. He had missed a lot of that, and it felt bad.

After a pause, Minna looked back and answered in a steady voice, "No, I was trying to face my fear. That's what Dr. Holinshed said I had to do."

"Congratulations," Harry told her, gently patting Katherine's back. "You just picked the wrong test."

The door opened and Wetherell Clampett, dressed in bib overalls, boots, and a blue work shirt, came into the room, followed by Doreen with her arm in a sling. Her usually ruddy face was pale and somber, making Harry think she was in pain.

"How's the girl doing?" Wetherell asked without preliminaries.

Before anyone could answer, Minna said, "Doreen, was your shoulder broken?"

"No," Doreen said, somehow managing a smile, "but it was dislocated, and it hurts like hell." She walked straight to the bed and leaned over Minna and kissed her on the forehead.

"Are you all sewed up?" she asked.

"I think so. You saved my life, Doreen. I want to thank you."

"It's all right. That was one scary pig."

"And I'm sorry I've been so mean."

"Was you? I didn't notice none of that. Anybody called Tucker, to say you're out of the woods?" Doreen asked.

"I called," Harry said. "That shotgun had some kick."

"Her own fault," Wetherell said in his usual loud voice. "She didn't pull the stock tight before she fired. Soon as I get her home, I'm going to begin rubbing Tuttle's Liniment into that shoulder. She'll be all right in no time."

He put his arm around Doreen and gave her a squeeze. She flinched and blushed at the same time. Harry couldn't have suppressed his smile if his life had depended on it.

Esther Benson kept Minna in the hospital for two days, making sure her wounds were clean and she was stable. Holinshed came down from the psychiatric wing on the second day and said with obvious satisfaction, "Take her home."

"She's making solid progress," Holinshed told Katherine and Harry later in the hall.

"Will she be ready for school when the time comes?" Katherine asked.

"I think so," Holinshed said, "but it will depend on her."

On the way back to the Hammock, Minna answered Katherine's question.

"I've got to have some new school clothes," she said from the back seat after a period of silence. "I've grown out of about everything I own."

"We can deal with that," Harry said, anticipating taking her shopping.

"You don't know what you're in for," Katherine told him later. "I'd rather wrestle an alligator."

Not believing her, Harry laughed.

Katherine looked at him appraisingly and said, "It's amazing what you don't know."

"Then you'll have to teach me," he replied complacently.

Within a few days Minna was limping around in the garden with Tucker and even trying to work a little. She was feeding Pearl Jam again but had stopped talking to him. She had begun talking with Harry and Katherine and only went into her bedroom to sleep or read. Katherine seemed to have moved beyond needing to engage Harry on the matter of his job, and Harry was considering having another try at persuading her to stay. Then Jim called him.

"Here's the situation," he began. "Five of those seven women are illegals. Technically, I'm not obliged to hand them over to Immigration, but it's getting harder not to. There's a lot of pressure on the Sheriff."

"The Lou Dobbs effect?" Harry asked.

Jim laughed.

"And the right-wing electorate effect," he added. "They're seeing to it that Fisher feels their pain. Anyway, the longer I keep them here, the more likely it is that they'll be deported."

"How can I help?"

"I need somebody to take them off my hands."

"Soñadora," Harry said. "I'll make the call."

But instead of calling he drove to *Salvamento*. The building was roofed and closed in. Harry followed the sounds of hammering and sawing and went inside. Soñadora was carrying tiles for the men putting in a shower stall.

"We have had money from St. Jude's," she said, pulling off her bandanna and shaking out the tumble of hair. "It has been a big help. Rowena is a good woman. I like her."

She started to say more but stopped herself.

"Even if she is an Anglo," Harry finished for her.

She could not entirely suppress the grin.

"Jim Snyder's got a problem," Harry said.

310

"Who doesn't?" she asked.

"Have you heard that, thanks to Rigoberta, we found the house where she and Hazel had been kept?"

"I heard, and I suspect that all the illegals are on their way out of the country or to jail."

"Wrong. Jim has five women that he needs to get out of his detention section and put somewhere safe before the Sheriff buckles and hands them over to Immigration. Can you help?"

Soñadora sighed and said, "It will not be easy. There is the space left by Hazel, but everything else is full. I'll need a little time."

"How much?" Harry asked.

"Can you give me two hours?"

"Yes, but I have an idea the window is closing."

"What?"

There was instant anxiety in her voice.

"Be as quick as you can," Harry told her. "Moving five women out of the detention wing of the county jail has to be done in a way that gives the Sheriff plausible deniability regarding their disappearance."

She hurried away and returned with a young black woman in tow, then took a moment to show her where to find the tiles and where to take them.

"Come back in two hours," she said to Harry.

"OK," he said and, stung because she had expressed so little interest in the women's rescue, he turned to walk away.

"Harry," she said, stopping him, "Thank you. You saved those women's lives."

He had turned to face her, and in that rough space of the half-finished building, she looked very small, very vulnerable, and very alone. With her hair tumbling around her shoulders, she might, from a distance, have been mistaken for a girl, but Harry was uncomfortably aware that she was a woman.

"I'm glad I was there," he said, unexpectedly moved by her words, "and thanks to you and Rigoberta they are no longer enslaved."

Her expression softened, and she said quietly but with apparent feeling something he could not understand.

He waited, perplexed. She was looking at him in an odd way, and he knew that whatever it was she had said she was not making a joke.

"It means . . ." her hesitation lasted until Harry wondered what was wrong. "Go with God," she said quietly. "I wanted to say it in Quiche so that you would know I meant it."

"And you," he replied, dissatisfied with his response.

She lifted her hand in an ambiguous gesture that left him wondering what it was she had really said.

Coming home to the safehouse from work, Rigoberta found a postcard waiting for her. It had been mailed in Atlanta. The message was printed in a large, childish hand, and Rigoberta, who was learning to read and write, found she could easily read the words.

Hi, Riggs

Sorry I ran off without saying goodbye. I'm working in Costco. The money's all right and they need more people. I got a place to live, and it will hold two. If you want to come up, I'll meet you at the bus station. If you ain't got any money, I'll send you some. I didn't know if I could get out of Florida, but I did, and you won't have no trouble coming from Avola to here on the bus. I hope you're OK. I miss you.

Hazel

Rigoberta read and then reread the message, the address, and the telephone number. Then she put the card into the pocket of her slacks and went to her room where she took the card out of her pocket, sat on the bed holding it, not thinking, just holding the card and feeling Hazel with her. Gradually, the sadness that had been weighing heavily on her heart since Hazel's leaving began to lift. And she allowed herself to cry. But she did not allow herself to cry long. She wiped her eyes and thought about her situation. She found the work endurable. She was grateful to have a comfortable place to live, but she knew she was not safe, and she knew that one day soon they would ask her to find another place to live. She got up and counted her money.

Four days later, carrying only her old bag, she stepped off the bus in Atlanta, and Hazel was there. She had combed her hair and even put on lip gloss.

"Welcome to Atlanta, Riggs," she said.

Rigoberta stood looking at her for a moment, waiting, and then, seeing she would have to do it herself, stepped forward and pulled Hazel into her arms. Hazel squawked and tried to pull herself free.

"No," Rigoberta said, tightening her embrace. "You listen."

Hazel, having no choice, wrapped in Rigoberta's strong arms, stopped wriggling.

"Better," Rigoberta said. "Kissing and hugging friend after long time away is old Indian custom. I will teach you."

And she planted a warm, soft kiss on Hazel's cheek.

35

Minna's wounds healed quickly.

"The miracle of youth," Tucker told Harry with a laugh.

Harry had found Tucker in the garden with Sanchez and Oh, Brother! maintaining a perimeter.

"Which reminds me," Tucker said, mopping his face with a blue bandanna. "Wetherell called me to say sitting around waiting for that shoulder to heal had made Doreen mean as a bear with a sore jaw and wanted to know if I'd take her off his hands."

"What did you tell him?"

"She's in the kitchen," Tucker said with a chuckle, "complaining to Minna about my housekeeping. Those two have become thick as thieves."

"I think you got used to having her around," Harry said, helping Tucker to raise a tripod over a new hill of pole beans.

"It's true," Tucker said, "there's a comfort that comes with having a woman's company."

"Especially one that goes home at night," Harry said.

"You want to be careful," Tucker said, "or you'll turn into a sour old man."

"Already am," Harry replied. "Ernesto Piedra tells me that Rigoberta has left Avola."

"Where has she gone?" Tucker asked.

"No one's sure, but the woman running the safehouse thinks she went to Atlanta. A few days before she left, Rigoberta got a card with an Atlanta postmark on it. It was from Hazel."

"Ah," Tucker said, "Hazel got out of the state without being spotted. Good for her."

"My sentiments exactly, and I hope Rigoberta finds her. I think they had become good friends, something new, I'd bet, for Hazel, maybe Rigoberta too. I think they'll be a lot safer in Atlanta."

"Enemies of the people, according to some," Tucker said.

"Two courageous women," Harry said as he and Tucker hoisted another tripod upright and spread its legs over the newly planted earth.

"A new beginning," Tucker said, resting a hand on one of the legs.

"It takes faith and courage to plant a garden," Harry said.

Tucker nodded, "Or start a new life."

"Well, you know," Jim complained, sitting in a lounge chair on Harry's lanai with his long legs thrust out, "catching those people has been like trying to net smoke."

"I thought you rolled over the man we caught," Harry said in surprise, passing Jim a cup of Katherine's coffee.

"We did, and, facing the possibility of life sentences, he and that woman gave us names and places, but when we got there everyone was gone. Half a dozen houses in La Ramada were stripped of everything including fingerprints and left with the doors open. Smoke, like I said."

"But you dismantled the organization," Harry said.

"The Avola part of it," Jim said. "That's all our man and the woman had any knowledge of."

"It's a beginning," Harry said. "Did you get any blowback for letting the women go?"

"Some, but Fisher's heart wasn't in it. He's not too fond of Immigration, thinks they're unprofessional, unnecessarily brutal, and a bureaucratic nightmare."

"He's not alone."

Jim took a tentative sip of his coffee and smiled.

"You didn't make this."

"No."

"Where is Katherine?" Jim asked in an elaborately casual way.

"Gone shopping with Minna for school clothes."

"They staying?" Jim asked, then waved his hand and said, "Wait, I don't need to be asking that question."

"It's all right," Harry said. "The answer is I don't know. I wish I did."

"I gather from that you want them to stay?"

"Yes."

"Cora?" Jim asked.

"Finished. She's staying in Europe. Found an Italian count, which in any poker game beats a Florida P.I."

"I'm sorry."

"Don't be," Harry said, trying to keep any traces of bitterness out of his voice. "The world keeps turning. How are you and Kathleen doing?"

"All right," Jim replied, hesitated, and said, "I guess I'm still holding onto Colleen. It's kind of clouding things."

"She was a good woman, Jim," Harry said quietly, "and so is Kathleen."

"Yes. I'm doing my best to let her know that and get it through my head that Colleen's not coming back."

"It's what Colleen would want. You don't have to forget her, you know."

"I couldn't if I wanted to, and I don't."

"No," Harry said. "We don't forget any of them."

Harry and Katherine had been discussing Minna. With Minna taking more of an interest in their lives and spending more time at home, they were finding less time to talk seriously with one another. They began taking late-afternoon walks to the bridge and were trying in their differing and deeply entrenched ways to find some common ground on the subject of Minna and, much more tentatively, their own relationship.

"I agree with Dr. Holinshed," Katherine said, "Minna should go home and go back to school there. Added to that, I don't want Jesse in his last year of high school risk losing that scholarship he's been fighting for. We both owe him better than that."

"Let him stay where he is," Harry replied. "He's going to be so busy he won't know you're not there, and you said yourself that your sister dotes on him."

"That's part of the problem," Katherine said a little sharply. "The other part is Thornton."

Thornton. The son Harry barely even knew. "Bring him here," Harry said.

She made no response to that, and Harry was beginning to feel as if he was drowning in complications.

They had reached the bridge and were leaning companionably on the plank rail with the red sun sinking behind them, spreading crimson slashes of light across the Puc Puggy and the marshes beyond. Flights of ibis and herons were winging westward to roost in the Stickpen Preserve that bordered the Hammock.

"Sometimes I wish the Hammock wasn't so beautiful," Katherine said, watching a low-flying flock of herons pass over them so low she and Harry could hear the rustle of their wings.

"My last line of defense," Harry said, watching her upturned face and thinking how much he wished he could persuade her to stay.

Katherine turned to him and said, "I can deal with the Hammock. It's you that's giving me trouble."

Harry's cell began to vibrate.

"I think Minna's getting hungry," Harry said, taking the phone out of his pocket.

It was Ernesto Piedra.

"Harry," he said, "they've found out where Soñadora is staying. I have told her but she will not listen. She says, 'Maybe I have lived long enough.' Please talk to her."

Harry, thinking of his conversation with Jim, asked, "Who's they? I thought the police had pretty well cleaned that stable."

"Those who weren't caught wish to settle some old scores. You should watch yourself as well. Will you talk to her?"

"Yes," Harry said, "but I can't promise she'll listen to me."

"Do your best."

"OK."

"It was Ernesto Piedra," he told Katherine. "It looks as though Jim and his people didn't get all the people involved in that human trafficking ring. Ernesto thinks Soñadora is in danger."

"And he wants you to do something about it," she said sourly.

"He wants me to talk to her, yes."

"But you can't call her."

"Not always. Sometimes I can. When we get back to the house, I'll try."

"Five will get you ten," she told him, "Minna and I will be eating alone."

"Let's hope not," Harry said. "I'm hungry."

It was a lame response because, he thought guiltily, she was probably right. They walked the rest of the way home in silence.

He had to wait over an hour for Soñadora to call after he reached the go-between, and he actually ate at home. Over dessert he asked Minna whether she would rather go back to Georgia or stay on the Hammock.

"Harry!" Katherine protested. "You weren't supposed to ask her that."

"I don't mind answering," Minna said, pausing a minute before going on. "OK, it's not an easy question to answer."

"Then don't try," Katherine said. "You don't have to."

"Mom, lighten up. It's not that hard, and the problem isn't with me, it's with you two."

"Isn't it always?" Harry asked, wanting to hear what she was going to say next.

"I don't see that at all," Katherine said, sounding a bit defensive. "We just want . . ."

"What's best for me," Minna said.

She had been talking between swallows, and continued eating, showing, Harry thought, no sign of being stressed.

"But whether I want to go back to Georgia or stay here," she said calmly, "is going to become part of what you two can't decide."

"Which is?" Harry asked.

"Whether or not you're going to go on living together."

Katherine blushed deeply. "We are not," Katherine exclaimed, *"living together."*

"Well then," Minna said, "my eyes and ears are liars."

"You're right," Harry said. "Your mother and I are having a difficult time deciding what we're going to do."

"What's your opinion?"

"Don't have one," Minna said, pushing away her empty plate.

That was when Harry's phone jiggled.

Soñadora was not happy with Harry.

"What do you want?" she demanded, slamming the car door.

"To find some easier way of meeting you away from *Salvamento.*"

It was a warm, humid night, and she was dressed in a green

cotton skirt and white blouse, white sandals, and had tied back her hair with a green ribbon.

"You look good, you smell good," he added, "and there's no plaster dust on your nose."

"Stop changing the subject."

"Where's your gun?"

"In my satchel."

"Nobody has carried a satchel since 1910. What good is it going to do you in your bag?"

"I don't know why I bother to carry it at all."

"Because some part of your brain is still functioning."

"Where are we going?"

Harry had pulled away from the Piggly Wiggly's on the ill-lighted corner in East Avola where Soñadora had insisted on being picked up and turned west toward 41. "I'm taking you home," Harry said.

"Are you making a joke?" she demanded.

"I don't know where your home is, of course, so it has to be mine."

"Your house?" she said as if she could not have heard correctly.

"Yes. If you won't look after yourself, I'll have to do it for you."

She sniffed. "Are you drunk?" she asked.

"No."

"Then what makes you think I need you to look after me?"

"Because Ernesto Piedra says you do."

"Ernesto is worse than a mother hen." She paused, straightened her back, and said, "Harry, are you making a move on me?"

"As you know, my ex-wife and my daughter are at the house, so my answer has to be no. If they weren't, well, that might change things."

She slumped back against the seat as if someone had cut the string holding her erect.

"Katherine and Minna," she said without enthusiasm.

"Someone intends to kill you . . . maybe tonight," he said. "I don't want that to happen."

"It is not a thing I look forward to myself," she answered, "but I have grown used to living with threats."

She made a few more feeble efforts to get him to give up on his plan, but Harry saw that she was at least resigned and possibly relieved to be with him. Not for the first time, he thought that as hard and challenging as her life had been and fraught with pain and danger, it had not really hardened her.

Harry parked under the big live oak on the front corner of his yard, bathed in moonlight. He had run down the windows and shut off the air conditioning as soon as he crossed the bridge onto the Hammock. As soon as the engine died, the cab filled with the chiming of the colony frogs along the creek and in the trees surrounding the house.

"How peaceful and beautiful," she said, staring out her window. "If I lived here, I would never leave, and I would always come out at night to watch the moon."

"I'd give you a week," Harry said, opening his door. "Then you'd go in search of someone to save."

"You spoil my dream," she said, looking up at the sky with a rueful laugh, "just as the clouds are dimming the moon."

They were walking together, talking quietly about how the women whom she had taken off Jim's hands were settling into their new homes, and had almost reached the lanai door when Soñadora gave a gasping cry and fell into Harry as if a giant hand had shoved her. At the same instant a muzzle blast shattered the night. Harry caught her and pulled her to the ground, falling on her and drawing his gun as he fell. The shooter fired again and missed.

Harry had seen the first flame in the darkness and confirmed its location with the second.

Beneath him, Soñadora was groaning.

Whoever was shooting at them was standing at the corner of the lanai, shrouded by the wisteria. Harry waited, knowing that in the bad light and lying as close to the ground as they were, they made a very difficult target.

A moment later a figure detached itself from the darkness and moved out onto the lawn, trying to find a better shot. Harry waited, sure that if he did not move, the man would come closer, thinking he had hit both of them. Soñadora continued to moan. The man took another step, and Harry shot him twice.

The man collapsed, and silence hung like a shroud.

"Harry!" Katherine shouted. "I'm right behind him. Don't fire. I'm coming out."

"Do you have the shotgun?"

"Yes."

"Keep it on him. If he moves, shoot him."

Katherine stepped into the pale light, but the man did not move. Harry stepped around his head and kicked away the pistol lying near his hand, then picked it up. Even in the weak light Harry saw the blood soaking down the side of his face into his collar. He pressed his finger against the man's neck and said, "He's alive."

Katherine had run across the lawn to Soñadora and dropped onto her knees beside her.

"Katherine?" she said through gritted teeth.

"Yes. Don't move. I'll call for help."

"You were right," Soñadora whispered when Harry replaced Katherine.

"Just hold on," Harry said. "Help's coming. Katherine will bring a light and something to stop the bleeding. Is the pain bad?"

"Do you know any pain that isn't?" she gasped.

"Encouraging," Harry said, "you can still be unpleasant."

She started to laugh and groaned.

"No making jokes," she whispered.

With a lantern standing beside them, Katherine and Harry eased her onto a blanket and from her left side peeled away her blood-soaked shirt.

"I think your ribs took most of the abuse," Harry said. "You're bleeding, but from what I can see nothing major has been severed. Take a deep breath. We're going to turn you so we can press it on the wound."

Harry lifted her, and Soñadora fainted.

"That was a forty-five-caliber slug that tore into her," Harry said as he and Katherine bent over her. "It did some damage."

By that time Minna had come out of the house in defiance of Katherine's orders.

"What about him?" Minna demanded, standing over Katherine and Harry and pointing at the man lying on the grass to their right.

"I'll look in a minute," Harry said.

He was a big man with a heavy gut, a mustache, and thick shoulders. He was sprawled on his back, his face running with blood. He was muttering something. Harry knelt over him and said, "Hang on. Help is coming."

The man made a growling sound and swung his right fist at Harry's head. Harry caught the fist with his left hand and pressed it down against the man's chest. His shirt was also soaked with blood.

"*No moverse,*" Harry said, slaughtering the language.

The man groaned and faded into silence, his body slackening like a punctured balloon.

Jim and Hodges arrived with the ambulance and a cruiser full of deputies.

"Oh, mother of us all!" Jim said when Katherine told him one of the victims was Soñadora. "How bad is she?"

"She'll live," Katherine said, setting Jim back on his heels.

"And the other one?"

"In need of attention," she said with her usual laconic response.

"He doesn't look too good to me," Minna told him.

Jim and Hodges looked at the young girl standing straight and tall before them.

"Some of each, I say," Hodges observed.

"A little more of the mother," Jim replied, looking at Katherine.

Harry came back from the wounded man. The medics were already working on Soñadora, and Harry hovered, ignoring Jim and Hodges. The team leader asked Harry to please step back. Rebuked, Harry drifted back to Jim and the little group clustered around him.

"I'd forgotten how beautiful she is," Katherine said.

Jim and Hodges exchanged quick looks.

"Is she? It never came up," Harry said.

"Harry," Minna said with a laugh, "you are so busted."

"And the hair," Katherine said in the same tone of voice, strangely flat and monotonous.

"Wait, wait," Jim said, "Let me do some work. Frank, keep that man company until the medics can get to him. Now, you two," he said to Katherine and Harry, "what happened out here?"

"Ivanhoe was bringing Rebecca home for safekeeping and walked straight into an ambush."

"Rebecca?" Jim said. "Katherine, I thought . . . ?"

"It's OK," Harry said quickly. "After the first shot was fired, Calamity Jane here grabbed the shotgun, slipped out the back door, walked up on the shooter, and was about to blow him away when I dropped him."

"And what prompted you to bring Soñadora out here?" Jim asked, clearly unsatisfied with what he'd heard so far.

"I got a call telling me that some of the gang members you didn't catch had decided to kill her, and they were going to do it tonight."

Harry wanted very much to go back and stand near Soñadora but between Jim and Katherine he could feel the leash tightening.

"And you're not going to tell me who called you."

"Jim, she's bleeding." There was no real reason not to say that Ernesto had provided the warning. Jim knew Ernesto. And yet . . . Harry held his tongue.

Jim turned to Katherine.

"Katherine, do you know?"

"No."

"How did they know you were bringing her out here?" Jim asked, not wasting time on a lost cause.

"There's no way they could have known," Harry insisted. "No one but Katherine and I knew, and I didn't tell Soñadora what I'd planned. So that means the shooter had come out here to kill me."

"I'm coming back to this later," Jim said.

A bulky woman from the first response team came over to Jim and said, "She's still conscious, and we've got her stabilized and sedated. If you want to talk to her, do it now because she's going out very soon."

Jim watched the team stream away from Soñadora, running toward the downed man.

"I've got to go," the woman said, "but Carl asked for an armed officer to ride with the casualties. He doesn't like the look of that one."

She jerked her thumb toward the downed man as she backed away.

"Tell him he's got it," Jim said.

"Harry?" a feeble voice called.

"Isn't that touching?" Katherine asked Jim as Harry hurried toward Soñadora.

36

Soñadora's wound was messy, splintered bone from two ribs had blasted through the surrounding tissue like shrapnel, tearing up a piece of her left lung and collapsing it. The surgical team worked three hours, repairing the damage.

"She'll be sore but fine," Bradley Post told Harry the next morning, but she's not going to be working on the *Salvamento* building for some time."

"How did you know about that?" Harry asked, surprised that anyone outside of Rowena Farnham and her women in the Anglo community had learned of it.

"I'm on a committee set up by the hospital to try to deal with the health issues in the immigrant population. The *Salvamento* name came up. While she was coming out of the anesthetic, the recovery room nurse said she kept saying, '*Salvamento, Salvamento.*' I put two and two together."

"You'd be doing her a favor if you kept that to yourself," Harry said.

"I'd already figured that out. Undocumented?"

Harry shrugged. Post nodded.

"The world is getting complicated," he said, getting to his feet.

"Tell me about it," Harry said. "When can I see her?"

"Let's make it tomorrow," Post told him.

Earlier that morning, Katherine and Minna had gone on

another shopping trip. They were back by two. Harry was working on reports and, as usual when he had to sit at a desk for any extended period of time, he began feeling very sorry for himself. Their return gave him the excuse he had been looking for to get up.

"We jumped over the moon," Minna told him, coming into the house loaded down with plastic bags.

"Meaning?"

"We bought the store out."

"So I see. Where's your mother?"

"She's sitting out in the car. Watch yourself if you go out there. Driving back put her in a rotten mood."

"Well, let's see if I can do anything to make her feel better."

"Good luck," Minna said and ran upstairs, calling back that she was going to try on clothes.

Katherine was getting out of the car.

"Minna says you're in a rotten mood. You were OK when you left. What happened?"

"Nothing," she said. "I feel like walking. Want to go with me?"

"I'll go if you'll talk to me."

"OK."

But they walked toward the bridge a full five minutes before Katherine spoke. "Minna and I are leaving tomorrow," she said finally, staring down at the white sand road.

"Any special reason?"

"Yes. Let's start with last night. What if it had been you instead of Soñadora who had been hit?"

"I guess you would have had to shoot him," Harry answered without enthusiasm.

"And wouldn't that have been fun."

Harry was beginning to feel very bad. "No, I suppose it wouldn't have been fun at all."

"And if something had gone a little differently, every one of us might have died because I don't think he would have left anyone alive."

"No, he wouldn't, and he would probably have burned the house before he left."

"Are you being smart?"

"I'm telling you what probably would have happened."

Katherine stopped, and they faced each other. "It's no way to live, Harry," she said.

"I suppose it isn't."

"And you're not going to quit."

"No."

"Then I'll confirm the reservations, and Minna and I will leave in the morning."

"Telling you I love you won't change your mind."

"No," Katherine said softly, putting her arms around his neck. "I love you, Harry, but I can't live the way you do."

"But we're still OK?"

"Are we?"

"Yes and no."

"That's probably right," she said and kissed him.

Katherine and Minna left as Katherine had said they would. She turned in her car and Harry drove them to the departure terminal.

"Are you going to be all right, Minna?" he asked her, hugging her gingerly and briefly at their gate.

"I think so, Harry," she said. "What about you?"

"Sure," he said.

Then he kissed Katherine, who kissed him back and gave him a look that twisted his heart, but Minna had the last word.

As she and her mother were going through the gate, she

turned back and said, shaking her head, "I think you two are nuts."

Harry managed a feeble smile, but at that moment an old song of Kris Kristofferson's began playing in his head: "Don't look so sad, I know it's over. / But life goes on, and this old world will keep on turning."

They disappeared into the crowd, and Harry heard the line, "There'll be time enough for sadness when you leave me," before he hit the delete button. He was halfway back to the Hammock before he remembered he was supposed to visit Soñadora in the hospital.

He pulled off the road and sat for a while, staring, without really seeing it, into a pasture overrun with scrub growth and weeds, its snake fence rotting into the ground. When his mind finally registered what he was looking at, he thought with a shiver that the place looked like an abandoned burial ground.

Another line of poetry further darkened his mind: "It is like this/ In death's other kingdom . . ." Pushing back against the darkness, he stifled the voice, wrenched the car around, and drove toward Avola.

ABOUT THE AUTHOR

Kinley Roby lives in Virginia with his wife, novelist and editor Mary Linn Roby.